Romancing the Rake

An Allingham Regency Classic

Merryn Allingham

ROMANCING THE RAKE

First published in Great Britain 2019 by The Verrall Press

Cover art: Berni Stevens Book Cover Design

Chapter One

Marianna Marquez raised her face to the warm sun and breathed a sigh of contentment. The gentlest of waves whispered along the pebbles at her feet and the wide blue dome of the sky spread itself to meet a distant horizon. She closed her eyes in pleasure. For a short time at least she was free: all too soon she would have to return to the house on Marine Parade and her cousin's inevitable questioning. If only her father would send Carmela back to Spain, she might truly enjoy this last summer before the dreary future that lay in front of her. But Papa would not do that. Her stern aunts back in Madrid had only agreed to her coming to Brighton if Carmela came too.

'You seem to have dropped this.'

She was startled from her reverie by a deep voice, disturbing in its intimacy. Shading her eyes against the sun's strong rays, she detected the outline of a slim but muscular form. The man appeared to be offering her a crumpled cambric handkerchief bearing all the marks of having been trampled in sand and sea.

She shook her head decisively. 'Thank you, but no. The

handkerchief is not mine.'

'Are you quite sure?'

'I think I should know my own possessions,' she responded a little tartly.

'Naturally. But you had fallen into such an abstraction, I thought you might not realise if you *had* dropped something.'

Marianna felt herself becoming ruffled. Whoever the man was, he was intruding on the few moments of solitude that were hers.

'As I said, sir, you are mistaken.'

Her voice was edged with ice but it seemed not to perturb him for he took the opportunity to move nearer. She became aware of a pair of shapely legs encased in skin tight fawn pantaloons, and a coat of blue superfine that perfectly fitted his powerful shoulders. Hessian boots of dazzling gloss completed an ensemble ill-adapted to a provincial beach.

'It would seem I *was* mistaken,' he admitted, 'but I shan't repine. It's given me the chance of speaking to a vastly pretty girl.'

She was astonished at his audacity. His voice and dress spoke the gentleman, but no gentleman of her acquaintance would have addressed a lady so.

'I would be glad, sir,' she said in the most frigid of voices, 'if you would leave me in peace to enjoy this wonderful view.'

He let out a low chuckle and for the first time her gaze moved upwards towards his face and she was unnerved by what she saw. She hadn't realised how young he was or how good looking. His fair hair fell carelessly over his forehead and a pair of golden brown eyes lingered over her in a way that made her flush with annoyance. A small scar on his left cheek only enhanced his attraction.

The gold-flecked eyes considered her with lazy amusement. 'I'm not impervious to your request,' he drawled, 'but it places me in an awkward situation.'

'How is that?' Marianna found herself responding though every instinct told her to turn tail.

'It puts my desire to gratify a lady at odds with my strong sense of duty. If I wish to oblige you, I must walk away this minute and leave you to your solitude.'

'Please do!'

'If only it were that simple,' he exclaimed mournfully, 'but chivalry requires I put my duty first. Since you appear to be entirely without an escort, it clearly behoves me to stay as your chaperon.'

'How fortunate then that I can put your mind at rest! You must trouble yourself no further. I am used to walking alone and am well able to take care of myself.' At that moment, however, she was feeling far from able. Her desire to venture out alone had never before exposed her to such persistent harassment.

'You are a mere slip of a girl,' he continued blithely, 'and have much to learn. How best to escape unwanted attentions, for instance.' There was a slight pause. 'Though a most comely slip of a girl, I grant you.' His eyes, glinting amber in the sunlight, danced with laughter.

There was nothing for it but to walk away. This man was impervious to disapproval and entreaty alike. She turned quickly to make her way back across the beach and her sudden movement impaled the flounce of her dress on a twisted piece of iron which had detached itself from the groyne. She was well and truly caught.

'Allow me.'

And before she could protest he was down on his knees, carefully unhooking the frill of delicate cream lace from the iron stanchion. She stood rigid with mortification, thankful for the cooling breeze on her heated cheeks. But there was worse to come. Before she could stop him his hands began to rearrange the crumpled hem of her silk gown and for an instant alighted on her ankle.

'Thank you, sir,' she said in a stifled voice and fled towards the safety of Marine Parade.

'Must you go already,' he called after her. 'I feel we are only just getting acquainted.' He grinned at her departing figure. 'It's not every lady's ankles I get to see before luncheon, you know.'

She hurried away more shocked than she cared to admit. That would teach her to walk out unaccompanied. She *must* stop breaking the rules: within a year she would be married and there would be no more solitary strolls, no more escapes by the sea. And no chance meetings with impertinent strangers. Relieved, she reached the promenade and looked back to the spot she had just vacated. The man was still there, watching her every step it seemed. He saw her pause and gave a cheerful wave. Impossible! She turned abruptly from the beach and hurried home.

⌒

Joshua Marchmain watched her for some time as she strode

rapidly over the wet pebbles and began to climb the worn stone steps to the promenade. He had not meant her to flee quite so precipitately and just as things were getting interesting. He would have liked to spar a little more for it was an unusual young lady who walked alone and disputed with strangers. And she had cut a most charming figure. The encounter had certainly provided a welcome break from the tedium of ministering to George's whims. How he had become so indispensable to the Regent he hardly knew. For years he had exiled himself from life among the *ton* and it seemed unlikely that on his return he would become a palace favourite. But he had and quickly. At first it had been amusing to supplant long serving courtiers in the prince's favour, though now it was simply a dead bore.

A summer spent in Brighton had promised new interest, but the reality had proved very different. Or at least not different at all, that was the problem. The prince's life revolved around food and gambling, music and his love affairs, whether he was in London or Brighton. The sound of the sea was the only novelty. Joshua had spent that morning, as so many others, idling in the hothouse that was the Royal Pavilion but, faced with the six course luncheon the Regent felt an appropriate midday snack, he had rebelled to play truant in the salt-tanged air.

Almost immediately he had seen her, a small, trim figure in cream silk and lace, with a saucy villager bonnet on the back of her head, its enormous bow of blue ribbon failing to keep the unruly dark curls from bursting forth. Her face, when she'd raised it, had more than matched the promise of her figure. The eyes, dark and tragic, set in a heart-shaped countenance had sent an unaccustomed longing through him. She would never be a diamond of the first water, but her youth and vulnerability spoke to him in a way that perfect beauty no longer did. The ripple of emotion was over in a trice. Just as well, he thought breezily. Suppressing inconvenient sentiment had made life a good deal simpler over the years. It might have been amusing to dally a while but, in the event, the flirtation was over before it had really begun. Regretfully, he retraced his steps; it was time to resume his duties before the Regent noticed his absence.

～

As soon as Marston opened the door to her, Marianna knew she was in trouble. Her cousin was in the hall, an apron wrapped around one of the black dresses she habitually wore, and a furious expression on her face. The butler made a strategic exit, winking conspiratorially at the young girl as he retired to the servants' quarters.

'And where exactly have you been?' Carmela's tone was as angry as her face.

Marianna did not answer immediately. She had meant to provide herself with an excuse, a frippery purchased from the stalls in Bartholomews perhaps, but in the flight from the beach she had completely forgotten.

It hardly mattered. Her cousin was launched into the tirade she had been keeping for this moment. 'You do realise that your papa is to host a reception here this very evening, and you were supposed to help with the hundred and one things that have to be done.'

Marianna did realise and felt a twinge of guilt. She knew

that as the new ambassador for Spain, Ernesto Marquez was setting great store by tonight's entertainment. He had only recently presented his credentials at St James's and though the Court had abandoned a hot and dusty capital for the sea, it was vital that he continue his work among those who surrounded the Prince Regent. Only a few days ago her father had confided a rumour to her that even George himself might attend this evening's event.

'I'm sorry, Carmela,' she said quietly, trying in vain to mollify the angry woman. 'I felt a little unwell – you know how stuffy this house gets in the hot weather – and I thought it would do me good to take a short walk in the fresh air.'

Her cousin seemed unable to decide whether to look sceptical or shocked. In the end she managed a mixture of both.

'It's even stuffier outside,' she scolded, 'and how many times have I told you that you must not walk alone? You are imprudent, Marianna. Why do you have a personal maid if it is not to accompany you wherever you wish to go? And why go anywhere today?'

'I'm here now so tell me what I can do to help.'

'Nothing.'

'Nothing?'

'Everything is done. As always, I have worked myself to a standstill.'

It was difficult to see how Carmela had worked so very hard. Marianna herself had planned the event days ago and had left the maids to arrange flowers and set tables. The catering firm and their own kitchen had prepared every morsel of food and drink considered necessary to entertain the cream of the *ton*. But she said none of this, unwilling to upset her cousin further.

She was sharply aware of the sacrifice Carmela had made. Her cousin had not wanted to come to England, least of all to a scandalous resort known throughout Europe as a den of extravagance, if not downright immorality. But come she had, putting her loyalty to the family before her own comfort and leaving behind the pleasing pieties of her Madrid home. Marianna might wish she were alone with her father but Carmela was part of the bargain, part of the price she had to pay for a few months' freedom.

Hurrying up the stairs to her bedroom, she locked the door. Marriage was unwelcome, but at least it would deliver her from the endless scoldings of relatives. Her aunts had already presented her with the names of three suitors they considered eligible and all she had to do, they urged, was choose one of them. Any of the three would make a highly suitable husband, able to oversee and conserve the vast estate she would inherit at twenty-one and certain to be assiduous in keeping the inevitable fortune hunters at bay.

It didn't matter who she married. After Luke Trelawny, it was utterly unimportant. She had loved and lost and she knew, even at this young age, that she would never feel so deeply for a man again. It was enough now to know that he was happy with the wife he should always have had, and that she was in some small way responsible for bringing them together. But if only...

Chapter Two

She was sunk in the familiar forlorn dream when a knock at the door roused her. Fearing a resurgent Carmela, she opened it cautiously, but it was Ernesto Marquez who stood on the threshold, a beaming smile on his face and his arms outstretched in greeting.

'*Querida*, come with me,' he ordered, having hugged her until her ribs almost buckled beneath the strain. 'I have a little present for you.'

'I fear I don't deserve a present, Papa. Ask Carmela.'

'Oh, Carmela, what does she know of deserving? I intend to spoil you to death now that you are with me again. I've missed you more than you will ever know.'

Her father was hustling her along the landing to his own room where the door stood open and a stunning gown of the deepest rose pink spread itself invitingly on the bed. Eagerly she snatched it up and held it against her body. A glance in the cheval mirror which stood in one corner reflected back creamy olive skin and burnished curls, their beauty heightened by the rich rose of the satin and gauze gown. Still holding the dress tightly, she waltzed around the bed laughing with delight.

'Thank you, thank you so much. It's quite lovely. But far too good for a mere reception, Papa. We should save it for a grand ball at the very least!'

'A ball? No, indeed. You can be sure that when the time comes, I will find something even better,' her father said proudly. 'Wear the rose pink tonight and your mother's amethysts. They will be perfect for the dress and perfect for you – you look so like Elena.'

His voice faltered a little and Marianna took his hand and squeezed it comfortingly. 'I love being spoiled, but you are much too kind to me.'

'You should know, my dear, that I have an ulterior motive. In that dress you will entrance all my guests and then they will say how lucky Spain is to have such an excellent ambassador!'

Marianna felt deep pleasure that she had returned from Spain to be with her father, despite the warnings she'd had from her English relative. Lady Serena Foyle had refused point blank to continue as Ernesto's hostess once he left London – Brighton had been a step too far for her. *Raffish, my dear*, Lady Foyle had counselled Marianna in a letter to Spain, *please consider carefully whether you will be comfortable entertaining in such a place.* Marianna had considered, but the prospect of living again with a much loved parent, free of her aunts' strictures, had been too appealing.

⟿

At six o'clock, her abigail arrived in a fizz of excitement at the prospect of dressing her mistress for the evening's entertainment. Flora, the best of a mediocre selection according to Lady Serena, who had despatched her from

London, had never before acted as a lady's maid and this evening would be a test of the skills she had been practising so assiduously.

The rose pink gown with its assorted underpinnings was soon in place, then very carefully Flora applied the slightest brush of rouge to both Mariana's cheeks and a smear of rose salve to her lips. Taming the luxuriant curls into the popular Roman style, though, took a little longer and it was some considerable time before the maid pronounced herself satisfied with the result. Her mistress's dark locks now cascaded from a carefully arranged topknot to rest lightly in two glistening ringlets on the soft cream of her neck. The delicate necklace of amethysts that had belonged to Marianna's mother, with earrings to match, completed the toilette.

Both young ladies viewed the finished result in the mirror and smiled with pleasure. Whatever Marianna might lack in willowy elegance, she made up for in sheer prettiness.

'I'm determined to enjoy this evening, Flora,' she pronounced, deep brown eyes sparkling. She had begun to feel the old excitement returning, even though English society had once proved a threatening place and tonight she was entering the lion's den again.

'Of course, you are miss, why ever wouldn't you?'

'I'm a little nervous,' she admitted. 'When I agreed to come to Brighton in Lady Foyle's place, the prospect of helping my father entertain seemed nicely distant. But now!'

'You'll be fine, Miss Marianna, you always know the right thing to say and do.' Flora was soothing.

'My aunts have schooled me well, it's true, but this is the very first *ton* party I have ever hosted.'

And it had arrived rather too quickly, she thought. It seemed as though they had hardly settled themselves in the elegant townhouse on Marine Parade before Ernesto announced that he wished to give a reception. But it was more than that. Her last foray into the social life of England's top one hundred families had ended in disaster. She could still see the young girl she had been, so open to all the pleasures of that first London Season: balls, picnics, exhibitions, ridottos, Venetian breakfasts. How young and foolish she had been! She had fallen in love with the wrong man and fallen foul of one who meant her nothing but dishonour.

'It's time you went downstairs, miss. I've just heard Miss Carmela's door close.'

The maid fussed around her, adjusting a tendril here, a fold of the dress there. Marianna bestowed a warm smile on her. 'Thank you so much, Flora. You've had magic in your fingers this evening. I hope I shall live up to your handiwork.'

'You will Miss Marianna, for sure. You look fair 'ansome,' Flora said joyfully, betraying her rural heritage, and forgetting for the moment the town bronze she had been painfully acquiring.

The hall had been sumptuously decorated with tall vases of early summer lilac and, as Marianna walked slowly down the marble staircase, their sensual perfume rose to meet her. The main doors were open and in the still of the evening she could hear the rhythmic beating of a high tide against the stone parapet. Her father and Carmela were already waiting by the front entrance to receive the first of their guests, her cousin having forsaken her usual black gown for a slightly less funereal mauve. They looked up at her approach and Ernesto glowed with pride; even Carmela gave her a tight smile of approval. So far, so good, but her nerves were taut. Would her planning stand up to the *ton's* stringent demands? Could she perform the role of hostess with aplomb? She had not long to find out.

Lord Albermarle was the first to arrive, and his bluff good nature put Marianna immediately at ease. Most of their guests that evening would be men, an inevitable imbalance in a diplomatic reception, and she had not been certain whether to feel this an advantage or not. But Lord Albermarle's gentle compliments and genial smile decided her. Far better to make her debut without female whispers to disparage her efforts.

Soon the ground floor of Marine Parade was throbbing with life. Most of the guests were involved in some way with the Court or with parliament, but there were a few who had little diplomatic or political interest and had come simply to look over the new ambassador and his household. They appeared to like what they saw.

Sir Henry Bridlington spoke for many when he observed, 'Señor Marquez seems a good sort of chap and his daughter is bound to make a stir this summer.' He took a long pinch of snuff. 'The girl has looks, breeding, and she's no fool. Refreshing to meet a woman with opinions!'

'It depends on the opinions, I imagine.' The man who

spoke was flaxen haired and his tawny eyes glittered with amusement.

'Nothing outlandish, I swear,' Bridlington responded. 'In fact I thought she spoke most sensibly. And a very attractive face and figure, don't you know.'

'Now it's you who is talking sense. A woman's opinions are as changeable as the sea. But her looks! That's a different matter entirely. I must ensure I make the acquaintance of this *nonpareil*.'

So it was that Marianna, busily circulating among her guests, came face to face with her tormentor.

He smiled lazily down at her while a flush gradually suffused her entire body as she realised who was barring her way. He had looked complete to a shade during this morning's encounter. Now he looked simply splendid. He was dressed in the satin knee breeches and black long-tailed coat befitting a gentleman attending an evening party, but the way he wore them singled him out from every other man in the room. His clothes fitted him impeccably, the work she surmised of a master tailor, and suggested very clearly the perfect male body beneath. A dandyish silk waistcoat of maroon and grey stripes was countered by the crisp white neckcloth, tied in an elegant *trône d'amour* and fastened by a single diamond stud. Marianna felt his amber eyes fix on her, sensual and appraising, and was conscious she had been gazing at him far too long.

'Miss Marquez, I imagine? Joshua Marchmain, at your servicr.' His bow had a languid grace.

She bobbed a small curtsy and inclined her head very slightly. His smile deepened at her evident reluctance to speak to him. 'Forgive my somewhat unorthodox approach,' he said. 'I lack a sponsor to introduce me at the very moment I need one. And I would not wish to leave this delightful party without thanking my hostess – that would be grossly discourteous.'

She had remained silent and unsmiling, but his arrogance had set every fibre jangling. 'Discourtesy should not concern you, sir,' she said sharply. 'You seem to have a fine stock of it.'

Her high colour was fading fast and she felt control returning. She would make this man acknowledge his earlier impertinence.

'But how is that?' He was looking genuinely puzzled and she was reduced to saying weakly, 'I think you know very well.'

'Ah!' He beamed at her. 'I understand you now. I would not, though, have been so discourteous as to mention our delightful,' he paused for a moment, 'rendezvous.'

'It was not a rendezvous. It was harassment, and you were abominably rude. How dare you accost a lady in that fashion?'

'But Miss Marquez, consider for one moment. How was I to know that I was accosting a lady? No *lady* of my acquaintance would ever walk alone.'

'So you feel you have *carte blanche* with any woman you do not consider a lady?'

'Shall we say that solitary females are not usually averse to my company.'

Marianna seethed – he was truly an insufferable man. 'You deliberately trespassed on my seclusion,' she said wrathfully. 'And despite my entreaties, you refused to go away.'

'But naturally,' he said in a voice of the softest velvet. 'How could I? You were far too tempting.'

The golden eyes held a look that made her blood heat. She felt the tell-tale flush creeping upwards and longed to flee. But her aunts' strict schooling had her stiffen her shoulders and say in an even tone, 'I believe, Mr Marchmain, that we have finished our conversation.'

He bent his head to hers and said softly, 'Surely not, Miss Marquez. I have a feeling that it's only just beginning.'

In her coldest voice she made one last attempt to put him out of countenance. 'I don't recall my father mentioning your name in connection with his work. Do tell me what your interest in this evening's event might be.'

He moved away from her slightly but his manner remained as relaxed as ever. 'Which is a polite way of saying, what am I doing here without an invitation? You are right, I have no invitation. However I believe the Prince Regent's presence *was* expected and I am here as his humble representative.'

'Then he's not coming this evening?' She felt a keen disappointment and, despite her dislike of Joshua Marchmain, found herself wanting to ask more.

'Did you expect him to?'

'My father was told that he might attend.'

'Then I'm sorry to disappoint you.' Joshua smiled his lazy smile again. 'George is a somewhat indolent prince, I fear, and only rouses himself to action when he anticipates some pleasure from it.'

Marianna was taken aback by his irreverence. 'You are a member of the prince's household?'

'For my sins and at the moment, yes.'

'Then how can you speak so of a royal prince?'

'Believe me, it is quite easy. If one knows the prince.'

'It would seem that you hold the Regent in some aversion. If that is so, why do you stay?'

'Your candour is refreshing, Miss Marquez. It's a question I ask myself most days. So far I haven't found an answer. Perhaps you might provide me with one.'

She looked puzzled. 'I cannot see how.'

'One never can at the time,' he replied cryptically.

She was rapidly tiring of the continual fencing that Mr Marchmain appeared to find essential to conversation, but was too eager to learn of life in the Pavilion to walk away immediately.

'Is the palace very grand inside?' she asked impulsively, and then wished she hadn't. She had no wish to betray her gaucheness in front of this overly assured man.

He smiled indulgently, seeming to find her innocence amusing. 'Yes, I suppose you could call it grand although I'd say rather that it's eccentric. But surely you will be seeing the Pavilion for yourself very soon and will be able to make up your own mind?'

'My father has not yet told me of his plans.'

'Then I shall hope they include a visit to the palace. If so, allow me to offer my services as your guide.'

She had no intention of ever seeking his company, but made the expected polite response. At least for the moment he was conducting himself unexceptionally. Then out of nowhere he disconcerted her once more.

'I understand you have been living in Madrid.'

'How did you know that?' she demanded.

'I ask questions and get a few answers,' he murmured. 'There is a wonderful art gallery in Madrid, the Prado. Do you know it?'

'The Marquez family home is close by.'

'Then you are most fortunate. To be able to look on the genius of Velásquez any day you choose.'

She stared at him in astonishment. 'You are interested in art?'

'A little. I collect when I can. I've recently acquired a small da Vinci – a *very* small one – but I'm quite puffed with pride. When you visit the Pavilion, I would like to show you the studio I have set up.'

'You're an artist yourself?'

'I am a dauber, no more, but painting is a solace.'

If she wondered why a man such as Joshua Marchmain should need solace, she had little time to ponder it. Carmela had arrived at her elbow and was hissing urgently in her ear that they were running out of champagne and would she like to find a solution. The party had been more successful than they had hoped and people had stopped for longer to drink, eat and gossip.

Marianna excused herself and Joshua swept them both a deep bow. Carmela glared at him fiercely before following in her cousin's wake.

'You should keep your distance from that man,' she said in a low voice.

'Do you know him then?' Marianna was surprised.

'No,' her cousin said baldly, 'but every instinct tells me he is not to be trusted and you have spent far too long talking to him.'

'I tried to get away, but he was insistent.' It was only half a lie, she thought guiltily. 'In any case, I doubt I'll meet him again.'

'That is to the good. You must remember always, Marianna, that you are to be married next year.'

'And remember that it's your job to guard me until such time as I have a wedding ring on my finger,' she retorted.

Carmela did not dispute this but hurried her charge into the kitchen.

⌐

Joshua watched them out of sight, smiling wryly. He knew Carmela's type well. How many such duennas had he taken on and vanquished in the course of an inglorious career? But Marianna appeared to have a mind of her own. That and her youthful charm made her a prize worth pursuing; the next few weeks could prove more interesting than he'd expected. He weaved his way through the chattering guests to receive his hat from a bored footman before sauntering through the front door of eight Marine Parade, his step a little livelier than when he had entered.

Chapter Three

The next morning was overcast, the sun hiding behind clouds and the sea a dull grey. It was not a day for walking, but attendance at the Chapel Royal on a Sabbath was essential for the ambassador and his daughter. Carmela had refused point blank to accompany them: nothing would induce her to attend a Protestant church, she said repressively. She would stay at home and perform her own private devotions.

If Marianna and her father felt a little jaded from the previous evening's exertions, a vigorous walk along the promenade on their way to church soon blew away any megrims. Tired they might be, but they were also in good spirits. The reception had gone without a hitch and Ernesto was feeling increasingly optimistic for the success of his mission. Marianna, too, was cheerful, seeing her father so buoyant. To be sure entertaining the *ton* had been daunting, but she had come through her first test with flying colours.

Apart from the impossible Mr Marchmain, nothing had occurred to spoil her pleasure. And even he had intrigued her. He was an enigma, a man of contradictions. She had thought him nothing more than a highly attractive predator, but then he'd announced himself a lover of great art. And an artist himself. He was sufficiently wealthy to laze the summer away in the Prince Regent's very expensive retinue, but seemed to lack the responsibilities that accompanied such wealth. And far from enjoying his exalted position, it appeared to give him little joy.

By the time they had passed the newly opened Chain Pier, a wind had sprung up, blowing from the west. Marianna was forced with one hand to hang on to the Angoulême bonnet with its fetching decoration of golden acorns, while with the other striving to keep under control the delicate confection of peach sarcenet and creamy tulle that billowed around her legs.

'We should perhaps have hired a carriage this morning,' her father said, stopping to help her adjust her bonnet. 'At this rate, your hat is like to be whisked into the sea and travel all the way to France!'

Marianna laughed. 'The wind is certainly tricky but at least I'm now wide awake.'

They walked on again, while her father began to enumerate his plans for the week. She tried to concentrate on what he was telling her, but all the time her mind was busy elsewhere.

'Papa,' she said suddenly, when he fell silent for a moment. 'What do you know of Mr Marchmain?'

'Very little. He is one of the Regent's courtiers, I understand, so no doubt expensive, idle, possibly dissolute.'

Marianna felt dismay at her father's description. Marchmain had been arrogant, patronising and certainly persistent in his unwanted attentions. But dissolute!

'Do not concern yourself, my dear.' Her father patted her hand. 'Members of the Prince Regent's entourage are a law unto themselves. We will have dealings with them only when we must.'

She tried another tack. 'How is it that Joshua Marchmain is only a plain mister? Surely if he belongs to the Regent's company, he should have a title.'

'I believe the young man is related in one way or another to any number of the nobility and has inherited a wealthy estate. He will certainly need it if he keeps company with the Regent for long. But why this interest, *querida?*'

'No real interest, Papa,' she said hastily. 'It was simply that I thought it strange he came to our house last night. He seemed a fish out of water – isn't that the phrase?'

'I think we can say that Mr Marchmain's appearance at our small entertainment was the Regent's overture to Spain. We must accept the overture politely, but still maintain a distance.' He took her arm firmly in his. 'Come, we should step out smartly if we are not to be shamed by our lateness at church.'

They redoubled their pace, the summer wind skirling around their feet and sending up dust and abandoned news sheets into a choking cloud. Brighton was a fashionable resort, almost too fashionable Marianna reflected, and Marine Parade was a less than ideal residence. It was too near the centre of town and attracted promenading society far too readily. She had quickly realised that lodgings close to the Pavilion were in general reserved for young bucks looking forward to a lively few months by the sea, and for the sprinkling of dandies with their pencilled eyebrows and curled mustachios who were always ready to ogle any stray female who crossed their path. She had come to wish that her father had chosen a house on the outskirts of town, but this morning proximity meant they had only a short way to travel before they arrived at the church a few minutes before the last bell ceased tolling.

The Chapel Royal was a square building in the classical style, with rounded sash windows and a row of Doric columns flanking the main door. It was the custom for visitors without their own pew to be charged an entrance fee and Marianna and her father obediently joined a straggling line of worshippers, all waiting to pay their shilling. The queue was moving slowly and they waited for some while to disburse their fee, but as they neared the imposing front door of the church, there was a sudden commotion behind them, a servant pushing his way forward to clear a pathway for his master. She turned to discover who this grand personage might be and received the most appalling shock. Marianna found herself staring into the eyes of the man she had come to loathe when last she was in England.

Robert Amesbury smiled grimly at her. 'Miss Marquez? Imagine that. And there was I thinking never to see you again.'

Her father had turned around and was looking with surprise at the sneering stranger. 'Is this gentleman annoying you, Marianna?' he asked her quietly. She was quick to reassure him and he turned back to pay their shillings.

'I see you have brought reinforcements with you this

time.' The sneer became more pronounced. 'And is your aunt here also, ready to spring to your defence?'

'Lady Foyle remains in London, sir, although I see no reason why that should interest you.'

'On the contrary, Miss Marquez, everything to do with you interests me. I have a long memory even if you do not.'

And with that he pushed in front of her, passing beneath the pediment displaying the Prince Regent's coat of arms and into the church. Marianna was left trembling from the encounter, but anxious that her father should not suspect anything amiss. She linked arms with him and smiled as bravely as she could. 'Shall we go in?'

Seeing Robert Amesbury had been a crippling blow. When she'd agreed to play hostess for her father, she had never for one moment imagined she would meet the man who'd harmed her so badly. If she'd been thinking sensibly, though, she might have known he could well be here and living at the Pavilion. Amesbury was an inveterate gambler and it was said that fortunes were won and lost on a nightly basis at the Regent's tables. Where better for such a man to spend his summer?

It was clear that his malevolence remained unabated, despite Lady Foyle paying him in full her niece's gambling debt. Of course, he had not wanted the money. It was herself, or rather her body, that he'd wanted. That was the prize of which he'd been cheated.

But how could she ever have thought him attractive? A shiver ran through her as though she'd been tiptoeing over a grave, desperate not to disturb dark layers of memory. Her only comfort was her father's assertion that they need have little to do with the Prince Regent or any of his cronies. George, she saw, was not in evidence this morning. Although he had laid the church's foundation stone some twenty-five years ago, Marianna had heard from Marston that the prince had stopped worshipping at the Chapel Royal when a sermon on immorality had offended him.

But there was some compensation to be had. An enormous man with creaking corsets was heaving himself into the pews reserved for the Royal Family a few rows in front of her: the Regent's brother, the Duke of York. He kept up a constant muttering, hardly audible, but nevertheless highly embarrassing to his companions. Their attempts to stifle him made her smile and, for the moment, she forgot the dreadful meeting she had just endured and was emboldened to look about her.

The galleried church was filled with decoration, its supporting columns and pulpit highly embellished, while a large organ in burnished copper thundered from above the altar. It was a rich man's building. She looked sideways across the aisle, scanning a busy canvas of faces, but hoping to stay out of Amesbury's sight.

Immediately beneath one of the galleries, a countenance she was beginning to know swam into view. Joshua was gazing at her, an appreciative smile on his face. He was dressed more soberly this morning, she noticed, but the familiar lock of bright hair swept his brow and the sprawl of his figure spoke his usual confidence.

Marianna's glance moved on to the woman who sat next to him – there was something proprietorial in her attitude.

She was richly dressed in an ensemble of emerald green Venetian silk and her hair was covered with a headpiece of ostrich feathers. The feathers swayed slightly in the current of air, their height ensuring that those who sat immediately behind could see little of the service at the altar.

The rector spoke at length that morning but Marianna felt unable to profit from his homily. She was too uncomfortable, too conscious that she shared the church with men she wished at all costs to avoid, and was relieved when the final hymn reverberated through the high ceiling beams and she was able to walk from the church into a burst of sunshine. The rector was at the door to greet his parishioners and, once again, they were forced to wait patiently in line before they could pass through the narrow entrance.

'Pious as well as pretty,' a voice said quietly in her ear. 'It gets better all the time.'

She turned to face him, grateful that her father was engaged in talking to a fellow communicant. 'Still accosting unwilling women, Mr Marchmain?' she snapped back.

'Never unwilling, Miss Marquez.'

Her face flushed scarlet as she realised the implication of his remark. She was about to retort angrily when a different voice cut across their interchange.

'Joshua, why don't you introduce me to your delightful new friend?'

It was the richly dressed woman she had seen sitting next to him in the pew. A look of irritation flitted across his face but it was gone in a moment.

'But of course. Miss Marquez, may I present the Duchess

of Severn. Charlotte, Miss Marquez – the daughter of our new ambassador from Spain.'

'How delightful to have you in Brighton, my dear.'

She wasn't sure she liked the woman. The duchess seemed to purr when she spoke and the glances she cast towards the waiting Joshua verged on the covetous. But Marianna curtsied decorously and made her father known to the lady.

'You must both come to one of my small *soirées* as soon as possible,' Charlotte Severn said smoothly. 'I will send an invitation this very week. I am sure Joshua will know your direction.'

Marianna sensed a hidden meaning, but managed to smile politely and hope that her father would conjure some excuse for their not attending.

'She is a very fine lady, is she not, Papa?' she asked, as they made their way back along the promenade.

'Who?'

'The Duchess of Severn.'

'She is finely dressed at least.'

'You don't sound as though you like her.'

'I don't know her, Marianna, but I dislike the set she moves in. I would prefer you to have as little to do with her as possible.'

'Mr Marchmain seems to know her well,' she ventured.

'Indeed he does,' her father said grimly, then abruptly changed the subject.

Marianna was left to puzzle over just what had vexed him so badly.

Chapter Four

Joshua turned abruptly on his heels and headed back towards the Pavilion, his temper fraying. He needed to be alone and Charlotte Severn could easily be left to the escort of Amesbury, whom he'd noticed in the distance. He was annoyed with her for intervening in his conversation with Marianna and angry that she had promised an invitation to one of her celebrated *soirées.* He wasn't sure why but he wanted to keep Marianna to himself, or at the very least not expose her to the intimacies of the Severn household. He had no intention of seducing the young girl, that was not his style, but neither did he want her knowing a woman such as Charlotte. That lady might be the wife of one of the premier dukes of the land, but she had the soul of a courtesan.

The role suited her well and she should stick to it rather than attempting to befriend the young and inexperienced. The Royal Pavilion was a suitable milieu for her, boasting every kind of dubious pleasure – and she had a husband happy to look away while she played. His Grace was content in his declining years to puff off his wife's beauty and retire to the lure of the gaming table, being one of the

Regent's most assiduous companions, not least because he was so wealthy that it mattered little to him how much money he lost.

Charlotte had access to wealth untold but that was not enough, Joshua reflected wryly. It hardly compensated for a dull and ageing husband. He remembered when he'd first seen her two years ago. Wiesbaden it was, at the town's most opulent casino, and seated at the hazard table. She had looked across at him, her eyes staring straight into his, their porcelain blue still and expressionless, but nevertheless saying all they needed to say.

That very night they had become lovers – from time to time they still continued to meet. But for long stretches of the year the duchess was unable to avoid the duties incumbent on her position and that suited Joshua well. There were always others happy to keep him company, and lengthy periods of absence had until recently staved off the inevitable *ennui* that acquaintance with any woman eventually produced. Or any woman since that first disastrous love affair.

But things were changing. Was it the sea air stirring his blood and making him restless? Charlotte Severn no longer beguiled him and his frustration at being part of the Regent's sycophantic court had acquired a sharper edge. That girl – she had something to do with it. It wasn't just that he wanted to bed her; that was as certain as it was unlikely. It was, he thought, that he'd begun to enjoy their encounters, enjoy her vitality, her verve, the zest with which she resisted his raillery. He'd met her on three occasions and each time behind his mockery he'd wanted to explore, to discover more, to know her.

Today she had looked enchanting in peaches and cream and yet another rakish bonnet, and beneath its brim, those dark tragic eyes looking out at him. Eyes filled with scorn. They could be made to wear another expression, he was sure. If ever he felt mad enough to risk exile again, he would savour the challenge. Instead he'd thought to seek her out whenever possible, enjoy the small delights of chaste encounters.

But now Charlotte had stepped between them, muddying the waters, and placing her footprint where only his had previously been. The woman's company had never seemed more irksome.

⌒

The duchess was waiting for him in the outer vestibule of the Pavilion. If his temper had improved with the circuitous route he had taken, hers certainly had not. He barely had a foot through the door when she addressed him in a voice crisp with indignation.

'There you are Mr Marchmain. I had begun to think I had lost you.'

'Why is that Your Grace?' He would be as formal as she.

'Not unnaturally I awaited your escort from the Chapel Royal. But when I turned to call on your services, you had gone.'

'Forgive me. I felt in need of a longer walk and I am aware that it is not a pastime you favour.'

'A walk with you is always a pleasure, Joshua,' she replied in a more conciliatory tone.

'Then forgive me once more. Had I known, I would

certainly have requested your company.' It was a lie that he knew she would not believe.

She fixed him with a cold eye. 'How is that you know the ambassador's daughter?'

'I was representing the Regent last night, if you remember,' he said indifferently. 'We met at her father's diplomatic reception.'

'You seem already to be on good terms with her.'

'Why should I not be? I understand the need for England to maintain a good relationship with Spain.'

'Ah, so that's what it is,' she responded waspishly.

Robert Amesbury had strode into the Octagon Hall while they stood talking and viewed the two tense figures with satirical amusement.

'Quite a breeze blowing out there,' he offered, with an assumed bonhomie. 'That's the problem with the sea, you're never without a wind. Hopefully Prinny will soon get bored with his coastal delights and leave for Carlton House within the month.'

His audience remained resolutely silent and his eyebrows rose enquiringly. 'Am I guilty of interrupting a private conversation? If so, my profuse apologies.'

'Apologies are unnecessary. Your manners are never anything but perfect, Amesbury,' Joshua remarked acidly, unable to conceal his dislike. 'Her Grace and I were just about to part.'

And with that he strode off to his rooms, leaving Robert Amesbury looking quizzically at the duchess.

'I realise I am hardly a favourite of Marchmain's but beyond my unwelcome presence, what ails him?'

'I imagine no more than a tedious sermon and a cold walk from the Chapel Royal.'

'He seemed ruffled – uncharacteristically so.'

'I may have annoyed him,' the duchess admitted, her voice carefully neutral.

'How so?'

'I invited a young woman who appears to have become his *protégée* to one of my *soirées*. That apparently is not something to be done.'

'And why not exactly?'

'Possibly he thinks I may corrupt her innocence.' Charlotte said the words with a knowing little smile. 'Would you be so good, Robert, as to escort me back to Steine House, a trifling distance I know, but I prefer to have a reliable man by my side.'

Lord Amesbury was swift to offer his arm and they sailed past the waiting footman and out into the Pavilion Gardens. He was not to be put off the scent, however.

'How innocent exactly is this young woman?' he asked. 'It seems unlikely if she knows Joshua Marchmain well.'

'Don't be so crude, Robert. Joshua is a gentleman.'

'You think so? Never trust a man not to sully innocence.'

'I suppose you should know,' she answered in a bored voice. 'Your reputation goes before you.'

'At least I make no pretence to be other than I am,' he responded harshly. 'Marchmain is as much a rake; his pretence is to be something else.'

'Joshua is a man of the world but he is not a rake. He has discrimination.'

'In seeking *you* out, dear lady?'

'In seeking out a woman who is mature and experienced and with whom he can enjoy life to the full.'

'As opposed to a girl who is young and naïve, yet sends his heartstrings singing.'

She bit her lip viciously and seeing it, Amesbury said slyly, 'Don't say, my dear, that you've fallen in love with him. Not a good policy, not at all.'

'Joshua and I understand each other very well.'

'I wonder.'

'What do you mean by that?'

'I wonder how well. After all you knew nothing about this girl until today.'

They had arrived at Steine House and Amesbury stood back for his companion to ascend the steps to the front door. But the duchess paused, a frown on her otherwise unblemished forehead.

'That is because he made her acquaintance only last night.'

Amesbury's expression was bland. 'And who is this paragon of unsullied innocence?'

'Her name is Marianna Marquez.' The man beside her stiffened imperceptibly. 'Why, what is the matter?'

'Marquez you say?'

'Yes, do you know her?'

'Shall we say I've had dealings with her.'

'It sounds as though they were not entirely to your liking.' Charlotte's frown had vanished, replaced by a small smile.

'They were not. I have a score to settle.'

'I see.' She glanced covertly at the man beside her, but he took his time before he spoke again.

'Are you perhaps interested? We might work well together.'

'We might,' she replied consideringly, 'but for the moment I prefer to see what I can accomplish alone.'

'Then let me give you a hint. Gaming.'

'Gaming? In what way?'

'A small chink in the armour. It is fatally easy is it not, when you are young and inexperienced, to find yourself adrift in a world you do not understand? Fatally easy to lose money, for instance, that you do not have. Think of the shame if that were made public, the scandal that would follow, the necessity instantly to withdraw from society.'

'You are a wicked man, Robert.'

'A practical man, my dear. And practical is what you should be. Marchmain may be the gentleman you profess but he *is* a man and women find him very attractive. Think of that.'

The duchess did think of it. She hurried into the house and up to her bedchamber, calling immediately for paper and pen.

Chapter Five

Marianna thought little more of Charlotte Severn. If the woman's invitation ever materialised she was sure she could depend on her father to rescue her. But Ernesto was busier than ever and it seemed to Marianna that days passed when she barely saw him. Looking for occupation, she decided to seek out one of the many art galleries that had sprung up in and around Brighton under the Regent's patronage. Prince George loved art and so by default did his courtiers, or at least maintained the pretence that they did. But rather than attend the Picture Gallery on Grand Parade, which boasted an unrivalled collection of Italian and French art, she chose a newer and much quieter gallery situated to the north of the town.

It was an unfashionable area and little visited by the nobility, but Marianna had recently seen a flyer advertising the Grove Gallery's latest exhibition and had been intrigued by the more experimental art it was offering for sale. Mindful of Carmela's repeated injunctions, she took Flora with her.

It was a beautiful early July morning when they struck

inland towards New England farm and the scattering of modern houses that had been built nearby. A delighted Flora chattered incessantly as they walked. Accompanying her mistress was a rare treat and she was determined to provide whatever entertainment she could on the arduous walk uphill. Marianna listened with only one ear, hoping her maid would run out of words well before they reached their destination.

Thirty minutes walking brought them to the top of the Dyke Road, the main thoroughfare north out of Brighton – and Flora was still talking. They found the gallery easily enough, the only building apart from a scattering of new villas, set amongst fields in which a large herd of cows was grazing placidly. Not even Carmela could find dangers lurking in such a tranquil setting, Marianna thought, and felt justified in asking the garrulous Flora to await her outside.

As she trod over the threshold, a grateful silence fell like a cloak. The interior of the building was bright and airy, a large rectangular space, its walls hung with green baize and its floor covered by a rough drugget. The paintings were displayed seemingly at random, but the brilliant light emanating high up from latticed casements that encircled the entire top of the rectangle, provided sufficient illumination. Marianna looked around her with pleasure.

The paintings were certainly unusual. She wasn't at all sure she liked them, though for the most part they were ingeniously executed. But there was one landscape that caught her eye and slowed her steps: the Downs on a tempestuous day, the grass, the bushes, the trees, all bending seawards in the southerly wind, seeming to tumble unstoppably towards the racing waters in the distance. The painting brought to life a glorious sense of freedom, so strong that she felt her breath catch with excitement.

She wanted to wake every morning to that wild landscape, feel its thrum, its energy, but the price tag was way beyond her means. Perhaps, she thought wistfully, she could return next year when she would have inherited the large fortune that awaited her. But then someone else would hold the purse strings.

Perhaps that someone else would have a love of art, too, would see how very special this picture was. But no, that was too fanciful. If her new husband took any pleasure in painting, it would not be an English landscape that would hang in his bedroom. *Our* bedroom, she thought, and quaked at the thought of the intimacies she must share with a virtual stranger.

'Are you going to buy it?'

Joshua Marchmain! The man seemed for ever destined to disturb her peace. He had expressed a strong interest in art, but why had he chosen to visit this morning and this gallery? The latter was soon explained.

'You would be doing a friend of mine a favour if you did – buy it, I mean.'

His voice was light and amused. She looked at him smiling easily down at her, a shaft of sunlight pouring through the glass atrium above and reflecting pinpoints of light in the gold of his hair. As always he was immaculately dressed: a perfectly cut coat of dark blue superfine, an embroidered waistcoat of paler blue and close fitting cream pantaloons.

Despite the fashionable dress, he was no dandy. Marianna was acutely aware of his body, taut and hard. A body a woman could melt against. A wave of desire suddenly knotted her stomach and began its destructive trail through every fibre. She was genuinely shocked at her response and there was an uncomfortable pause before she was able to gather her wits and wish him a prim good morning.

'I take it that your friend is the painter and this is his exhibition.'

'It is and he is doing the painterly thing and starving in a garret.'

'Then surely, you should be helping him.'

'I'm very willing but he won't hear of it. He maintains that he must live by his brush and his brush alone, and there are only so many paintings an individual can buy. So you see how important it is that you purchase his most treasured work. It's a splendid scene, is it not?'

Alarm bells were ringing loudly in her head and had been since she'd first heard his voice. She should murmur something innocuous and move on, but somehow found herself replying with genuine warmth.

'I think it wonderful – so wild and natural, so full of energy and joy.'

'Now I wonder why those qualities should appeal to you?'

The familiar flush flamed her cheeks and seeing it, he made a vow to tread more carefully. He was intrigued by this delightful girl and, if he wanted to know her better, he must be sure to confine his remarks to the unexceptional.

He offered her his arm. 'Since we are both here, Miss Marquez, do allow me to escort you around the rest of the exhibition.'

She hesitated for a fraction and he was relieved when her good manners triumphed. A lace-mittened hand was placed lightly on his arm and they began a stately progress around the gallery, stopping at a picture here, a pciture there, while he shared all he knew about his friend's art.

She was simply dressed in sprig muslin, he noticed, but its soft folds and pleats revealed an exquisite young figure. As they walked slowly side by side around the vast space, her warm limbs occasionally touched his and he felt his body stiffen in response. He wondered what those delightful curves would feel like beneath his hands and how soft that full mouth would be in meeting his.

'How have you become so knowledgeable, Mr Marchmain?'

Her words cut through the fantasy and he was forced to administer a sharp mental shake before he could reply. 'I think you might find the experts would quarrel with that word knowledgeable. But I've travelled widely in Europe and have always made a point of seeking out the very best art each city could offer.'

'And are you always travelling?' she asked.

His voice when he answered was unusually sombre. 'There were a few years when I stayed put, years when I rented rooms in a Venetian palazzo. I found that an ideal location for painting.'

'It must have been. I've only ever seen pictures of Venice and I long to visit myself.'

'Then you must, and as soon as possible. I would say that you were made for the city.' His gaze lingered on her: the creamy olive skin, upturned nose, sorrowful dark eyes, did not make a classical beauty, but something infinitely more charming.

She blushed again and he silently chided himself. She was bewitching, that was the problem. She was so serious and yet so full of youthful zest that he wanted to open up the world for her and watch her smile. He was surprised by the force of his feelings.

'And do you still stay in Venice?'

'No longer, I fear. I inherited a property in England and it became necessary to return and become a responsible proprietor.'

'So where is your home now?'

'I would hardly call it home but the house is known as Castle March. It's in Norfolk. Do you know it?'

When she shook her head, he said, 'It's a large estate and needs managing. I ought to spend more time there but ruralising in the depths of the English countryside is not my *forte*.'

'I am sure that country living must have its own attraction.'

'Possibly, but only I imagine if you have someone with whom to share it.' Instantly, he wished he'd remained silent. It was the kind of remark that sent her into retreat and he tried to retrieve the situation. 'It can be pretty bleak in the fens for much of the year so company is always welcome,' he offered.

But Marianna had taken fright and detached herself

from his arm. She adjusted the ribbons of her bonnet and thanked him prettily but firmly for his escort. In a minute she had disappeared out of the door and he was left to fume at his clumsiness. For a man of his address he was managing extremely poorly. What was it about her that made him as maladroit as an untried adolescent? It could only be the enchantment of youth. For years he had strictly confined his most intimate attentions to experienced women – he had forgotten how utterly disarming innocent beauty could be.

⌒

As soon as Marianna stepped through the front door of Marine Parade she saw the letter. It sat, almost menacingly, on the hall table, and she knew immediately from whom it came. The envelope was of thick cream vellum and bore a ducal crest. Charlotte Severn's invitation had arrived. The duchess's words uttered in the heat of the moment had been made good, but Marianna had no wish to open the letter. She had taken the woman in dislike, why exactly she was unsure, but her father's condemnation had served only to underline the distaste she felt.

It was clear that the duchess was a close friend of Joshua Marchmain and was certain to attend her social events. For that reason alone, Marianna would be reluctant to go. She had spent an engaging hour with him this afternoon, but he was a man she needed to avoid. He was dangerous to her peace of mind: his languorous gaze had made her whole body burn in shameful response, promising the kind of pleasure she dared not think of.

And he was most definitely not a gentleman. He might

dress as one and mix with ease in *ton* society, but he was too bold, too reckless, and he constantly put her out of countenance. How very unlike her dear Luke, who was just as handsome but mindful of the proprieties, and careful never to overstep the line. Joshua would not even recognise the existence of a line. He was undoubtedly a libertine, a charming one, but someone with whom she must have no further commerce.

But her assumption that her father would prevent her attending the entertainment at Steine House proved false. When Ernesto walked into the dining room that evening, he was waving the duchess's card in his hand.

'The Duchess of Severn.' Then seeing his daughter's long face, he said firmly, 'I think we must attend, Marianna.'

'Could you not go alone, Papa?'

'I would prefer to, certainly. I am not at all eager that you further your acquaintance with the lady. But I fear we would give grave offence if you were to refuse.'

'But I'm of no importance,' she said persuasively. 'It is your position as ambassador that has prompted her to write.'

'I think not. The invitation was issued directly to you at the Chapel Royal. And my position, as you put it, means that I dare not offend anyone as influential as the Severns. The duke belongs to the Regent's inner circle.'

Marianna made no reply but sat erect, hands in her lap, and looked blankly ahead.

'Will it be such a trial, *querida*? We will stay no more than a couple of hours, I promise. And you will have me by your side the whole time.'

'I'm sorry, Papa, I'm being a goose.' Marianna leaned across the table and gave his hands a loving squeeze. 'I'd thought the duchess had forgotten me.'

'Unfortunately not. I only hope her remembrance does not signify that she wishes "to take you up", as they say here. Your standing would not be enhanced by her favour.' Ernesto sighed deeply. 'I always knew that negotiating our way successfully through the English court would not be easy, but I may have underestimated the difficulties.'

Then a thought struck him and he brightened. 'Carmela can attend with us, then your being singled out for an invitation will not look so particular.'

Carmela, who had retired from the table and was sitting on the cushioned window seat reading an improving work, put her book down with a sharp slap. Her face glowered.

'I mean no disrespect to you, cousin, but nothing on earth would induce me to attend that woman's party.'

'Carmela, how is this? She may not be precisely to our taste but she is a great noblewoman,' Ernesto chided her.

'Is that what you call it? We have a different word for it in Spain.'

He looked warningly at her and then back to Marianna.

'What is that, Carmela?' Marianna asked innocently.

er cousinHer cousin compressed her lips. 'Suffice to say that she is a married woman but does not behave as one. She would not be welcome at any house belonging to our family.'

Marianna looked shocked. 'You mean she has lovers?'

Carmela appeared to struggle with herself for a moment, but then decided where her duty lay. 'I do not generally indulge in idle gossip, as I hope you know,' she said repressively, 'but I think it right that you should be on your guard. In the few weeks we have been in Brighton I have heard disquieting things of the Duchess of Severn. I believe that her current lover has followed her here and is even now residing at the Pavilion.'

Marianna glanced at her father, urgently seeking his reassurance, but no denial was forthcoming. His face was set and he refused to meet her eyes. Suddenly she understood. Joshua Marchmain was that lover. That was why he had been so irritated at the Chapel Royal. He had not wanted her to make the duchess's acquaintance, had not wanted her to know the truth of their supposed friendship. She felt herself flushing hotly, embarrassed at having been so naïve. Flushing, too, with a kind of pain. But why on earth did she feel that? Had she been stupid enough to think there was any kind of connection between them?

She should remember her first encounter with him as she walked by the sea: his conduct had been predatory – light-hearted and amusing, it was true – but nevertheless predatory. And outside the church on Sunday, he'd not been able to resist throwing out lures to her. He was a womaniser for whom every female was fair game, even as his mistress was living a mere stone's throw away. The thought of visiting Steine House was loathsome.

Chapter Six

A few days later an unwelcome message arrived at Marine Parade. Señor Marquez was required to return to London immediately. News had arrived from Spain too confidential to be entrusted to a messenger and it was necessary for the ambassador to post up to Manchester House. He would spend only one night away, but it looked unlikely that he would return to Brighton in time for Charlotte Severn's *soirée*.

Ernesto was faced with a quandary. He had no wish to expose his daughter to the malign influence of Steine House without his protection but, at the same time, he knew it essential that he was represented at what would be a prestigious affair.

'I hardly like to ask this of you, *querida*,' he began tentatively, 'but would you be willing to go alone to the duchess's concert and stay for a short while without me? I will be home by evening and will make haste to join you at Steine House.' He paused for a while, and then took a deep breath. 'Or perhaps Carmela might swallow her misgivings? Cousin, if you would agree to attend, it would make things a great deal more comfortable.'

The despondent look on both the women's faces promised little comfort. Attending the event without the support of Señor Marquez was the last thing either of them wished to contemplate. But after a tense few minutes they found themselves agreeing to his suggestion, Marianna because she loved her father dearly and knew he would not ask this of her unless it was necessary and Carmela because the family's honour was at stake and that was sufficient to call forth her loyalty.

⌒

So it was that at six o'clock on a balmy Friday evening the two of them set off in a hired carriage for Steine House. It had an infamous reputation since it was the home the Regent had purchased for his long standing mistress and unofficial wife, Maria Fitzherbert. She still resided there and was hardly ever seen beyond its walls, though the Prince was said even now to visit her frequently, despite a legal marriage and many subsequent lovers – rumour insisted that a tunnel ran via the adjoining Marlborough House to the basement of the royal palace.

The Duke of Severn was an old friend of Mrs Fitzherbert and he and his wife were always made welcome in her home when they visited the town. The duke in particular could not bear to live permanently in the overheated Pavilion and always availed himself of this hospitality.

The whispers that swirled around Steine House could only sharpen the aversion both Marianna and her cousin felt at having to enter its portals. But when their carriage stopped outside, they saw only a graceful white stucco building with an Italian style façade and trellised balconies.

A balustrade of carved ironwork led up a single flight of steps and a heavily ornamented glass door. Marianna pinned on what she hoped was a polite smile and made ready to greet her hosts.

She received a courteous welcome, the duke seeming to her young eyes horribly withered and old. No wonder the duchess looked elsewhere she mused, and then promptly castigated herself for such an appalling thought – it seemed Steine House was already having a noxious effect. Once inside the main door they were directed up a bamboo and iron staircase to a salon from which the strains of music could already be heard.

'This is the staircase Lord Barrymore once rode his horse up for a bet,' Carmela hissed in her ear.

Marianna paused on the stairs, startled for a moment by her staid cousin's incongruous knowledge of *ton* gossip. Where on earth did she hear such stories? But then her attention was deflected as she caught sight of her reflection in the long pier glass that hung at the top of the stairs. She was pleased with what she saw. The apricot silk she had chosen, trimmed with gold edging and worn with an overdress of vanilla gauze, was the perfect foil for her skin. Dark, glossy curls fell to her neck in natural ringlets and her eyes, she noticed, were sparkling, if only in apprehension. Carmela leaned forward and tapped her wrist sharply with her fan, a painful reminder that in her cousin's book any sign of vanity was sinful.

In a few moments they were in the large salon, a huge scarlet cavern of a room hung with red satin drapes and upholstered in red plush velvet. A uniformed footman ushered them to one of the rows of little gold chairs that had been arranged in the shape of a wide semi-circle. Marianna lowered herself gingerly onto one of the tiny seats.

'Be careful, Carmela,' she warned, 'these chair legs are so thin that one false fidget and the sound of breaking wood will drown out the string quartet.'

Carmela permitted herself a slight smile and looked searchingly around the room. 'I see nobody who came to our reception,' she remarked disappointedly. 'How strange when a most famous soprano is to sing.'

'Evidently our guests have decided to miss whatever pleasures the duchess has arranged.' Including Joshua Marchmain, Marianna noted.

She told herself that she was glad that at least this evening she would not have to face *him*. Yet unaccountably she felt a pang of disappointment. She had enjoyed her tour of the Grove Gallery. True, she'd been put out of countenance once or twice, but she had spent nigh on an hour in Joshua's company discussing nothing more incendiary than art and European travel. He was interesting and intelligent and, though he had visited places she could only dream of, he'd not made her feel the gauche girl she knew herself to be.

But she must put him out of her mind – completely. Rumour had named him the lover of any number of married women, including Charlotte Severn. Could rumour have possibly lied? In her heart she knew it had not. Mr Marchmain was a thorough going rake and if the sensations of her own unruly body were anything to judge by, he did not have to work too hard for his success. The shaft of intense desire that had pierced her so suddenly and so unexpectedly signalled clearly that she was in danger of being drawn into a whirlpool of feeling, with him at its centre. It was well for her that he was not here this evening.

There was a sudden hush as the duke led the famous singer, who had journeyed from Milan at his request, to a raised platform, kissing her hand enthusiastically. 'My lords, ladies and gentlemen,' he declaimed. 'I give you the illustrious soprano, Bianca Bonelli.'

The string quartet began to play the opening piece of music and Marianna set herself to listen with what she hoped was a thoughtful expression.

A late-arriving Joshua, hovering in the doorway, spotted her immediately and almost laughed aloud when he saw her face, screwed up in concentration. Or was it pain? If so, it was a pain he shared. He made a swift escape to the library where he would not be disturbed, but from where he could still hear the concert's end.

And end it did, with a great deal of relief on Marianna's part. But Carmela's spontaneous applause made clear how much she had enjoyed the performance, despite her severe expression never wavering. Marianna was not surprised – the music had evinced a moral seriousness sufficient even for her cousin. The latter seemed eager to meet the musicians personally and, when the duchess suddenly appeared at their side, Carmela was whisked away for introductions and Marianna found herself led by Charlotte into an adjoining salon where liveried footmen were circulating with drinks and canapés.

Her Grace deftly lifted two large flutes of champagne from a passing tray and handed one to her guest, saying warmly, 'I am so pleased you were able to come, Miss Marquez. I collect your father has been forced to post back to London on urgent business.'

'Indeed, Your Grace. He sends his most sincere apologies and will make every effort to join us later this evening.'

'I understand,' she cooed, 'and really it matters not. You are my prize after all. I was entranced when we met at the Chapel Royal on Sunday and have spent all week wishing to know more of you.'

Marianna doubted that very much. The woman's insincerity was blatant, but she managed a gentle smile in response.

'Tell me do,' the duchess continued, 'how long are we to have the pleasure of your company in Brighton?'

'For the summer, ma'am. I have undertaken to stay with my father while the Court is absent from London.'

For a moment the expression on her hostess's face suggested she was not best pleased by this news, but she rallied immediately. 'How delightful, for we are also destined to be here until the prince returns to Carlton House. Let us toast our new acquaintanceship, Miss Marquez. I am sure we will be the best of friends.'

Marianna could not think so but politely raised her glass. Champagne bubbles shot up her nose and she had difficulty in preventing herself from sneezing.

'You see,' Charlotte continued, 'one meets so few new people in Brighton, the same dreary crowd year after year. So when a bright new star appears, one is drawn immediately towards them.'

Marianna concluded that she must be the bright star,

but was at a loss how to answer. She need not have worried since the duchess was now in full flow.

'You are so beautiful, my dear, and have such charming manners, that I prophesy prodigious success for you – you will be the toast of the town.'

This was so patently absurd that Marianna was hard put not to laugh aloud. She knew herself to be well enough but, against the duchess's blonde perfection, she was nothing. And she certainly had no ambition to take Brighton by storm. Quite the opposite. She looked forward to several agreeable months by the sea, spent quietly in her father's company, before she returned to Spain to make the decision of her life.

The duchess continued to talk while Marianna sipped her champagne. The drink was gradually becoming more acceptable so that when her companion substituted her empty glass for another fizzing to the brim, she hardly noticed. And when the older woman took her by the hand, she allowed herself to be expertly steered through the crowd towards a smaller chamber at the far end of the salon.

'In proof of my friendship, Miss Marquez – but may I call you Marianna, such a sweet name – I would very much like you to meet some particular friends of mine. Just a few congenial spirits whom I know you will appreciate.'

Her head had begun to spin a little, but she retained enough caution to remind her hostess that Carmela should be with them.

'But naturally, my dear. I shall introduce you to a few dear companions and then collect your cousin and bring her instantly to you.'

They were through the door before Marianna could protest further. The room they entered, though smaller than the last salon, was still a substantial size, thickly carpeted and curtained in a way that deadened all sound and cut the space adrift from the outside world. A number of people were gathered around three large tables set at different angles in the room and even in Marianna's befuddled state, she knew instantly that this was a gaming room. She pulled back sharply.

'I am honoured, Your Grace, that you should wish to introduce me to your friends,' she stumbled, 'but I do not play cards.'

'Allow me to advise you, my dear, since you are still so very young.' The duchess's voice was honey. 'You have undertaken to play the role of hostess for your father, I believe. In England polite society expects always to have the opportunity to indulge in games of chance and a hostess must be as well-versed in them as her guests.'

'I thank you again, Your Grace, but I do not gamble.'

'Who said anything about gambling? Just a few friendly games, my dear.'

Marianna felt deeply uncomfortable. She was finding it very difficult to gainsay her hostess but games of chance, whether money passed hands or not, were something she had sworn never again to engage in. She had learned her lesson all too well the last time she was in England. Gambling had a fatal attraction for her and she could not risk getting involved. But she could hardly say this to someone she barely knew, and to a woman who occupied such an exalted position.

Her head was definitely swimming now and her legs feeling decidedly unsafe. She felt the duchess's hand on her shoulder and began to sink downwards to the waiting chair. The faces around the table looked up at her expectantly. In the distance, other faces at other tables blurred into a misty vision. She longed to get away but could not in politeness leave. Surely just one hand of cards would not matter. She would satisfy the demands of hospitality and then depart straight away. She took hold of the arms of the chair, making ready to sit down, and the support made her feel slightly less shaky. She smiled hazily at the assembled company and then out of the blur, a face swam into her vision. A dark, wolfish, horribly familiar face. Robert Amesbury!

Chapter Seven

Marianna felt her limbs tremble, shaken by a sudden, irrational panic, and would have collapsed but for a supportive hand at her elbow.

'Miss Marquez? How nice to see you here.' Joshua Marchmain's voice penetrated her fear. 'I hope you found the music to your taste.'

'Yes, indeed, thank you,' she stuttered.

He was holding his arm out to her and she took it. Nervously she glanced at the woman who stood at her left side. Charlotte Severn's eyes were narrowed, but there was no mistaking the daggers she was sending forth.

'The concert *was* delightful, was it not, and such a privilege to hear Signora Bonelli?' Joshua continued. 'I believe she is judged one of the finest sopranos of our day.' His voice was unruffled, but even as he spoke he was skilfully extricating her apricot silk from the entanglement of chair and table.

By now the duchess had regained her composure and, in a gesture of seeming warmth, clasped hold of Marianna's other arm.

'But must you go already?' She addressed the girl directly,

excluding Joshua from the conversation. 'I am delighted that you enjoyed our small concert, but do stay for the rest of the evening's entertainment.'

Her head still whirling, Marianna was caught between the two and had no idea how to cope with such a dreadful situation. It was one scenario the etiquette books had failed to mention. She saw Joshua lock glances with the duchess. His voice was imperturbable as ever, but there was an edge of steel that Marianna had never heard before.

'It does not seem, Your Grace, that card playing holds much attraction for Miss Marquez. In which case, I will engage to reunite her with her cousin.'

Leaving their hostess stranded with outstretched hand, he propelled Marianna firmly towards the door and whisked her through it. Once on the other side, he cut a swathe through the milling crowd to arrive unerringly at Carmela's side. Her cousin wore a worried expression which turned rapidly to exasperation once she saw Marianna safe and well. Nodding curtly to Joshua, she grabbed Marianna by the arm, and brushing social politeness aside, made for the bamboo staircase without waiting to bid their hosts goodbye.

'I've ordered the carriage,' she muttered. 'It will be waiting for us.'

Catching her breath at the head of the stairs, Marianna had only time to glance briefly over her shoulder. Joshua Marchmain had not spoken a word as they'd threaded their way through the crowded room, but now she saw him in conversation with the duchess, their heads close and talking animatedly. Her heart lurched as she took in the intimacy of the little tableau.

But why did the image cause her such distress? While Carmela was bundling her down the stairs and into the coach, she struggled to find an answer. Why on earth should Joshua's relationship with the duchess matter? She knew them to be lovers and naturally they would have much to say to each other. He would be keen to explain his absence from the concert and his intervention with Marianna, even keener no doubt to make an assignation with his mistress for later that evening. It all made perfect sense but only served to intensify her misery.

~

Unknown to Marianna, however, her departure had left the two locked in a furious exchange.

'What exactly were you thinking of?' Cold anger permeated Joshua's voice.

'I don't pretend to understand you.'

'I think you understand me perfectly. Miss Marquez is still a minor and yet you were encouraging her to break the law by gambling.'

'Don't be ridiculous.' The duchess fairly spat the words. 'I merely suggested to her that she might like to join a select gathering and play a few rounds of loo.'

'A select gathering – is that what you call it?' He snorted derisively.

'Is it possible you decided to put in an appearance this evening for reasons other than to be unpleasant?'

'It's as well I did. It was clear the girl did not want to stay and just as clear that you were intent on forcing her.'

'What rubbish. How could I ever force her to do

anything she didn't wish? If you had not interrupted us in that nonsensical manner, she would be happily playing cards right now.'

'Playing cards I am sure, but happily I don't believe.'

'I say again, how could I make her play cards if she did not wish it?' The duchess's expression was scornful.

'I imagine a few judicious glasses of champagne might help to do the trick, together with pressure from her hostess that she would find difficult to resist.'

'You talk as though she were an innocent. It won't have been the first time she has supped champagne, I'm sure, and from what I hear she has been more than happy to engage in games of chance in the past. Even dare I say, to accrue considerable debts.'

'How can that be?'

For an instant, Joshua appeared less composed and the duchess watched him with a gloating expression. 'Why don't you ask her? The two of you seem remarkably thick with each other. And why *are* you so late? The concert is long finished.'

'I am devastated to have missed it,' he said with barely concealed irony, 'and naturally I apologise. I was visiting a friend – a fellow artist – and was detained unexpectedly.'

'Your visit must have been important,' came the brittle rejoinder and giving him a final cold stare, she walked away to mingle with her guests in the inner sanctum. Robert Amesbury was waiting for her.

'I can see why you wanted to handle the matter yourself.' His smile was sardonic.

'I was wrong. She was far more stubborn than I gave

her credit for. But I think I'd have succeeded in the end if Marchmain had not turned up and spoilt the game.'

'And you still feel she is of no interest to him?'

The duchess did not answer him directly, but said slowly and deliberately, 'I need to get rid of her.'

There was a slight pause before Amesbury said in a heartening voice, 'Don't be too discouraged, Charlotte. It would have been difficult to coax her to stay once she saw my face. There must be more subtle ways to catch our little bird.'

'You have some ideas?'

'I have some ideas. Shall we now work together?'

Charlotte Severn's nod was almost imperceptible, but Lord Amesbury retired that night a contented man.

⌒

Marianna slept fitfully that night and woke unrefreshed to a new day. The events at Steine House still crowded her mind, jangled impressions only half understood, but all of them contributing to her unhappiness. How was she to make sense of the dreadful evening? The concert had evoked stifled yawns, but at least it had been innocuous. It was the Duchess of Severn herself who appeared far from innocent, yet she'd seemed so friendly, so keen to make Marianna's acquaintance. Despite her dubious reputation, Charlotte Severn was enormously influential and her notice of a mere ambassador's daughter would for most be a cause of pleasure and gratitude. But Marianna had felt neither pleased nor grateful.

Instead she had felt manipulated, even coerced. She'd not wanted to abandon Carmela but the Duchess had been insistent. She'd not wanted to enter the inner room, yet had found herself propelled through its doors unable to protest. And once there her fears had multiplied. Seeing Robert Amesbury had been the final straw. His malevolent face still plagued her dreams. Three years ago he had been her bad genius and here he was once more, ready to do her harm if he possibly could.

Safety had come, but at what cost. Just when she'd decided that on no account must she have further dealings with Joshua Marchmain, he had made her beholden to him. How shameful to be dependent on a rake for rescue! He must have thought her foolish and naïve, a girl out of her depth and drowning. It was evident that he'd been angry with the duchess – at one point Marianna had felt literally pulled between the two of them – and she might have found comfort in that, but for the last glimpse she'd had of the pair.

They had stood closeted, their heads so close that his cheek was almost grazing the woman's hair. Any animosity seemed to have vanished. They had been talking easily together and Marianna had a sinking feeling that she had been the main subject of their conversation. Her face burned: they would decide she was a stupid young girl who had become hysterical when invited to partake in a game of chance. Then a worse thought struck, making her face burn hotter. What if she really had been that stupid – stupid enough to imagine the whole thing and misinterpret the duchess's conduct? This high-born lady had gone out of her way to be friendly and her seeming coercion might simply be a desire to encourage a reluctant young guest to enjoy herself. The duchess would know nothing of her unfortunate history with Lord Amesbury; she would be ignorant of the dread he evoked. And what had been her response to Charlotte's overtures? Blind, inexplicable panic, and a dreadful lapse of good manners. She and Carmela had left the party without a word of thanks or indeed a word of farewell. It was appalling.

She told herself that she must not dwell on such harrowing thoughts, but still she did. The evening's events continued to revolve in her mind until they began to assume hideous proportions. She wished that her mother was by her side to guide her. She knew she could have told Mama everything, well nearly everything, she amended inwardly. Her feelings towards Joshua would remain under wraps. She hardly understood them herself. How could she feel this strong attraction to him when Luke Trelawny had been the only man she had ever loved?

Remember him, remember him, she told herself fiercely. Luke and she, a whirling figure in pale blue, dancing with him at Almack's for the very first time. How wonderful that had been. She hugged the memory to herself, warmed by its still powerful glow, chasing confusion away.

But then another image emerged. Luke dancing that very same night with Cassandra, the woman he swore he despised, the woman who had so cruelly jilted him, but the one he still loved. Marianna had known even then, deep in her innermost self, that his feelings for the flame-haired beauty had not died and that he was deceiving himself in thinking he was free of her power.

But she had deceived herself just as much. How resolute

she had been in refusing to see the truth of the situation, wishing, hoping that he would turn his head and see the girl who, through those long summer months, was so often by his side. The girl who idolised him. But all he saw was a scrubby schoolgirl, without guile or wisdom, too spontaneous for her own good. Is that what Joshua saw? Was this another time when she was refusing to see the truth?

Chapter Eight

For much of the day Marianna stayed cloistered in her room, venturing downstairs only at mealtimes, though in truth she had little appetite. At the table, Carmela made no mention of yesterday's tribulations and she could only assume that her cousin had vowed herself to silence. Señor Marquez seemed to have taken the same vow.

He had arrived from London in the early hours of the morning and Marianna had expected to find him eager to hear details of their visit to Steine House. But not one question had he asked. Perhaps Carmela had alerted him to the wretchedness of the evening. It certainly seemed so. His daughter had committed a serious impropriety in disappearing without a chaperon, yet there were no words of censure from him. Indeed both he and her cousin treated Marianna with unaccustomed gentleness and, during the days that followed, were careful never to comment on her fondness for her room or her refusal to venture out for even a short walk.

It was Ernesto who finally broke the impasse on a morning which sparkled with light.

'The weather is so fine, *querida*,' he said heartily,

embracing her in one of his bear hugs. 'Why do we not walk on the Downs, perhaps even take a picnic?'

Carmela nodded silent approval and he continued persuasively, 'There is a good breeze blowing and we will easily find shade in which to enjoy our meal.'

Marianna said nothing, but her father was not to be defeated. 'Just you and I,' he coaxed.

She did not wish to disappoint him, but shrank at the idea of walking on the Downs or indeed anywhere in the vicinity. What she wanted most was to hide away – from the duchess, from Amesbury, and particularly from Joshua Marchmain. Every time she stepped outside the front door, she risked meeting with one or other of them. Brighton was not a large town.

'If that is too far for you, we could take a short walk through the Lanes.' Ernesto was not giving up and she saw how concerned he was. 'It's not good, Marianna, to be confined in these four walls for too long.'

He was right. Eventually she would have to emerge from her refuge and face whatever was in store. By hiding away, she was compounding her folly at Steine House. And exhibiting a drastic lack of spirit, too, she castigated herself. She needed to show the world that she was ashamed of nothing. She could do that. If she met Charlotte Severn, she would smile and curtsy and leave it to the other woman to set the tone. If she met Lord Amesbury, her father would be there to defend her. And if she met Joshua – but she would not, she was sure. She had been shut away in Marine Parade for nearly a week and had heard nothing of him. He socialised within his own tight little circle and would not have noticed her absence.

'I need to change my books at the library, Papa,' she offered, 'and if you're agreeable, we could walk there.'

The library she patronised, one of the many that were dotted across Brighton, was in the west of the town and would furnish a satisfying stroll. On the way, there was the distraction of any number of tempting shop windows filled with exquisite silks and laces, almost certainly smuggled from France. She chose her dress with care, searching for as plain a gown as possible and ended by donning a simple but stylish jaconet muslin. Once out of the house, she kept her eyes lowered beneath the deep brim of her straw bonnet, but she need not have worried for the *ton* were out of town that day it seemed, enjoying themselves elsewhere. They walked through near deserted streets while her father told her of his trip to London and the worrying news from Spain.

'A change of government usually means a change of everything,' he confided to her. 'I am no longer certain of my position. It could be that I will be recalled to Madrid very soon and perhaps reassigned elsewhere. I am sorry, if that happens. Your holiday by the sea will come to an abrupt end, my dear.'

She squeezed his arm reassuringly, but felt a tremor of foreboding. Leaving Brighton would mean separation from her father when they had so recently been reunited. It meant an inevitable return to Spain and the future that awaited her there. The life she had contemplated only a few weeks ago seemed increasingly dreary. Nothing had changed and yet everything had. She was still pondering this paradox when they arrived at the fashionable new subscription library which fronted the western end of the promenade.

Usually its coffee rooms and lounges were filled with residents and fashionable visitors, but as with the rest of the town today, it was nearly empty. A few ladies were browsing the bookshelves and a small card game was in play at one end of the smallest salon. Another gentleman was busy sifting through music sheets, evidently keen to find something new for the musical evening he was planning.

'All at the Race Ground,' he explained succinctly when Ernesto mentioned the scarcity of people. 'The Regent's Cup today, y' know. Big prize money.'

Her father turned to Marianna. 'I wish we had known – you would have enjoyed the meeting. That's what comes of staying too close to home.'

She could only feel gratitude that her father had not heard the news. At the race course she would have been sure to see everyone she most wished to avoid.

Thirty minutes of browsing the floor to ceiling bookshelves secured a neat pile of small volumes and they made ready to leave. They were almost out of the door when her father spied a tattered poster taped insecurely to the wall.

'Look, Marianna. Henry Angelo has set up a new fencing academy here in Brighton. I was tempted in London to try a lesson or two with him.'

She could not help but smile. Her father's physique in middle age was hardly conducive to fencing.

'Why do you smile, little one? You think I couldn't do it?'

'No, Papa, I am sure you could, but wouldn't you prefer to watch rather than participate?'

'Perhaps you are right, though in my youth I was a match for anyone.'

'Yes?'

'I actually beat the legendary Don Roderiguez.'

She looked at him questioningly. 'You wouldn't know of him. It was well before you were born, but he was worshipped in Madrid for his skill. I took him on as a wager and nobody expected me to win, but I did.'

'And Don Roderiguez?'

'I have to admit he was probably not quite himself. I managed to fight him after a particularly boisterous party.'

They both laughed and she said wistfully, 'Gentlemen are lucky – they have so many channels for their energy. All we have is embroidery or the pianoforte.'

'I don't notice either of those featuring heavily in *your* life, Marianna.'

'That's exactly what I mean. Fencing would be far more enjoyable.'

It would get rid of some of my restlessness, she thought, perhaps even beat the blue-devils plaguing me. Yes, men were lucky that their lives were so much freer.

Unbeknown to her, Ernesto had taken note of his daughter's interest and promptly committed to memory the address of the new fencing school. He would arrange a small treat for her. He knew the evening at Steine House had not gone to plan, but he was in the dark about his daughter's true state of mind. Anything that would distract her could only be good.

So it was that Henry Angelo had an early morning visitor the next day. The request was unusual and certainly unconventional, but he had a business to establish and an ambassador was too important a personage to offend in these early days. His school had already attracted the attention of a number of the *ton* spending the summer in Brighton, but Señor Marquez could prove useful in bringing new clients from the diplomatic circles in which he moved.

Summoned to an early breakfast the next day, Marianna found her father already at the table, seething with barely suppressed excitement.

'What have you been doing, Papa?' she asked guardedly. 'You look like a naughty schoolboy.'

'This morning I have important papers to clear but this afternoon, Marianna, we are to play truant together!'

'And Carmela?' Her cousin had not yet put in an appearance.

'Carmela and playing truant are not compatible, I think.' Señor Marquez smiled happily. 'This is just for you and me.'

'Not a picnic?' she asked in some alarm. Riding on the Downs was popular with the *ton* and despite Marianna's resolve to be brave, she still feared places where she risked meeting the world and his wife.

'No. No picnic. The wind today is too strong even for the English to eat outdoors.'

Through the windows she saw the grey surf breaking harshly on the sea wall and spilling through the iron railings which defended the promenade. A few hardy souls, determined to complete their daily constitutional, were making slow progress along the seafront. Heading into the fierce wind and clutching wildly at flying garments, they were bent nearly double.

'Then indoors somewhere?'

'Indeed. But you must probe no further. It is to be a great surprise!'

Marianna had hoped to spend the day curled on the sofa reading her way through some of the library's offerings, but it was evident her father had made special plans and she was sufficiently intrigued to hurry upstairs after a modest nuncheon and change her dress. Choosing suitable raiment proved difficult for she had no idea where she was going. Eventually she settled on a primrose sarsnet flounced with French trimmings – it was modest enough for an informal outing, yet not too plain. She quickly threaded a matching primrose ribbon through her tangle of curls and joined her father in the hall.

'We will go by carriage,' Ernesto announced, as Marston battled to hold the front door ajar. 'The weather is far too rough to walk.'

Chapter Nine

They were soon bowling past fishing boats pulled high onto the beach, past fishermen's wives tending the nets and then past Mahomed's much patronised Vapour Baths, until they reached the end of East Cliff. The imposing mansions which lined the road gradually became far less in number, but just before they reached open countryside, the carriage pulled up at a small establishment tucked between two large white-washed dwellings. An arched wooden door painted in luminescent green beckoned a greeting and, even before they had taken a step out of the vehicle, a sprightly, dark-haired man bounded out to greet them.

'Welcome, welcome,' he enthused, executing a deep bow. 'I am most honoured by your visit.' Marianna supposed him to be the proprietor. But what was this place?

'Follow me, please.' The man ushered them into the house, fairly dancing down a narrow passageway to a small but comfortable sitting room. All the time he kept up a stream of lively chatter.

Looking around her, she saw a pair of highly polished rapiers hanging cross-wise above the fireplace and all four walls dotted with prints of sword fighting. Her father had brought her to none other than the fencing academy they had seen advertised! It was hardly the outing she would have chosen, but she owed it to him to look pleased. For days he had good humouredly tolerated the Friday face she'd been wearing and must have gone to some trouble to arrange what he clearly thought an interesting diversion.

Henry Angelo proved an attentive host. Marianna had to suppress a smile as this most Italian of men solemnly observed the rituals of an English tea and did it with aplomb, pouring the steaming liquid himself and handing around the Crown Derby teacups with a flourish. Small delicate scones with a selection of jams were offered, followed by pastries and fruit cake. The whole time Signor Angelo bubbled along with his tea.

'My father moved from Paris forty years ago to set up a fencing school in London. It was a gamble for him but a very successful one!'

'So I understand,' Ernesto acknowledged. 'And now you are continuing the family tradition in Brighton?'

'A new venture, señor, but I am gradually becoming known here. It helps that my father has many powerful friends. He knows the great boxer, Gentleman Jackson.'

'Really?' Ernesto appeared impressed.

The Italian nodded vigorously. 'He numbers Mr Jackson among his closest friends, you know. Years ago he helped him establish a boxing club in Bond Street – next door to our Fencing Academy.'

Reminiscences of the Gentleman's many successful prize fights and a listing of all the great and the good that frequented both establishments, followed at break-neck speed.

'The Regent himself honoured us with a visit to Bond Street,' the younger Henry announced breathlessly. 'We hosted an exhibition of fencing just for him and he asked for a set of foils used by the master fencer of the day. Masks and gloves, too!'

The heat of the small sitting room, combined with the unbroken flow of small talk, was making Marianna's head swim and she was heartily glad when their host danced once more to his feet and made ready to show them around the Academy of which he was inordinately proud.

Once in the school proper there was far more space and air and she breathed freely again. Signor Angelo led them from one practice room to another. The building was far larger than appeared from outside, stretching seawards a considerable distance. Each room was flooded with natural light, the ceiling consisting almost entirely of glass panels open to the sky. Collections of foils, their guards decorated with acanthus leaves, anchors, cherubs and serpents, filled the corners of each room. Still voluble, their host was explaining at length the distinctive style of French *epées*, Italian rapiers and English swords. From a large oak cupboard in the final room, face masks and padded bibs spilled onto the floor.

'Señor, please, try one of these,' he invited Ernesto, holding up a stiff white corset. 'It is the very latest in design.'

The body padding was a cause of some humour since Señor Marquez's rotund figure defeated all attempts at accommodating him. Ernesto smiled ruefully. 'My dream of fencing again is dashed!'

'Can I try?' Marianna asked.

Both men turned to look at her, their mouths open, but she stared boldly back at them. 'I'm here, Papa, because I said how much I wished women could follow the same pastimes as men,' she reminded her father. 'Isn't that so?'

'Well, yes,' Ernesto said guardedly. 'But I did not for one moment mean – '

'I wish only to try on a bib,' she interrupted. 'And see how it feels to hold a rapier. That can't be too scandalous, surely?'

Her father looked bewildered, taken aback by this sudden turn of events, but Signor Angelo found his smile and delved back into the pile of corsets. 'Here, signorina, I think this may be a good fit.'

With his assistance, Marianna donned the bib. It felt strange to be encased in something so rigid after the free flowing dresses she wore daily. But a new strength seemed to flow from the garment – in it she felt defended. More than that. She felt ready to challenge. 'And a sword?' she asked.

She heard her father mutter something beneath his breath. He was looking increasingly dismayed, but Signor Angelo had begun rifling through his cache of foils, all the time talking to himself, as he weighed up the benefits or otherwise of the various swords. 'Ah! The very one for a lady. Light, sharp, a beautiful balance. Try this, signorina.'

Marianna grasped hold of the foil and immediately her wrist buckled.

'No, no.' Signor Angelo danced around to her right side. 'Like this.' Very delicately, he adjusted her wrist. 'The grip is not too tight. You must have the loose wrist – the flexible wrist,' he said, drawing out every syllable.

The foil felt a good deal better now and Marianna tried a few experimental wafts with the blade. Then Angelo was beside her again, masks in hand.

'Here,' he offered her one. 'You have the skirts and that is difficult. But no matter. We will try. First we learn the *En Garde* position.'

He arranged himself side on, leading with his sword hand, and with his foot pointing towards her, while the other was angled at ninety degrees.

She tried to copy him, though her skirts were as difficult as Angelo had predicted. 'Now,' he said, 'when you advance, the front foot leads, and when you retreat, it is the back foot leading.' She nodded her understanding. 'But before we start, you must be sure to be balanced. Have your weight spread evenly and stand on the balls of your feet. So you can move quickly either way.'

There seemed a great number of things to remember all at the same time but Marianna tried to comply. It took several shiftings of position before she felt sufficiently balanced, but then with knees bent and sword outstretched, she was ready.

'First we learn the straight thrust,' Angelo said, 'and then the basic parry. These are simple moves to attack and defend. We try now.'

Marianna tried a simple attack. It took several attempts to get close to what the signor had demonstrated, but the power she felt as she lunged and retreated and lunged once more was astonishing. It was the power of movement, of strength, of freedom.

'I think – ' her father began. But before he could impart his thoughts, the door was thrust open and a voice called out, 'It was a good bout, Angelo, but – now what have we here?'

Marianna turned, dropping her foil, and lifting her face mask. Of course, it had to be him. It was the first time she had seen him since the Severn *soirée* and shameful memory flooded her mind.

Joshua Marchmain smiled across the length of the room and walked slowly towards her, a smattering of sweat still on his forehead. As he walked, she felt herself absorbing his shapely form. Really fencing garments left little to the imagination.

'Miss Marquez! A convert to the sport, I see.' He grinned in sheer pleasure. 'Have you come to fight me?' He thrust his mask down to cover his face and took up the *En Garde* position in the space Angelo had occupied. He was mocking her. She must appear idiotic in long skirts with sword outstretched, playing at being a man. His smile said that he would show her how foolish she looked. Well, let him. She stilled her pulse and took up the position Angelo had showed her.

How she would have fared if he'd really crossed swords with her, she was not destined to know. Ernesto had jumped up from his chair and stepped between them. 'I think that sufficient, Marianna. Give Signor Angelo the foil and remove the bib.'

She knew the voice and knew she dared not disobey, though she would have dearly loved to land at least one strike on Marchmain.

'We give you an exhibition instead,' Angelo said, realising the afternoon might not turn out the money spinner he'd anticipated, and trying to rescue the situation. 'Mr Marchmain is a most talented amateur.'

'Have a heart, Henry,' Joshua protested. 'I've just this minute survived a bout with one of your best instructors. And now you're expecting me to take *you* on!'

'It is only the demonstration,' Angelo coaxed. 'The signorina is most interested.'

'Most interested,' Marianna repeated. Her eyebrows arched, daring him to refuse. Joshua looked at her for a moment, then slid down his mask and raised his foil.

She sat quietly beside her father while the two white-clothed figures circled each other, lunging, parrying, occasionally retreating to recover position. Energy crackled through the air and for a while, it was impossible to tell who was the expert and who the pupil, since they were so well-matched. First one man, then the other, gained the advantage.

Marianna found herself being pulled into the drama of the fight. It was a demonstration only and the buttons were firmly fixed to the top of the men's foils, yet there was a sense of restrained danger. Both men were in the prime of fitness: one small and angular, buzzing forwards and backwards like an angry bee, the other slim but muscular, agile and menacing in his weavings.

She watched his figure tauten and slacken in response to the other's constant teasing, his muscles hardening and contouring his body. He had such natural grace that she was mesmerised into following every movement, imbibing his strength almost like a drug. She would have liked to reach out and touch him, stroke the line of his rippling arm, his slim waist, his powerful thigh. For a moment she found herself breathless, liquid with desire.

Then she shook herself awake. She had not felt such a powerful emotion since Luke had smiled at her and turned her body to water. With a shock she realised she had not thought of Luke once during the past few days. Somehow he'd begun to drift into the distance, remote from the pressing concerns of her life. And thinking of him now no longer evoked the same eager yearning that it had always done. What could that mean? That she was ready to give herself to another, ready perhaps for the husband who was even now awaiting her return to Spain. Would he evoke the same intense desire that had just shaken her? It seemed unlikely.

The bout was over and the opponents shaking hands. Signor Angelo wrung his pupil's hand. 'That was *magnifico*, signor. You get better all the time.'

'With such an audience, I had to be magnificent!' He bowed to Angelo and then crossed to where they were seated and raised Marianna's hand to his lips, just grazing the surface. 'I hope I kept you interested,' he murmured.

She found herself unable to speak. There was a fire raging inside her and she was helpless to dampen its ravages. It was left to her father to fill the silence that spread between them.

'Thank you for a splendid display, sir. I have not seen such skill for many years.'

'You fence yourself?'

'I used to.' Despite his annoyance at the way the afternoon had progressed, Ernesto smiled wryly. 'But tell me, was that the Italian style?'

'Always the Italian style,' Henry Angelo put in. 'Mr Marchmain fences like a professional.'

'I had to wait until I reached Italy before I learned the true art of fencing,' Joshua said in explanation.

'But now you don't have to do it for real, eh?' Henry chuckled. 'English husbands are more complacent.' He waved his hand at the scar that Joshua bore on his cheek.

The barely disguised reminder that this man was an out-and-out womaniser brought Marianna back to her senses. 'How often do you fence, Mr Marchmain?' she asked in a neutral voice.

Joshua had flushed with annoyance at Angelo's intervention but, turning to her, he smiled so sweetly that hammer blows again began to afflict her heart.

'As often as I can, Miss Marquez. It is a great pity you cannot participate yourself – you would find it exciting.'

'I'm sure if women enjoyed the same freedom as men, I would not be alone in finding it exciting.'

'Any time you wish to bid for freedom and would like a lesson, I am at your service.'

The golden eyes darkened and she felt his voice caressing her. It wasn't only fencing he had in mind, she was sure. Her father frowned, looking from one to the other, and when he spoke his tone was brisk.

'I'm sure it is an excellent way of keeping fit, but my daughter is a keen rider. That is sufficient. In Argentina she lived in the saddle.'

'And in England?'

'I rode in London, but Rotten Row was far too tame,' Marianna said.

'Then ride on the Downs. I guarantee you'll not find that tame. Or perhaps try sea bathing.'

'I hardly think that would be suitable,' Ernesto said heavily.

'I assure you it is all the fashion. The ladies have their own part of the beach and are well looked after by 'dippers' – they are the bathing attendants.'

Her father shook his head. 'It would not do. Your aunts...' He left the sentence unfinished.

'They would certainly not contemplate sea bathing.' Marianna's face lit with amusement at what those very proper ladies would make of such an activity.

'A suggestion only.' Joshua's expression was bland. 'But Miss Marquez should savour all Brighton has to offer before she returns to London.'

'My daughter will not be returning there,' Ernesto said decisively.

Joshua fixed her with an intense gaze. 'You will not be staying in town this autumn?'

'I will be returning to Spain,' she said quietly.

'That is sad news.' His voice held genuine regret. 'Before you leave England, though, can you not spend a few weeks in London?'

Her father once more intervened. 'I regret not. My daughter has a most important date to keep. She must leave for Spain immediately the Brighton season ends.'

Joshua looked enquiringly at her.

'I am to be married, Mr Marchmain, and must return to Spain to meet my bridegroom.'

She touched her father's arm and, with a brief bow in his direction, they were gone.

Chapter Ten

For a moment Joshua stood motionless, hardly able to believe her words. Then he wheeled around abruptly and made for the changing room. Married? But to whom? She had said that she was going to Spain to meet her bridegroom which meant, dear God, that she did not yet know the man. She did not know the man with whom she was destined to spend the rest of her life. An arranged marriage! Fury welled up in him and he slashed blindly at the walls as he strode along the passageway. Whatever Charlotte had intimated, the girl was an innocent. How could her father dream of sacrificing her in such a way. How could *she* think of agreeing to give herself to a stranger?

The idea that any young woman might marry a man she'd never met was discomfiting, but this was Marianna! A girl so enchanting, so full of youthful joy, that he could have wept. When he'd seen her in fighting pose and ready to attack, his heart had applauded. All she had needed was breeches and she'd have been complete. If she were his, he would order her a pair and teach her to fight. If she were his? What was he thinking?

He dressed quickly, his hands shaking in fury. Every layer of clothing was donned in rage. He couldn't remember ever feeling so angry, yet he to get himself under control. He hardly knew the girl and it was madness to react so strongly to an arranged marriage. In his world they were frequent; indeed his personal world was built on them, he thought cynically. Loveless partnerships were the hunting ground for any self-respecting rake. And that was what he was, an ugly label but one that suited him.

A rake never pondered the past for he had no past. He suffered no confusion since he knew exactly who he was, and so did the women who chose to tangle with him. And what he also knew was that innocent buds such as Marianna were best avoided. That particular lesson had been seared early on his prodigal soul. He should need no reminding.

⤳

Seated beside her father as they rattled their way home, Marianna felt pleased she had startled Joshua from his customary calm. He had looked genuinely shocked when her father announced she was to be married. Could it be that he cared or was it simply that he found the idea of an arranged marriage appalling? Hardly. Over the years he must have benefited from any number of such alliances, the comforter of wives who had no love for their husbands. Yet his face had shadowed with the news, as though he would wish to save her from that fate.

Or preserve her for his own dishonourable intentions – that was more likely. He could not have developed a *tendre* for her, she reasoned. Rakes did not do that – it was more than their career was worth to care for the women they made their lovers.

Her father's words, though, had brought home to her how swiftly the weeks were passing. Marriage was ceasing to be an abstract notion and rapidly becoming reality. When Luke Trelawny disappeared from her life, she'd not cared whom she wed, and resigned herself to going through the intimacies of married life impassive and acquiescent. But the events of this morning suggested differently.

Joshua Marchmain's face and body was his stock in trade but, despite knowing that, her response had been intense. Hungry even. She'd loved Luke passionately, but had never experienced the sheer elemental need that just a short while ago had swept through her. And it wasn't the first time. Whenever Joshua came on the scene, she had to exercise the tightest control over her emotions. Today she had lost that control. Surely she could not be seriously attracted to such an arrogant user of women? Yet those golden eyes had only to settle on her, that lazy smile flicker her way, the hard muscular body be close to her, and she became someone she hardly recognised.

The next few days found Marianna restless. She forgot her earlier reluctance to be seen abroad and needed constantly to be on the move. Every morning she set off with her maid in tow to explore an unknown part of the Sussex landscape, winding through the town and up the hills to a viewpoint far above the sea, or along the shoreline itself or following the pathways which circled the foot of the Downs. Poor Flora was hard put to keep up with her mistress. On one of their walks along the seafront, they came to the ladies' beach that Joshua had spoken of.

'Look, Flora.' She drew her maid's attention to the horse-drawn bathing machines carrying the swimmers into shallow waters. From there the professional dippers helped their female customers into the sea.

Her maid shuddered. 'It's not proper, miss.'

'The women change in the carriages and then just slip into the sea. It seems quite modest,' Marianna said thoughtfully.

Flora sniffed, unconvinced. 'Mebbe, but I don't reckon Señor Marquez would be too keen, nor Miss Carmela neither.'

'But if so many women take part, it must be acceptable,' Marianna pursued, her interest now thoroughly aroused.

'You're never thinking of joining them, Miss Marianna.' Flora's tone was scandalised. 'And think how dangerous it must be.'

Several women, clad in flannel gowns and caps, emerged at that moment from the carriages and cautiously dipped their bare toes in the water. Courage gained, they were soon venturing further out and in no time at all a flurry of bonneted heads were bobbing up and down in the waves.

'I don't think there can be too much danger. The water is shallow close to the shore,' Marianna reasoned, 'and the dippers are there to provide security. Once the women are used to the sea, they're fine. Just look at them.'

She had a sudden longing to be with them, to ride the waves rolling into the distance, to cleave her way through the surf out to the far horizon, to swim to an escape. But seeing Flora's concerned expression, she laughed and said reassuringly, 'Don't fret, it's only a silly fancy.'

The next day she excused herself from accompanying Carmela to a lunchtime recital at St Nicholas's church. Her father, too, was engaged, dealing with the daily round of official business, and she was able to slip out of the house unseen. And Flora had been given the afternoon off and was already deep in the excitements of the stalls at Bartholomews. A ten minute walk brought Marianna to the ladies' bathing beach and another five saw her slipping into the flannel bathing costume provided by the attendant. She gave a little gasp as she glimpsed her bare arms and legs but, peering out of the carriage doorway, she saw other women happily disporting themselves, seemingly without anxiety for their unclad state. It was female territory, she comforted herself, and the water looked delightful.

It was. Soon she was luxuriating in the flow of the tide, her body tingling to its touch. At first she bobbed up and down amid the waves, allowing the foam to swirl and curl around her toes. But then, more daringly, she began to cut a path through the water, feeling the sun warm on her bare face and arms. How fortunate that life in Argentina had been so much freer, allowing her to swim in private and become strong in the water. Effortlessly she swam on, feeling lighter than air, her body and mind at one, all trouble and confusion suspended. But there was a strict time limit imposed on the bathers and all too soon she was forced to turn back to the shore.

The horse-drawn carriages once more loomed into close view, lined up on the shore like so many sentries watching over precious treasure. Reaching the shallows, she found her feet and picked her way carefully over the pebbled seabed. The wet costume clung tenaciously to her body and a thrill of womanly pleasure passed through her at the sensuous form it revealed. Tearing the cap from her head, she waded the last few yards ashore, wild black curls streaming. For an instant before she reached the shelter of the bathing machine she looked towards the promenade – and turned scarlet with vexation.

Joshua Marchmain! How dare he! This was an area reserved only for ladies and all men were banned. Of course, he would not care for that. He cared for no convention. He would embarrass anyone he wished for his own pleasure. He'd suggested to her that she should try sea bathing and now it was clear why. Not from any wish to afford her enjoyment but so that he could view her better and nearly naked. Her anger turned to chagrin. How could she have imagined that he might harbour any genuine feeling? He was a libertine through and through.

Chapter Eleven

S he had looked like a water sprite from the deep and Joshua, watching her graceful progress ashore, had to restrain himself from wading out into the shallows and catching her in his arms. He had barely seen her since that evening at Steine House, just those few moments at Angelo's, when he'd reacted so angrily to news of her future marriage. He'd known then that he should put all thought of her out of his mind and had tried very hard to do so. Nevertheless he'd found himself looking for her at every social gathering since – and her absence had only increased his interest. His desire for her was becoming insistent. It was all too familiar, but this time complicated by something else, something deeper and unfathomable. Desire he knew but not this nagging need to take her in his arms, to protect her from harm, to kiss her awake to a passion he was sure lay within.

Caught by her magic, he had remained on the promenade and was still there when she emerged fully dressed from the land side of the bathing machine. She made to walk past him with a bare nod of acknowledgement, but he was too quick for her and barred the way.

'Did sea bathing live up to its promise, Miss Marquez?' he enquired, an appreciative smile on his face.

She turned abruptly. 'Did ogling female bathers live up to yours, Mr Marchmain?'

For an instant, he looked taken aback but soon recovered his poise. 'One bather certainly did!'

'You are insufferable!'

'Because I appreciate female beauty? That is hardly fair.'

'Because you seem intent on pressing your attentions on unwilling women.'

'Not always so unwilling,' he said drily.

'Let us be clear, sir.' Her tone was arctic. 'Whatever your customary experience, *I* find your attentions wholly distasteful.'

'And what attentions would they be? All I have done is stand on this small spot of promenade and enjoy the pleasurable sight of women for once free of the shackles imposed on them.'

Since she was so much in tune with this sentiment, Marianna found it difficult for the moment to continue the quarrel. But not for long.

'The only reason you told me of the sea bathing was to allow you to spy on me.'

'An over-dramatic interpretation, I think. I am no spy.' His voice no longer sounded amused.

'Call it what you will. I have no intention of being ogled by men, and particularly not by a man with your reputation.'

'And what reputation would that be?' A hint of danger lurked in his voice.

'I have no wish to continue this conversation. Please allow me to pass.'

He made no move but instead looked her fully in the face. 'You are a delightful girl, Marianna, but young and naïve. You know nothing of me or my life, so be careful in passing judgement.'

'I am not so naïve that I cannot recognise a rake when I see one.'

There, she had said the shocking word, and to his face. She waited for the explosion but none came. Instead he was smiling down at her, a condescending expression on his face.

'A rake am I?' he drawled. 'And all because I dared to see one second of your beautiful body in a bathing costume – and not a particularly revealing one at that.'

She flushed scarlet. 'You have done nothing but distress me since our paths first crossed.'

'Another somewhat overwrought statement. I've simply been going about my usual business. Why are you so eager to feel distress?'

'Are you suggesting I've no cause for complaint?' She was fuming.

'I'm suggesting that you may be prone to exaggerate my interest. Forgive me, but encouraging such fancies cannot be healthy.'

She longed to hit him very hard, but by a supreme force of will managed to stay her hand. Instead she took a cold, calm breath and launched the most wounding insult she could think of.

'You *claim* to be a gentleman. If you are indeed such,

then you will leave me alone, now and in the future.'

She saw him stiffen. It was one thing to call him rake but the insinuation that he was not a gentleman would cause the deepest rancour.

'I regret that you have found meeting me so distasteful, Miss Marquez.' His tone had acquired a new aloofness.

'I have.'

'Then I will no longer distress you with my presence. And as far as I'm able, will make sure I stay out of sight.'

'Please do.'

'Dare I enquire if you intend to be at the Lewes race meeting tomorrow?'

'I believe my father has reserved places for us.'

'In that case you can be certain I will spend the day a hundred miles from Lewes.'

'I'm delighted to hear it,' she flung at him and stormed past, her cheeks still flaming and her head held high.

A blind rage sustained Marianna on the short walk back to Marine Parade and it was only when she was in sight of the house that she began to question why Joshua Marchmain's conduct had so angered her. His blatant voyeurism was only what she would have predicted. Why then was she so out of temper? Was it that she'd expected better of him? Deep down she'd held a secret hope that the stories were exaggerated, that gossip had distorted his true nature. In short, she had wanted to believe he was the kind of man she could trust. How very stupid!

He was right, she *was* naïve. He was and always would be an inveterate womaniser since, even though she might acquit him of deliberately luring her to the bathing station, he'd still gazed his fill. An honourable man would have turned away; an honourable man would not even have been there! She wondered wearily how many disappointments she must endure before she finally accepted that she was a very poor judge of men. Once back in Spain, she would trust her aunts to choose her husband. They could do no worse.

'Good to see you, miss.' Marston opened the door to her. He sounded relieved and she wondered why, but then heard her father's voice raised in protest.

'It is simply a day out, Carmela, a social occasion, nothing more.'

'Naturally I realise that in *this* society a day at the races is just one more entertainment.' Carmela shuddered. 'But you cannot deny that a racecourse is a place of sin.'

'Come, my dear, I know that you have – definite views.' Her father phrased his words carefully. 'But in this instance, are you not being just a little severe?'

'I think not. Gambling wherever it occurs is sinful.'

'Marianna will not be gambling and neither will I. We will enjoy a day in the fresh air and the excitement of seeing horses compete.'

'But you will be surrounded by every kind of vice!' Fired by moral zeal, her cousin was not giving up easily. 'We should be doing all we can to protect Marianna from the work of the Devil, not exposing an innocent girl to temptation.'

'Enough!' Ernesto held up his hand. 'I am taking my daughter on an outing of pleasure whether you approve or not. And I will personally guarantee that she returns as innocent as she went.'

Shoulders stiff, he strode along the hallway to his office and closed the door noisily. Carmela sniffed just as noisily and hastened back to the purity of her bedroom. Even after both had disappeared, the atmosphere crackled with irritation and Marianna was left thinking that for all kinds of reasons it might be a good idea to return to Spain sooner than she'd hoped.

⁓

But the next morning she changed her mind. A perfect English summer day greeted her, cotton wool clouds drifting lazily across an azure sky, and the green perfection of ancient downland rolling out its smooth carpet to welcome them, as they drove the few miles inland to Lewes. The racecourse, some five hundred feet above sea level, was idyllic on a tranquil day such as this. Shaped like an elongated horseshoe, it ran along the crest of a valley and then downwards towards the sea, its natural undulations making it a test of stamina and tactics for both horses and riders.

A decidedly mixed crowd had already gathered by the side of the track and Ernesto silently wondered if he had dismissed Carmela's qualms too readily. Every type of person it seemed had come to the Lewes races that day: prosperous farmers and their wives; rural workers in smocks and gaiters; smartly dressed professional men and their clients; sellers of every kind of food and drink vociferously shouting their wares and any number of ragged urchins.

As their hired vehicle drove onto the course, he saw with relief that the cream of society had decided on keeping a comfortable distance from this ragbag of humanity. A large white-painted grandstand, with an unparalleled view of the entire course, was alive with a colourful swathe of silk gowns and feathered hats. It seemed that the Regent and his party had already arrived.

As the races began, Ernesto felt even greater relief. The gambling that Carmela had so feared was modest and conducted with decorum. So much so that towards the end of the programme, he was encouraged to place a wager on a likely looking horse. The result of the race was in doubt right up to the finishing line and Marianna, immersed in the spectacle, cheered on their horse

with such verve that her father was delighted they had come. For weeks he'd been aware his daughter was less than happy. In his presence she tried to be bright and talkative but whenever she thought herself unobserved, she fell back into a preoccupation he couldn't fathom. Now the sheer excitement of the chase had prompted her to throw herself into the moment as only she could. Her arms waved wildly in the air as their horse breasted the finishing post a few inches ahead of its nearest rival. Ernesto smiled. It was clear his daughter was finding it hard to stop herself from jumping up and down.

'I see you have been a clever girl and backed the winner. I fear that *my* luck is completely out today.'

Marianna looked round at the woman who'd spoken and her heart sank. Her father had chosen the worst moment to collect his winnings and now she was left to face the duchess alone. She had not met Charlotte Severn since that dreadful evening at Steine House, but the older woman, resplendent in sapphire satin, was smiling invitingly at her and patting her hand in what Marianna supposed to be a motherly fashion.

'Such exuberance needs sustaining.' The duchess's voice had taken on the cloying tone that was so discomfiting. 'Do accompany me to the marquee – we must take tea together.'

Marianna began to demur but her companion immediately linked arms with her and urged her forwards. 'Don't worry about your Papa. When he returns he will be sure to know where you have gone and will come to collect you.'

Very quickly Marianna found herself seated at one of the small ironwork tables that dotted the interior of the marquee, a waiter pouring the pale straw of China tea into delicate white porcelain.

The duchess fixed her with eyes which smiled out of a pool of ice. 'I am so pleased to see you again, Marianna,' she was saying sweetly. 'We are on first name terms, are we not?'

Marianna was hypnotised into assent.

'I was most upset by the way that we parted at Steine House. Such a dreadful misunderstanding on my part. I had no idea that you were so averse to cards – though obviously not to gambling in general.' Her voice momentarily lost its honey as she nodded pointedly towards the races still taking place.

Her victim squirmed, remembering her gauche behaviour that evening. And to be discovered now in the very pastime she had rejected so publicly!

But Her Grace was continuing smoothly, preparing her

ground with the girl she was seeking to undo. 'I am so very sorry,' she trilled, 'if anything I did or said at the time upset you.'

After such a show of contrition, Marianna could hardly reject the overture. The duchess's deep blue eyes held hers in a seemingly sincere appeal and she found herself softening towards their owner. Her natural good nature won over whatever reservations she still harboured and in a small voice she confessed, 'I am sorry, too – my conduct must have seemed a little strange.'

'No, my dear, absolutely not.' Charlotte Severn was determined on complete abasement. 'The fault was entirely mine. But I hope we can mend our fences. I so much wish us to be friends.'

Marianna would have liked to believe her but could not. An older female friend – someone she could confide in, someone with the maturity and experience to guide her through this difficult summer – was a luxury she must do without. Years ago she had lost the person who might have helped. Cassandra was long married and living many miles away.

'It is as I told you, my dear,' the duchess was saying pleasantly, 'there are very few new people in Brighton. An old hand like myself can become seriously *blasé*, not to say boring, if we are not kept on our toes. I adore young people and you are so bright and lovely.'

Charlotte was having an effect. Today she appeared more genuine and more approachable. 'You know, if Mr Marchmain had not interrupted us that evening, I'm sure we would have quickly resolved our differences. But Joshua is always so hot-headed.' She gave a soft sigh of pain. 'Have you not found that also?'

'I hardly know Mr Marchmain, Your Grace,' Marianna stammered.

'Really? I understood that you were a good friend of his.'

'Indeed no, ma'am.' She sounded indignant.

'I hope you are not too cross with him. I know he can be a little unconventional.'

'As I said, I hardly know him.'

Marianna was aware of the duchess watching her closely and felt herself flush. Her obvious discomfort must have decided Charlotte to abandon her line of questioning. Changing tack, she said, 'Tell me what you have been doing since we last met.'

Chapter Twelve

Marianna searched her mind urgently for something to report. Anything to leave the subject of Joshua behind. 'I've done little of note, I'm afraid – reading, walking – oh, and I tried sea bathing.'

'You are so brave, my dear. I would be utterly scared of immersing myself in water.'

'I learned to swim as a child – we lived by the sea in Buenos Aires.'

The duchess looked questioningly at her, no doubt hoping to probe more deeply.

'In Argentina.'

'Yes,' the duchess responded a trifle waspishly. 'I am aware of the city's location.' Then quickly recovering, she cooed, 'I have the greatest admiration for ladies who can boast such sporting prowess. As for myself, all I can claim is to ride well. I do pride myself on that.'

'I adore riding, too. Papa put me on my first horse when I was three. But riding in Argentina is very different.'

She sounded wistful and the duchess scented an opportunity. 'How is that?'

'Once out of the city you can gallop forever – the pampas stretches for miles. And you ride on a proper saddle. Like the ones gentlemen use here.'

Charlotte repressed a shudder and murmured encouragingly, 'How wonderful.'

'In England, one feels so constrained.' Marianna warmed to her theme. 'Always having to ride sidesaddle and so gently. Ladies are not permitted to gallop and certainly not to race.'

'If it were possible, would you do so?' the duchess asked cannily.

'It would certainly be fun!' Marianna threw back her head and laughed aloud.

Seeing the girl's dark eyes alight with merriment and her shining curls dancing in pleasure, the older woman felt a surge of envy.

'Of course, one would not race openly, but maybe a race in a more secluded place?' she suggested, apparently absorbed in stirring her tea.

'Wherever would that be, Your Grace?' Marianna's voice conveyed interest and the duchess moved in for the final scene of the little drama she had been busy staging.

'Have you heard of Prince George's famous wager?'

The girl shook her head.

'He bet that he could drive a coach and four down Keere Street, just a short way from here. It is the steepest and narrowest of roads in Lewes. And do you know, he won that waver!'

'He must be very expert.'

'Yes,' her companion said judiciously. 'But I have it in

mind that we women could undertake something even more masterly.'

'How could we do that?'

'Why, by racing our horses down Keere Street,' the duchess produced triumphantly.

Her companion at first looked nonplussed, and then her face fell. 'But surely that would be dangerous.'

'Skilful shall we say?' Charlotte's voice was smooth. 'We would not be hurtling down the road pell mell. It would take considerable expertise to negotiate the steep gradient and find a clear way over stones and cobbles. A very considerable feat!'

'It would certainly be a test of horsemanship.'

'So what do you think?'

'You mean that we should race?'

'Why not?' The duchess smiled as warmly as she could. 'I am longing to do something a little more daring than attending routs and receptions; and it seems that you feel similarly. You said a moment ago that you have been in the saddle since you were three years old, so maybe now is the chance to prove it.'

'I would love to, Your Grace, but I doubt that my father would allow me to undertake such a race.'

'Charlotte, my dear, call me Charlotte. And it's really quite simple. Say nothing to your father and I will tell no-one either. It will be our little secret.'

'But how could we prevent people knowing?'

The duchess's patience was wearing thin but she made one last effort. 'We ride over the Downs to Lewes very early in the morning before anyone stirs. It's sad we will never be able to boast of our exploit, but we'll have the satisfaction of knowing just how clever we have been.'

Marianna was seized with a sudden panic. 'Are you quite sure that it's possible to ride down this road?'

'I would not have suggested it if I thought otherwise, but if you're fearful then of course you must not attempt it, my dear.'

Annoyance rippled through Marianna as her courage was subtly brought into question. 'And we will tell no-one?' she asked, seeking more reassurance.

'Not a soul. No-one will ever know – just we two.'

'When shall we hold the race?'

A silent joy engulfed the duchess. She had caught her fish at last. 'How about the day after tomorrow? That will give us the opportunity to choose suitable horses.'

'And when shall we meet?'

'Just after dawn I think, around five o' clock. The Downs will be wonderful at that time.'

'And we will both come alone?'

'Completely alone,' Charlotte reassured her. 'We will meet at the crossroads which lead into the town and then ride the few paces to Keere Street together.'

She paused for a moment and then said musingly, 'I think I shall make a laurel crown for the victor – though whoever wins, will have to keep it hidden!'

Marianna laughed brightly but her determination to win the laurel crown was strong. She had agreed to the duchess's wild suggestion not wanting to appear cowardly, but now she was filled with a fierce desire to beat the woman. She felt a sharp frisson of pleasure at the thought that she might vanquish the duchess in this one thing, even though she could not rival her in love. It was not a thought she intended to examine too closely.

Her father was walking towards them and bowing to the duchess. 'Your Grace,' he murmured. Then to his daughter, 'The races are nearly over, *querida*. Shall we go?'

'You are not cross, Papa?' she enquired, as he led her back to their place in the grandstand.

'No my dear, I am not cross, but do not make a habit of spending time with that lady.'

Marianna said nothing but consoled herself with the thought that she would be spending only an hour or two with the duchess, and that in any case, no-one would ever know.

⤙

As the last folds of Marianna's jonquil gauze cleared the marquee, Robert Amesbury appeared from the shadows and took her vacated chair.

'Well?'

'It's fixed – I have caught her. The day after tomorrow.'

'So I can spread the good news?'

'As quickly as you can, Robert. Make sure one of your cronies opens a book and encourage all your acquaintance to wager on the result. When the scandal breaks, I want it to be as big as possible. But don't let the news get to her father.'

'Isn't *she* likely to mention it?'

The duchess smiled wryly. 'How little you know! Girls never divulge misdemeanours to their papas. In any case, it's to be *our little secret*.' She screwed up her face in distaste.

'The sooner I rid Brighton of the señorita, the better.'

'With men betting heavily on the race, her reputation will be destroyed,' Amesbury muttered grimly. 'She's likely to be the topic of gossip for months ahead.'

The duchess's smile creamed her face, until her companion continued, 'But what about you? You'll be subject to the same gossip.'

She looked stonily at him. 'I think, Robert, that my credit stands a little better than our young friend's.' Then shrugging her shoulders, she said, 'In any case, there is no way I will ride down that road. It's a death trap.'

'So you won't turn up?'

'I shall meet her as planned, but only to lead her straight to the audience waiting at Keere Street. *You* must invite the most inveterate gossips you can find. *I* will then be the good friend who is trying to protect her from scandal, outraged that she should have even considered such an exploit!'

Amesbury looked doubtful. 'That's all very well, but she's bound to expose your part in setting up the race.'

'She may try but nobody will believe her. I shall say that she was intent on persuading me to race. I tried to deter her but without success, and I've come to Keere Street only to make one last effort to save her.'

'I like it,' Robert mused, rubbing his chin thoughtfully. 'You will be seen as a saintly Samaritan and she a reckless girl, who cares nothing for her reputation and is happy to outrage the *ton* for some shocking spree.'

'Exactly. When she sees that everyone is against her, she will flee. I warrant she will be on the next ferry to Europe.'

'Very neat, Charlotte. It will destroy her utterly but leave you glowing with virtue.'

'Admit it, I am as good a conspirator as you!' The duchess blazed with pride.

'Don't forget that I was the one who revealed her weakness to you.'

'And how has that helped today?'

'Simple. With her predeliction for gambling, it was always probable she could be seduced by a wager.'

The duchess was in benevolent mood. 'Let us call it a draw. If all goes the way I've planned, we will both end content.'

⌒

Marianna started to entertain doubts even before she regained Marine Parade. This mad adventure offered her a last exhilarating grasp at freedom, but was it too mad? Still it had been Charlotte Severn who'd suggested this daring exploit and, though her father did not approve of the duchess, she was a great lady and moved in the very best circles. Nothing she did could ever be truly wrong or rather, Marianna corrected herself, ever be truly challenged. And the race would wrongfoot Joshua. While she was revelling in the company of his mistress, he would still be abed and unknowing.

But the more she considered the matter, the less sure she felt. She could not tell her father what was afoot and certainly not Carmela. And it would be wrong to involve Flora. It was a secret she must keep alone. She hugged the knowledge to herself, trying gradually to build the pleasures of the race in her mind. She was an accomplished horsewoman and there was a good chance she would beat the duchess – Charlotte Severn made a satisfying adversary. Try as she might, Marianna could not warm to the woman and the spectre of the duchess's liaison with Joshua was never far from mind.

And even if she were to lose, she told herself, there were forbidden pleasures: to ride at full stretch for the first time since she'd left Argentina, to feel the wind flow through her hair, hear the pound of hooves in her ear, see the ground swift beneath her. A risky adventure, but worth it!

Chapter Thirteen

Marianna had taken the precaution of ordering a horse from stables some way from Marine Parade. The building was situated at the start of Juggs Way, the winding path used by the Brighton fishwives on their way to sell their menfolk's catch to the good citizens of Lewes and surrounding villages. It was a lengthy walk from the seafront and meant she had to rise very early. The sun was only just emerging from a dawn mist when she swung herself up into the saddle and coaxed the neat bay over the courtyard cobbles and on to the Downs. She had been assured that the pretty mare was the swiftest in the stables.

It was a glorious morning, the air still and translucent, and the rays of an early sun beginning to warm her face as she headed eastwards. Small hedges fenced the lower slopes of the Downs and were filled with the scent of honeysuckle and the sound of birdsong. Once they were left behind, Marianna allowed the horse to fall into a canter over the close-cropped grass and rolling folds of the hills. She wanted the mare to be fresh for the race but not too fresh. The miles melted as though by magic and within half an hour she could see the roofs of Lewes beginning to appear. She wondered if the duchess was already at the crossroads.

A figure, she saw, was just breasting the misty line of the horizon – it must be Charlotte come to meet her. That was unexpected, but it would be companionable to ride into the town together. As the form drew nearer, though, she could see the figure was not that of a woman and began to feel uneasy. She was still a long way from any dwelling and there was not a soul in sight. The man was cloaked against the morning chill but bareheaded, and in a sudden shaft of sunlight, she saw the colour of gold. It could not be, but it was!

'Good morning, Miss Marquez.'

She found herself clenching her fists until her fingernails drew blood. Was she never to be free of him? As he drew closer, she saw his face. It was unsmiling and his bow was brusque.

'I hope you will forgive my trespass. I've been at pains to obey your command, but today I find I cannot.'

Marianna recovered from the shock of seeing him sufficiently to execute a minimal bow. By now they had both come to a halt, their horses beginning to sidle against each other.

'And why have you found it necessary to bother me again, Mr Marchmain?' she enquired in the coldest voice she could manage.

'I understand you have engaged yourself in a contest. I have come to warn you that you should not take part.'

Her eyebrows lifted. 'I was not aware I'd appointed you the arbiter of my conduct.'

'It will not be me who judges your conduct,' he said grimly. 'Although it will be judged – and harshly.'

'And why is that pray?' Her anger was tangible and filled the space between them.

He allowed himself a slight smile. 'Ladies do not engage in races, nor do they risk breaking their necks as you assuredly will.'

'What makes you so certain?' His smile was infuriating her. 'I find your arrogance breathtaking. You should know that I'm accounted an excellent horsewoman.'

He did not respond directly but instead said bluntly, 'Have you seen Keere Street?'

'No.'

'Then you should before you accuse me of arrogance. To race a horse there would place you in certain peril – and not just you but that delightful mare you are riding.'

'I understand it has been done before,' she retorted.

'You refer to Prinny's little escapade, I collect. That nearly ended in disaster and he had a coach behind him to act as a brake. He is also a prince of the realm and princes tend to be forgiven their foibles.'

'Are you saying it would be unseemly to follow his lead?'

'Not just unseemly, but quite shocking. If you value your reputation and that of your father, you should abandon this race. I cannot imagine how you ever agreed to such a foolhardy exploit.'

'I agreed because the proposal came from a person I considered trustworthy – someone *you* introduced me to,' she said bitingly.

'That does not absolve you from making sensible

decisions. I reiterate, give up this race immediately.'

She bristled with annoyance at his words, but his tone was urgent and carried conviction. Astride a powerful chestnut, he looked magnificent. He also looked serious. She had never previously encountered him in such a severe mood and, though she was still smarting, she took notice of what he said. But how on earth had he come upon her here, miles from anywhere. And how did he know about the race?

'This morning's arrangements were secret,' she protested, 'and I cannot understand how you know of them.'

'All of Brighton knows of them. The whole town is buzzing with the scandal. There is even a book being run.'

He saw her puzzlement. 'Wagers, Miss Marquez, bets on who will win. Regretfully, I have to report that you are seen as an unlikely victor.' His light tone did nothing to disguise the gravity of his news.

Marianna was appalled. 'I don't understand how this is,' she faltered. 'How could the race have become common knowledge?'

His gaze swept over her, at first sardonic and then with something approaching sympathy. 'No, I imagine you don't.'

'We had an agreement,' she stammered. 'It was to be between the two of us.'

He was silent but his face made plain that he knew everything.

'And the duchess – surely she would not be a part of anything openly scandalous?' Marianna was still groping her way through the dark, trying to make sense of the morning's bewilderments.

'I doubt that she would,' he replied, tight-lipped.

'But she is meeting me.'

'Yes?' he smiled derisively, his gold-flecked eyes glittering in the sunlight now flooding over the downland.

'I have an appointment with her at the crossroads in just a few minutes.'

'Then allow me to keep it for you.'

She gasped. 'But – '

'My advice,' he interrupted roughly, 'is to turn around and ride back to Brighton immediately. Return to Marine Parade as fast as you can and say nothing to anyone about this day's doings. To the world, you never left your father's house.'

'But nobody will believe that, especially not the people who have placed bets.' Her voice wavered.

He looked at the long dark lashes downcast over pale cheeks, the full lips trembling despite all her efforts at control, and had a strong desire to punch someone.

'It was a joke, was it not?' he suggested encouragingly. 'A joke got up between you and the duchess. You never meant it seriously. Why would you willingly risk your life in such a foolhardy escapade?'

'And the duchess?'

'She will tell her own tale no doubt.'

'But she will still be waiting for me.'

'I will undertake to put her mind at rest,' he said caustically. 'I'll ride to the crossroads this instant and tell her that you have reconsidered the propriety of taking part in such a race.'

'I see you have it pat.' Her fear and frustration came tumbling out.

'Don't be angry, Marianna.' His voice softened and she felt herself once more caressed by velvet. 'You have been misled but the situation is not irreparable. Allow me to be of some small service.'

His sincerity was evident and, battered by what she had just learned, she could only acquiesce. 'I thank you sir,' she responded in a small voice.

She turned the horse to retrace her steps, all pleasure in the lovely morning gone. How could she have been so stupid as to involve herself in something so evidently scandalous? How could the whole town have known of her intentions? Joshua had lodged no accusation, but it was clear he believed Charlotte Severn to be the malign influence behind her troubles. If so, his intimacy with the woman made him the very man to deal with the problem.

She had been foolish enough to believe Charlotte's repeated assurances that their race would remain secret and in her innocence had trusted the older woman to be sincere. She had been betrayed but, if she were honest, she'd contributed richly to that betrayal. She'd been so intent on beating Charlotte, on avenging her humiliation at Steine House, her humiliation over Joshua, that she'd lost all sense of perspective. She must never again make such a mistake. In the meantime, all she could do was to rely on Joshua to stifle the gossip which must already be circulating.

⌒

As soon as he reached the crossroads, he saw Charlotte

pacing irritably up and down, her horse grazing by the roadside. At the sound of his approach she wheeled around, her face startled at the sight of this unexpected visitor.

Joshua reined in beside her. 'Your Grace, how charming to see you out and about on such a fine morning. I trust you are enjoying your ride.' His voice was calm and gave no hint of his feelings.

The duchess's eyes narrowed. 'And why are you riding so early, Joshua? It's most unusual.'

'I can rise with the best of people if I have reason.' His smile was ominous.

'And what would that be?' she enquired sweetly.

'Let us say, a little pre-emptive action.'

'I see.'

'I'm sure you do.'

'And since when have you played the shining knight?'

'Since I found myself wading through the festering garbage of a corrupt court.' She turned white and raised her whip hand in fury as though to strike. Unperturbed, he continued, 'But don't let me detain you. For myself, I have friends to meet – I believe our rendezvous is Keere Street, somewhat singular but one can never account for the whims of one's friends.'

And with that he rode off into Lewes, leaving the duchess furiously snatching at her horse's bridle.

A crowd of young bucks had already gathered at Keere Street and there were even a few grey heads among the crowd, Joshua noted. What people would do for a titbit of scandal in the hothouse environment the Regent created around him!

'Good morning, gentlemen.' He hailed them, relaxed as ever.

'Morning Marchmain, come to see the fun?' asked one budding young dandy, almost muffled by a shirt collar whose starched points reached to his cheek bones.

'I fear not.'

'Why ever not?'

Joshua glanced with distaste at the coarse-looking man who had spoken. His high colour signalled a partiality for claret. 'That Spanish filly – they say she's an out and outer on a horse, but I'm still backing the duchess. Tactics will win the day!'he rumbled floridly.

'Quite possibly, but not this day. Neither lady will be coming.'

'How can that be?' A sporting gentleman in a high-crowned beaver and a driving coat of many capes was indignant.

'It was all a joke, my dear fellows.' Joshua was at his negligent best. 'You cannot seriously imagine that two ladies of such impeccable virtue would engage in horse racing!'

'You mean the whole thing is a hum?' the dandy asked disconsolately.

'The joke is on us, I'm afraid. The ladies have proved that men will place a wager on just about anything.'

There were some disgruntled mutterings among the group, but Joshua cut it short by suggesting that one of the present company might like to pick up the gauntlet themselves. As one, they peered down the steep hill, watching it bump and curl on its way, finally to vanish in a dark pit of shade.

Lord Wivenhoe summed up what they were all thinking. 'We'd have to be mad! Let's get a heavy wet – the Lewes Arms should be open by now.'

Chapter Fourteen

Joshua rode slowly towards Brighton, well pleased with his morning's work. He was confident he had managed to quash the torrent of gossip that might have poured unhindered if Marianna had made an appearance at Keere Street. Now he'd had time to think, he could see Charlotte's strategy clearly. She would have delivered the girl into the lion's den, then stood back and protested her own innocence while the lions devoured the lamb. He smiled wryly. Marianna was hardly a lamb. She'd provoked him at every opportunity and by rights he should have left her to fend for herself. She'd made no secret of the fact that she despised him, had even called him a rake to his face. So why put himself out?

Was it her charm? Maybe, but he'd known more beautiful women. Was it that she was interesting and intelligent? But she was also young and untried. So what? She was a challenge perhaps, no simpering miss certainly. And though her impulsiveness led her into danger, it sprang from an unconstrained spirit. She still possessed the joy in life that he'd long ago lost, whether she was dreaming on a beach, learning to fence, carving a path through the waves or taking up this ridiculous wager. How long would that free spirit survive the bludgeoning of an arranged marriage?

She'd begun to penetrate his heart, he realised, and that was troubling. When she was close he found himself captivated, unable to think or act the man he'd been for so many years. He looked deep into those expressive eyes and wanted them to speak only to him, longed for them to sparkle with mischief, to cloud with passion just for him. He must put an end to such feelings, and ensure she made no further inroads into his life. He had no wish to be drawn into the kind of intimacy he'd been at pains to shun for years. It could only lead to disaster.

Once upon a time he'd been overpowered by youthful passion, had convinced himself that finally he'd found love in his life. He'd been heedless, inviting the spread of vicious gossip, piling further hurt on his despairing family and sacrificing the one friendship he'd learned to treasure. That first and last wretched experience of love had been a lesson for life: never tangle with innocence. He was fairly sure he need not fear Marianna's attachment – this morning's events would have done nothing to change her attitude. He would still be a man to avoid.

Charlotte Severn would avoid him, too. Their liaison had grown stale and unsavoury months ago and today's encounter was as good a way as any to draw a final line beneath it. He had suspected Charlotte to be venal, but not realised the depths to which she'd stoop. Ever since the *soirée*, he'd mistrusted her intentions towards Marianna and recently the duchess and that cur, Amesbury, had had their heads together a little too often. When news of the projcted race reached him, he'd guessed that the two of them were involved. But why Charlotte should wish to destroy the young girl mystified him. Even less understandable was why Amesbury should be privy to the plot. Joshua wondered if either of them would be waiting for him at the Pavilion – if so, it was likely to be an interesting conversation!

〜

The duchess, though, had ridden straight to Steine House and found Robert Amesbury pacing up and down the pavement, his face wolfishly eager. She swept past him and up the steps to the open front door. Together they walked into the drawing room and for the first time he had a clear view of her face and knew that something had gone badly amiss.

'She never came,' Charlotte said baldly. 'Marchmain must have intercepted her and persuaded her to return home.'

'And you let him!'

'What else could I do? She was already riding back when he met me at the crossroads. And it was clear he would expose my part in the plan if I did not also return to Brighton immediately.'

'And?'

'And he must have ridden onto Keere Street and told some tale to account for our absence,' she concluded wearily.

Amesbury began pacing the pale grey drawing room carpet, leaving a dark tread in his wake. His face was thunderous and he bit his lip constantly, his agitation finally spilling over into words.

'It is hard to see how you could have managed this more badly,' he exploded.

'What do you mean, *I* couldn't have managed it more badly.'

'You were the one who insisted that this would work. You would humiliate the girl, you said. Now look – she has humiliated you!'

'She has not. And let me remind you that you agreed to the plan. In fact, I recall that at the racecourse when we spoke of it, you expressed complete confidence.'

'Clearly I was wrong to rely on your ability to bring this tiresome girl to account. From now on, I will be the one making decisions.'

'As you wish. I have no further interest in the matter.'

'You had sufficient interest until today.'

'It's unlikely that after this morning's events I will enjoy any kind of friendship with Joshua,' she said dully. 'And since that's so, I no longer care what happens to the girl.'

Amesbury moved towards her and took her hands. 'Do you not think, Your Grace,' he said courteously, his tone markedly different, 'that Mr Marchmain might be persuaded back into the fold if this wretched girl were no longer around.'

The duchess broke free from his hold and walked towards the door.

'In any case, don't you want revenge?' he called after her retreating figure.

Charlotte stopped, her hand beating a tattoo with her riding crop against the velvet skirt of her modish ensemble.

'Can you deliver me revenge, Robert?' she asked slowly.

'I can. We have been too complicated. It needs something simple, something obvious.'

'You have an idea?'

'I have. Will you trust me with it?'

Her response was tart. 'As you've been at pains to point out, my plan has failed dismally. So what have I to lose?'

⌒

It had taken time for Marianna to return her horse to the stables and walk back along the seafront, and she was lucky to regain Marine Parade before anyone in the household became aware of her absence. Slipping into the house through the rear entrance, she heard distant sounds coming from the kitchen but managed to reach her bedroom unseen.

She was still unhooking the last gold fastenings of her riding dress when Flora knocked on the door with her morning chocolate. Seeing her maid's perplexed face, she gestured to the heavy gown she had just removed.

'I was going to ride this morning but have changed my mind. I find I'm too tired to go far today.'

The girl looked concerned. 'Then you must rest, miss. Maybe keep to your parlour this morning – you still have books to read. But make sure you drink your chocolate while it's still hot.' She closed the door quietly behind her and Marianna was left to her thoughts.

Few of them were pleasant. The irony of the situation was crushing: she was relying on a man of dubious reputation to save her own. Joshua would save her, but why? She'd not endeared herself to him, rejecting all his advances and making clear that she found his presence odious. He'd deserved her severity – his behaviour had been intolerable. But not this morning.

This morning his face had been grave, his tone abrupt and his words a million miles from seductive. There had been no trace of the libertine. Instead he'd been stern and insistent – his rebuke over her conduct could have come from Luke Trelawny himself. She thought she had discerned some sympathy in those gold-flecked eyes as he'd turned to go, maybe even a little tenderness. It seemed unlikely, but the thought made her feel slightly giddy. In her mind's eye she saw him again, handsome and unyielding. Astride the large chestnut, his caped greatcoat flung carelessly over his shoulders, he'd looked superb. He'd also looked like a man on whom she could depend. And so she had consigned her fate to his hands or rather to his silver tongue. She could not imagine the tale he would tell those eager scandalmongers waiting at Keere Street. But she knew without doubt that he would make her safe.

Chapter Fifteen

It was to be some days before she set eyes on Josdhua again. For a while, she kept close to home, a little afraid that gossip might still be bandied around the town. But no discomfiting news reached her, and she felt sure that if her name had become common currency, her father would know it. It was reasssuring but strangely dull. Joshua's continued absence from her daily round was naturally to be welcomed. It could do her no good to be in the company of a known womaniser but, if she were honest, life without him had become tedious.

Then the summons came. Piqued by the success of the duchess's evening, the Prince Regent had been persuaded to hold a *soirée* of his own. He was well-known as a devotee of music and was intent on outdoing Charlotte Severn's offering. Not just one Italian soprano but three had been invited to perform on the following Saturday. Robert Amesbury's suggestion that the same audience be invited that had flocked to Steine House had appealed to George's vanity and his desire to upstage the duchess.

The household at Marine Parade had therefore received an invitation, and despite reservations over the Regent's lifestyle, there was excitement in the house at the prospect of an evening at the Royal Pavilion. Even Carmela took to perusing fashion plates, a few years out of date to be sure, but with a view to having a new gown made for this very special event.

On the Friday morning a large parcel bearing Marianna's name arrived at the door – the dress promised by her father on the night of their own reception. She peeled back the layers of rustling tissue and pulled from the parcel an exquisite white satin underdress and an overskirt of the palest pink gauze, together with new pink kid slippers and a fillet of tiny pink blossoms to be woven though her curls. Flora was entranced: such possibilities for dressing her lady!

~

Saturday came and Marianna felt nervous. Not because she was likely to meet Joshua – if he knew she'd been invited, he was almost sure to keep away – and really, it was most disconcerting. But more worrisome was the strong possibility that her tormentor would be present at the Regent's entertainment. After hours of tortured thought, Marianna decided that all she could do was wear a brave face and refuse to allow the duchess to know how much she feared her.

The prospect of unknown splendours within the palace was an incentive to courage and punctually at eight o'clock, Marianna, her father and cousin, drove through the Pavilion gardens and alighted from their carriage in the shelter of a portico modelled on an Indian temple. Marianna had often walked around the perimeter of the palace looking with wonder at its oriental façade and she could scarcely believe that she was now about to penetrate its mysteries. An impassive footman ushered them through the octagonal vestibule into the entrance hall, a square apartment lit by a Chinese lantern suspended from a tented roof.

'Papa,' she whispered in amazement. 'Those statues are wearing real robes!' She pointed to the life-size Chinese mandarins that stood in each corner of the room.

Carmela took in this abomination and pronounced her verdict. 'Ridiculous! And it is so very hot in here,' she grumbled. Despite it being July, a roaring fire filled the marble fireplace.

From the Inner Hall they made their way into the Long Gallery which linked all the state rooms arranged along the east front of the building. Here, three further fireplaces threw out yet more heat into an atmosphere that was already sultry. Marianna was relieved that her dress was of the most delicate material and that both she and her cousin carried fans.

'Let us wait by the glass doors,' Ernesto suggested. 'They will be the coolest spot in the room.'

They made their way towards the long windows which looked out over lawns still dappled by sunshine even at this late hour, and waited for their turn to be presented to the Regent. She looked around her in awe. The Gallery walls were covered with painted canvas, a peach blossom background with rocks, trees, shrubs, birds and flowers pencilled in pale blue. A deep pile carpet patterned in matching tones spread beneath their feet.

The room was divided into five sections and the Regent

stood at its centre in order to welcome his guests. He caught Marianna's eyes immediately since he was dressed in the greatest of finery but with little consideration for his bulk. She had leisure to study him and saw the lines of dissipation etched on his face, a testimony to his selfishness and excess. But when she advanced to meet him to make a nervous curtsy, she was disarmed by the kindness he showed in seeking to put her at her ease.

The hum of conversation was gradually abating and people began to move towards the vast mirrored doors at one end of the Gallery.

'Everyone is making for the Music Room,' her father said quietly. 'We should do the same.'

A blaze of red and gold oriental splendour made Marianna gasp. If the Long Gallery had been superb, the Music Room was overwhelming. The ceiling was gilded, supported by pillars covered in gold leaf and decorated with carved dragons and serpents. A lamp made to resemble a huge water lily and coloured crimson, gold and white, hung from the centre with gilded dragons clinging to its underside. More dragons embellished the crimson canopies of the four doorways leading out of the room and still more writhed above the blue and crimson window drapes.

Large ottomans decorated with fluted silk and covered in enormous satin bolsters lined every wall and an Axminster carpet of spectacular design flooded the floor: a riot of golden suns, stars, serpents and dragons on a pale blue ground.

'Utterly vulgar,' Carmela announced, causing Ernesto to glance anxiously over his shoulder, fearing his forthright relative had been overheard.

His cousin, though, was unrepentant. 'To think of all the money wasted on such immoral foppery!' she exclaimed.

Ernesto made haste to usher his companions towards the yellow satin seats that had been set out for the audience. 'I think we should have a good view of the musicians from here,' he said soothingly.

Carmela made no reply but noisily unfurled her fan. The heat was even more oppressive than in the Gallery and many of the ladies were already cooling themselves vigorously.

The prince's own private band of wind and string instruments, formed from the cream of Europe's musical talent, accompanied each of the three fabled sopranos. Throughout the recital, the Regent who had learned to play the violincello in his youth, beat time with his foot. Marianna once more set herself to sit stoically through the entertainment. She hoped her reward might be to explore this strange and exotic building.

As the last note faded, an army of footmen whisked away the audience's small chairs and yet another army carried in tray after tray of refreshments. Marianna and her family began to walk around the room, taking in the expensive array of Chinese vases, pots, glasses and pot-pourris that decorated every available surface.

They had stopped in front of a particularly ugly ceramic jar when a modestly dressed grey-haired man came to her father's side and whispered a message in his ear. Ernesto looked surprised but immediately touched Marianna on the arm and signalled that they should go with the retainer. Equally surprised, she followed, and found herself confronting the Regent himself. The prince, large and perfumed, smiled graciously down at her, seeming to be pleased with what he saw.

'Señor Marquez, lend me your daughter for a few minutes.' The prince's languid tone did nothing to disguise that it was a command rather than a request.

Ernesto was uncertain, particularly as a faint aroma of chartreuse hung in the air, mixed imperceptibly with the heady scent the prince affected. The Regent seemed unimpaired, however, and the ambassador, mindful of his position, felt unable to quibble.

'I was wishful of speaking to you at greater length, my dear.' The prince smiled archly down at her and offered his arm. She found herself returning his smile.

'I love to welcome foreigners to my modest little abode and I am most interested in how you are enjoying your stay in Brighton.'

'Very much, sir,' she responded politely. 'I love living by the sea for in Madrid we are landlocked.'

George looked gratified. 'I remember when I first came to Brighthelmstone – that was Brighton's original name, you know. It was a small fishing village then, but I was captivated. I simply had to build myself a folly in sight of the sea.'

She smiled again. 'It is very beautiful,' she concurred dutifully, though not at all sure that it was.

'Come, let me show you.' And Marianna found herself once more walking around the Music Room while he described in detail every one of his purchases. She knew she should feel flattered, but the heat of the room, the proximity of the rotund prince and a slight but unexplained feeling of panic, made her wish that he would not be quite so gracious.

He steered her expertly back into the Long Gallery still talking smoothly about his possessions.

'This vase, you see, came from a most remote province of China. I had my envoy negotiate for months. Do you think it worth his effort?'

'Indeed, it is most striking, Your Highness.'

He looked satisfied. 'How delightful to find a young woman of such discernment. So different from some of your countrymen...' The sentence drifted away. 'But I have heard only the very best said of you, and tonight you have proved your champions right.'

Marianna was left little time to wonder what exactly he had heard and who could have spoken of her. They had left the Gallery by this time and traversed the library without stopping and were now in a room even hotter than anything she had so far experienced.

'The Yellow Drawing Room,' George announced. 'We can be private here.'

'Your Highness, should I not call my cousin?' She was fearful of offending such an important person, but becoming more anxious by the minute.

'Your cousin is occupied,' the prince returned cheerfully, 'and you have only to say that you were with me to escape a scolding.'

She felt doubtful on this point, but found it difficult to rebuff a man who was old enough to be her father and a royal prince, too.

'These are my private rooms,' George repeated, 'and so much more pleasant than the public areas, do you not think? So much more tranquil.'

Marianna had unfortunately to agree. As she looked around, there was not a person in sight. By now she had become accustomed to the assault on her senses and, without a flicker of surprise, she took in the room's array of mirrors, Chinese pictures, flying dragons and white and gold pillars wreathed by serpents. What was more disturbing, though, was the sight of an open doorway leading to another room beyond. This was clearly the prince's personal chamber and she was horrified by a glimpse of an enormous bed in the far reaches of the room, massive and mahogany-panelled, with at least five mattresses and crowded with satin bolsters and pillows.

A gnawing panic had been growing ever stronger. Now it overwhelmed her and, when she should have fled, she stayed transfixed. The light from a hundred candles bounced from mirror to mirror, reflection to reflection, disorientating her completely.

'I see you admiring yourself,' the prince joked heavily, as she turned this way and that to avoid the piercing light. 'And so you should. You are a taking little puss – my spies have not lied.'

Now thoroughly alarmed, Marianna tried to extricate herself as diplomatically as she could, but the prince was before her.

'I have brought you here to see some very special treasures,' he whispered hotly in her ear.

Her mind went into a tailspin at the thought of what treasures he meant, but she had little time to consider for he was pulling out a series of drawers from a small chest which sat on the nearby table. The drawers contained the most brilliant collection of jewellery she had ever seen.

'What do you think?' he asked grandly.

Shaken, all she could utter was, 'Magnificent!'

'And which of these gems would you choose above all others?'

The heat and light were making her dizzy and she tried to steady herself. 'It would be impossible to make such a choice, Your Highness. Every piece is exquisite.'

'Try,' he pressed.

Hoping to hasten her departure, she pointed to a small butterfly brooch studded in diamonds. 'This is very elegant, I think.'

He frowned; it was obviously the wrong choice. 'I agree, most elegant,' he said a little too heartily. 'But have you seen the other butterfly brooch? This one here.' He pointed to an item at the back of the drawer. 'Filigree – not as expensive, of course – but I would say far more fitting for a young girl.'

The prince lifted the filigree butterfly from its bed of satin. 'Here my dear. Take this as a small token of my friendship.'

Marianna had thought it could not get any worse, but it had. 'I am most grateful for your kindness,' she stuttered, 'but I cannot accept a gift.'

'Cannot?'

His frown deepened and his eyebrows rose haughtily.

He looked an entirely different prince and she was forced to reconsider. 'It is most kind of you,' she said faintly.

He beamed again. 'I am well known for my generosity, but you must think nothing of it. You are a delightful child and deserve to have pretty things. Now how about a little thanks?'

'Naturally, I thank you very much,' she stammered, unsure of just how effusive she had to be.

'You can do better than that surely!'

And with those words he lunged towards her, wrapping his arms around her in a bear-like clasp and pushing her towards the open door and the bed that lay beyond. The feel of his breath on her cheek and the overwhelming scent he wore repulsed her. She tried to struggle free, but the Regent was no lightweight and she was inexorably propelled towards danger.

'I like a little resistance, my dear. That is all to the good. But not too much, you know, not too much,' he was saying.

She felt herself reeling and tried desperately hard not to faint. That was the last thing she must do – she had to keep control. But she was losing the struggle.

Chapter Sixteen

A toneless voice spoke from the door. 'Excuse me, sir, but Signora Martinelli is about to leave and I know you will wish to thank her personally.'

Joshua Marchmain was dressed in the conventional dark coat, embroidered waistcoat and light-coloured satin breeches of a gentleman's evening attire, but to Marianna he wore angel's wings.

The Regent stopped pawing at her and looked annoyed, but then waved away the intruder. 'No, no, Marchmain, *you* must thank her for me. I am sure you will find just the right words. As you see, I am a little busy,' he finished irritably.

'I should perhaps mention, sir, that Señor Marquez is also waiting – he wishes to be reunited with his daughter.'

The Regent turned an angry red and reluctantly let go of his captive. 'We will speak later, Marchmain,' he barked. 'Leave me now.'

'Certainly, sir,' Joshua said smoothly. 'Miss Marquez?' and he ushered her out of the room and towards the library. As the door closed behind them, she heard the Regent mutter quite distinctly, 'Drat Amesbury, telling me the chit was a likely romp.'

At the sound of her enemy's name, she stumbled, and Joshua had to step quickly forward to offer a supporting arm. Marianna began to shake uncontrollably. All the time she had been in the Regent's apartment, she had managed – just – to keep her nerve, but rescue had brought with it reaction.

For a moment she clung to his arm, then drawing herself up straight, she said decisively, 'I cannot go back to the Gallery just now, Mr Marchmain. I need a few minutes alone.'

His gold-flecked eyes surprised her with their concern and, when he spoke, his voice lacked its usual mocking note. 'Will you allow me to escort you to my studio?' he asked gently. 'It is close by and I can promise solitude. You may be alone there for as long as you wish.'

She nodded agreement and he led her towards the western side of the Pavilion. It was not so lavishly furnished as the rooms she had previously seen, but a great deal cooler. At the entrance to his studio, he paused and waved her through the doorway, motioning her to take a seat. She noticed that he kept the door ajar.

'I will leave you to your thoughts. But before I do, tell me about Amesbury.'

The request came out of the blue and she looked at him, startled.

'It's evident that he was behind the unpleasantness you suffered tonight. I heard the Regent's words as clearly as you.'

Her face was bright red but she remained silent.

'Marianna, answer me,' he said a little less gently, 'Why

has Robert Amesbury been hawking you to the prince as a likely lady-bird?'

She still said nothing.

'He was also behind the Keere Street race,' he continued inexorably. 'He seems to be trying to ruin you. Why?'

She supposed Joshua deserved to know the truth since he had rescued her more than once from Amesbury's wickedness. But it was still painful to talk.

'I crossed him in the past and I think he is seeking revenge,' she managed.

'In what way did you cross him?'

'I met Lord Amesbury three years ago,' she began falteringly. 'It was when I came to England to stay with my aunt, Lady Foyle.'

'Yes,' he encouraged.

'I stupidly lost money to him at faro, money I couldn't repay. He took my handkerchief as a token of payment. I didn't realise that it was a scandalous thing to do and when I tried to get it back, he blackmailed me.'

'That sounds like the man. But could you not have confessed your troubles to your aunt and asked her to pay the debt?'

'He wouldn't take money,' she said, without elaborating further.

Joshua looked grim. She imagined that he must know Amesbury well enough to guess how deep the man's villainy ran. Aloud he said, 'Would it be indelicate to enquire how you resolved your difficulties?'

'I eloped.'

'What!?'

'Not exactly eloped,' she clarified. 'A friend helped me escape from England. The plan was to go to my father's friends in Paris and then on to Spain, but we only got as far as Dover.'

The innocence of the recital seemed to make him smile. 'What happened at Dover?'

'Dominic's sister arrived and made us return to London.'

'Dominic?' A frown passed swiftly across Joshua's face.

'Yes, Dominic Latimer. Do you know him?'

'I've heard of him,' Joshua said shortly.

'He got into immense trouble because of me and was sent back to Cornwall. But at least there was no scandal. And it turned out that as I was under age, Lord Amesbury could not insist on the debt. He had no hold over me, but my aunt paid him anyway.'

'You seem to have a lively ability to get into scrapes, Señorita Marquez.'

'I do, don't I?'

She looked so comically concerned, that he burst out laughing. 'A girl of my own heart! Come, let us forget Prinny and his dastardly ways. Will you let me show you around my workroom or would you prefer to remain alone?'

'I would enjoy seeing your workroom,' she said a little shyly.

Though small by palace standards, the room was bright and airy, the last rays of the evening sun flooding through the open doors that led to the gardens beyond. A breeze lifted the delicate voile drapes hanging either side of the long windows. It was a relief to breathe fresh air.

Feeling a great deal less shaky, Marianna walked slowly

around the room, looking with interest at the pictures hung four deep on the walls and the several piles of canvasses stacked against a large chest. A battered paint-splashed smock was thrown carelessly over an easel and to one side a tray held paint tubes of every conceivable hue.

'What do you think?'

'It's a real artist's studio,' she responded warmly.

'A studio at least – and I keep plenty of "real" art as a reminder of what I *should* be aiming for.'

She gazed around her. Works by the painter she'd admired at the Grove gallery were scattered across each wall. He was certainly a fine artist. She felt Joshua watching her as she wandered the room, every now and then pausing to look at a particular painting, viewing it from different angles until she was satisfied. He made no attempt to follow but, when she began to browse the canvasses stacked against the corner chest, he moved swiftly towards her and placed a restraining hand on her wrist. In the companionable silence, she'd regained much of her composure and his sudden prohibition jarred.

'They are mere daubings,' he explained smoothly. 'Without interest and not good enough to frame.'

'This looks a little more than daubing.' She gestured to the canvas which fronted the stack. 'It catches the light and the Sussex coast perfectly.'

'You are generous, but the remainder are much the same and hardly worth your attention.' His tone admitted no disagreement. 'Can I get you some refreshment before we return to the Gallery?'

'A glass of lemonade would be welcome.'

She tried for a neutral tone, but felt irritated at his determination to change the subject. It was strange that he was so opposed to her viewing the remaining works. Probably just vanity, she thought. No doubt the pictures deteriorated in quality the further one explored. But when he left her for a moment to pour the wine, she was sufficiently intrigued to defy his wishes and began surreptitiously to flick through them.

He'd been right about the similarity of the paintings; they were virtually all seascapes, the light clear, the atmosphere still and the meeting of sea and sky a hardly perceptible line. As she skimmed each canvas, it seemed their horizons grew more and more distant, attempting almost to span infinity. Something about them called to her, their sense of freedom perhaps, their suggestion of escape.

More and more seascapes, but then in the middle of the stack, a lone portrait. It was the image of a young girl. Dark eyes looked searchingly out at her, raven curls tumbled onto soft shoulders and the creamy skin of arms and breast gleamed translucent in the dying light of the day. She gasped: she was looking at herself.

⌒

He turned at the sound, a glass in his hand, and stood motionless as her eyes travelled from the painting to his face.

'This is me!'

Chapter Seventeen

'I'm glad that at least it's recognisable.' The joke fell a little flat.

'But why have you painted me?'

'I take my inspiration where I find it.' His tone was negligent. 'Your face intrigued me – it's not an English face and I wanted to capture it on canvas if I could.'

'It's very good,' she said slowly and looked back at the portrait.

The face was a study in radiance, the eyes sparkling with vitality, the curls glistening and tumbling with hidden life. Every line of the painting spoke feeling and she felt dazed at the thoughts that came unbidden to her mind. Was it possible that she stirred such emotions in him?

His brusque enquiry cut her reverie short. 'Your father mentioned you would shortly be travelling to Spain. How long do you stay in Brighton?'

She ceased dreaming immediately. The return to her aunts had been temporarily forgotten, lost in more pressing concerns. Now it recurred with unwelcome clarity.

'I'm not sure. For as long as my father thinks it worthwhile. I imagine that Papa will return to London when the Regent travels back to Carlton House.'

'And you will leave for Spain?' She found his questioning unsettling, but nodded assent.

'Then be on your guard during the weeks you remain here. You have attracted the enmity of people in high places, the Duchess of Severn as well as Amesbury.'

'I cannot understand why. Until I came to Brighton, I had never met the lady.'

'Charlotte Severn is a jealous woman,' he said obliquely.

She sipped at her wine, unsure of his meaning, but then Joshua enlightened her. 'It seems Her Grace feels my interest in you is too great, hence her rather clumsy attempts at your social humiliation.'

A ready blush flew to Marianna's cheeks and she dared not look at him.

'She is mistaken, however. You are a piece of perfection, but I'm not in the market for *ingenues*. I leave that to the connoisseurs of Spain.'

His words were unexpectedly biting. He seemed to be blaming her for a future over which she had no control.

'I'm sure the duchess will be delighted to hear the news,' she responded as witheringly as she could. 'Perhaps you should tell her yourself. But do it quickly – it will spare me any further "unpleasantness".' Indignantly, she began to pace up and down the room, her skirts swishing in noisy displeasure.

'What the duchess knows is of no concern to me.' He was equally withering. 'And I'm insulted that you believe me willing to consort with a woman capable of such baseness.'

'Your friendship is at an end?' Marianna could hardly

believe her ears.

'It has been at an end for some time.'

'I did not know that.'

'Why would you?' he responded acidly.

Her heart did a strange little dance. Whatever had tied him to the duchess, the knot was well and truly broken. It was time to call a truce.

'You've been good enough to rescue me,' she began with difficulty.

'On a number of occasions.'

'On a number of occasions,' she agreed. 'It would be unbecoming in me not to acknowledge that.'

'It would – and so...?'

'And so I should apologise for calling you a rake.'

'You should not,' he said unexpectedly. 'Since a rake is what I am.'

Marianna let out a long breath. Really he was impossible.

'But,' he continued, 'I give you my word that you will never find me other than an honourable man.'

She flushed again, his words seeming to hint at a deeper friendship. 'Why do you paint the sea so often?' she asked, eager to change the subject.

'I hardly know. Because the sea is ever changing and I'm equally restless?'

She considered this for a moment but, before she could reply, he went on, 'Perhaps because the sea offers a promise.'

'Of what?'

'Liberty, movement, transformation – all of these and more.'

She was intrigued. 'Why would you wish for such things?'

'Why not?'

'I can think of a dozen reasons. You already have the liberty to be or do what you wish. You are wealthy, popular with those you live among, a favourite with the Regent. Why would you want to change?'

His laugh rang a little hollow. 'Nothing in your list persuades me. The palace is a web of lies and popularity at Court is as transient as the gossip it feeds upon. As for wealth, it's certainly better to have money than not, but that is the sum of its importance.'

For a moment, she was taken aback until she recalled his words the very first day they'd met. She had wondered then why such an obviously successful man needed the solace of painting.

'It's always possible to change one's life,' she said tentatively. 'For a man, if not for a woman.'

'You think so? That is the innocence of youth talking. Once one's feet are set upon a path, Marianna, they are generally doomed to tread it for ever more.'

She was disconcerted by the weariness in his voice, but then he seemed to shrug off his depression and consider her intently. 'Why do you think a woman is not able to change her world, if she has enough spirit? I cannot believe you to be wholly powerless in deciding the course of *your* life.'

'There are circumstances,' she murmured.

'Really? And what are those circumstances?'

She had no answer. Instead she took refuge in a timeworn sentiment. 'Change isn't always for the best.'

'Ah yes, the old *cliché*. The trouble with truisms is that they are so often right. Change isn't always good, the sea doesn't always deliver its promise.'

For a second only, she glimpsed the deep well of disillusion beneath his customary calm.

'Your home in Suffolk – doesn't that hold promise?' she asked quickly. 'It would seem an ideal place to set up a permanent studio.'

'I have little interest in the house.' He had regained his nonchalance. 'I inherited Castle March from an uncle a few years back. It was not where I grew up: I hardly know the area.'

'Where did you grow up?'

'Oxfordshire.'

'And do you never visit the county?' They were talking as friends and she felt emboldened.

'I no longer have ties there, or indeed anywhere.'

'But your family?'

'Yes?' The monosyllable should have warned her that she was approaching dangerous ground, but she pressed on. She wanted to know as much as she could about him.

'Your family is still in Oxfordshire?'

'I have a brother living there.' His voice lacked emotion. 'I hardly know him – he is ten years older than I. My parents have been dead these five years.'

'I'm sorry to hear that.' She felt bad now at having obliged him to offer information he evidently wished to keep to himself, but he seemed unperturbed.

'Don't be. We were not a close family.'

'They didn't share your interest in art then?'

'They didn't share my interest in anything.' His laugh was laconic. 'I must confess to being an embarrassment to my family from the moment I was born. My parents were more than contented with one child and my arrival was inconvenient to say the least. And then I managed to continue the good work by becoming a permanent black sheep. My brother was the model son, while I spent my youth breaking every known prohibition. It's hardly surprising I was expelled from the family seat at an early age.'

She looked stricken and he said in a rousing voice, 'There's no need for tears. I hated my home whereas the time I spent travelling in Europe has given me lasting pleasure.'

'But you must have been very young when you were sent abroad.' Marianna felt a sadness settle on her heart.

'Young enough, but I survived. Families have to be negotiated, do they not?' he asked slyly. 'Yours, for instance, seem intent on marrying you to a man you do not even know.'

'They are not forcing me,' she protested, 'I've agreed.'

'But why would you do so?' He sounded genuinely perplexed.

'I have to marry.'

'Then choose someone you love.'

'As you have?' she retorted.

'Learn from my mistakes. Life without love is hardly worth living.'

'I have loved,' she returned with dignity, 'but it was not sufficient.'

For the first time, she found herself openly acknowledging the hurt she'd suffered. But somehow the memory of Luke was no longer as distressing.

'He must have been blind, deaf and insane to boot,' Joshua said roughly. Then catching her hands in his, he demanded, 'Tell me his name, and I will personally knock some sense into him!'

She smiled up at him, warmed by the sincerity of his voice and the glow from those leonine eyes.

'I fear you are too late.' And she allowed herself a small gurgle of laughter. 'He has already made his decision and married another.'

'Then he deserves even more of a kicking.'

Joshua let go of her hands to reach for a stray tendril of hair, then wrapped it around his finger and slowly brought it to his lips. She stood motionless as his fingers moved through her hair, lightly touched her cheek and then brushed her neck, coming to rest on her bare shoulders. A breathless, slow heat began to uncurl within her. He was looking hungrily down at her, his eyes molten brown, flecked with that golden intensity.

She felt herself mesmerised, falling into a vortex that was drawing her inexorably to his very centre, and hardly knowing what she was doing, she brushed a strand of hair from his forehead and allowed it to drift through her fingers. The gesture seemed to unleash in him the passion he'd so far restrained and he lowered his head and brought his mouth down on hers in a kiss of such aching pleasure that all rational thought vanished. She could think of nothing but the feel of him, the scent of him, the taste of him. He kissed her once more slowly and tenderly and then again, exploring, savouring, and finally allowing the full force of his desire to wash over her. She was reduced to trembling sensation.

When at last he lifted his lips, it was to trail kisses down her neck, her shoulders, and to settle whisperingly against the swell of her bosom. A burst of heat throbbed through her and she found her body arching, cleaving desperately to him. Somewhere in the distance she heard herself moan softly.

The sound seemed to bring him to his senses. In a moment he had stepped back, breathing heavily and looking considerably less polished. It was a while before he spoke and, when he did, his voice was ragged with passion.

'You should keep your distance from me. I can only bring you distress.' Then in a quieter tone. 'Forgive me, Marianna. You are a beautiful girl in all senses of the word, but that does not excuse my breaking the promise I made you – and so quickly.'

Still in a daze of desire, she managed to stammer a disclaimer, before silence fell between them, a silence filled with unexpressed longing.

In an attempt to make light of the situation, he tried a joke. 'As an experienced rake, I should advise you that now would be a good time to return to your family.'

As he spoke, he proffered his arm and she took it with as much dignity as she could muster, her head held high. Retracing their steps across the library and down the corridor, she saw their figures reflected in the wall of mirrors. Joshua might be dangerous to know, but what a comely couple we make, she thought. Almost respectable! She could have laughed aloud but for the mantra beating inside her head. She must *never* allow herself to lose control like that again. Her father must never know what had just occurred. Never guess at the force of her desire. Nor Carmela and her aunts – certainly not her aunts – and as for the unknown Spanish husband, he must stay for ever ignorant of such unmaidenly passion. But there was no reason that any of them should ever know. At least rakes did not kiss and tell or they would hardly be so successful.

Joshua caught sight of their reflection at the same time as she, and smiled back at her. The scar on his cheek was hardly noticeable but it gave him distinction. Not that he needed it, he was so beautifully made. Guiltily she caught herself up. From now on, such thoughts were taboo. She must focus on a very different future.

Once in the Long Gallery amid the noisy buzz of chatter, he stopped and turned to her, a serious expression on his face. 'Remember my warning. There are those close by who wish you ill. If you need me, I am here.'

She saw her father rapidly approaching, a worried look on his face, and had no time to reply.

'We have been looking for you everywhere.' Ernesto was clearly upset. 'Carmela is even now questioning every footman in the building.'

Marianna was startled. 'Please stop her, Papa. As you see, I am well. Mr Marchmain was kind enough to offer me his escort from the prince's apartments.'

It was Ernesto's turn to look startled. 'The prince's apartments?'

'His drawing room, sir,' Joshua said soothingly. 'He wished to show Miss Marquez his magnificent collection of brooches.'

145

Her father's expression remained uneasy. 'I am sure His Highness was most gracious, but the time has come to leave.'

It was short while only before they had collected Carmela and were bowling down the Pavilion driveway towards Marine Parade.

⤚

Joshua was left looking after them, a prey to uncertainty. Marianna was to be sacrificed on the altar of family duty. Indeed she was willing to be sacrificed, and there was little he could do to prevent it. He was a disreputable man and could have no voice in her future. That kiss – those kisses he corrected himself reminiscently – could only ever be an interlude, but what an interlude. It was ridiculous that his heart still sang. How many kisses had he known in his lifetime? Not like this, a small voice within argued, not like this. She had been a revelation, all her youth and vitality poured into those moments of pleasure.

He'd known instinctively that she was a girl of strong emotion, that beneath her modesty lay a passion waiting to be roused, and he'd been right. He had wanted to kiss her until she begged him never to stop. And she had wanted him to. She had desired him as much as he desired her. Another conquest to add to the many, he thought acidly. All the more reason then to keep his distance. Otherwise he would hurt her and hurt her badly. It was inevitable since didn't he damage everything that became dear to him?

An unbearable restlessness seized him and he knew he had to get away from the chattering foolishness all around. He turned on his heel and strode back the way he had come. Once in his studio, he threw off his black evening jacket and shrugged himself into the spattered smock. A blank canvas was before him and he picked up his brush. In his mind's eye, he saw her as she'd stood just minutes before. His painting would capture that moment, would capture her lovely young face as he kissed her into mutual submission. It was as close as he would ever get to possessing her, and with that he must be content. For her sake, his heart must remain well defended: she was too young, too trusting, too innocent. For his own sake, too. The life he'd fallen into was predictable, often unlovely, but always free from the pain of feeling. It was a life he intended to keep.

Chapter Eighteen

I t was a long time before Marianna fell asleep that night.
The visit to the Pavilion had proved a kaleidoscope of
sights, sounds, conversations, that tossed and tumbled
through her mind. The strange architecture, exotic
furnishings and an overpowering heat, had generated
a strong sense of disorientation even before she'd been
assailed by the Regent's clumsy advances. For a while she
had truly feared for her virtue. Yet it was her destiny, it
seemed, to be saved from disaster by the man who should
have spelt the greatest danger.

It was some time, though, since Joshua had played the
libertine, if indeed he ever had. When she thought back to
their first meeting on the beach, she had to acknowledge
it was her peace of mind that he'd threatened rather than
her person. In fact, she had never felt seriously threatened
in his company. Ruffled, irritated, occasionally shocked by
his unconventionality, but never genuinely alarmed. He
was simply adept at provoking her. But this evening he
hadn't provoked; he'd seemed almost a different person.
She'd always guessed there was more beneath the careless
exterior than was evident but seeing him in his studio

tonight, among the things he valued and so much a part of his setting, a serious and interesting man had come to the fore. She'd felt a powerful connection to the paintings he loved and a powerful connection to him.

More than powerful. Those kisses had turned her life upside down. She'd melted beneath their onslaught and all she'd felt or known in those moments was Joshua. She had never before experienced such emotion: her heart, her body, her whole being had shaken with the pulse of feeling. And though she'd left the Pavilion vowing never again to succumb so shamelessly to desire, here she was thinking of it again and again. Endlessly repeating those kisses, endlessly drowning in their delight.

Luke had never kissed her. If he had, she suspected it would have been a poor reflection of what she'd felt tonight. In retrospect, her feelings for Luke had been just what he'd always said they were – a schoolgirl crush, painfully deep, but a mere rehearsal for the real thing. Was tonight the real thing? The thought scared her mightily, for if so it blew to pieces the future she'd decided on.

After a restless night, she dragged herself from bed the next morning, feeling tired and dispirited. She no longer knew what to think or how to behave. When she could label Joshua a philanderer, it had been easy to ignore the promptings of her heart. But now her feelings lay exposed, raw and vulnerable. She tried to give them covering by dwelling on Joshua's past iniquities and telling herself how foolish it was to believe in his caress, but the attempt was flimsy.

Without doubt he was a sexual buccaneer. His name,

Carmela had warned, had been linked to half a dozen women currently residing in Brighton, and though she did not know the truth of these insinuations, the old adage of no smoke without fire came to mind. In short, he was a wholly unsuitable person with whom to consort. And how she had consorted! She had been utterly brazen.

With her mind torn this way and that, she was undecided whether to hide herself away at home or fight despondency by venturing into town. Carmela made the decision for her. Her cousin was in a particularly disagreeable mood and it looked likely to last for hours.

'I do not understand why you felt it necessary to disappear last night,' she greeted Marianna crossly, as the latter took her seat at the breakfast table.

'The Regent wished to show me his collection of jewellery,' she replied in a tired voice. 'Papa knew where I was.'

'He did not, or else why would he have been looking for you everywhere.'

'But he took me himself to meet the Regent.'

'In the Music Room, Marianna. You were to stay in the Music Room and not wander off to goodness knows where without a word.'

'The prince wished to escort me to his drawing-room. I could hardly refuse, and there was no chance to let you know where I was going.' She thought it wise not to disclose that the Regent had resisted her plea to send for her cousin.

But Carmela had not yet finished her scolding. 'Your lack of thought caused both your father and I much worry and also a great deal of talk. What must people have thought when you left the room with the Regent and without a chaperon?'

'I imagine my absence would have gone unnoticed if you'd not taken it on yourself to alert every footman in the palace.' Marianna's response was tart.

Her cousiner cousi appeared to bite back a retort, perhaps conceding silently that she had been at fault in broadcasting Marianna's truancy. But it was clear she blamed her charge for the evening's troubles and for falling once more into mischief. Doubtless she was counting the days until the family could leave Brighton and all its shocking attractions.

⌐

Marianna left the breakfast table before her cousin could continue the harangue but her father, encountered in the hall, proved no more benign. He was making his way to his office and the daily round of papers and, though he greeted her courteously enough, it was evident from his distant manner that he was far from happy. Her relatives appeared suspicious that she had conducted herself ill last night, but their suspicion fell squarely on the Regent. What would they say if they knew about Joshua?

eHe greeHIn an effort to brighten a day which had started so badly, she slipped on the white figured muslin newly arrived from the dressmaker, and chose a charming Gypsy straw bonnet, embellished with cherries and matching ribbons. Flora who was assisting her to dress was delighted to learn that she was to accompany her mistress.

'It will be good to be on one of our adventures again, miss,' she said.

Not much of an adventure, Marianna reflected, a walk to the Level and back would have to suffice, but at least she would be safe from further recrimination. And there would be plenty to see, since the Level was a popular leisure area frequented by local people as much as by visiting London society. It was spacious and grassed with a variety of attractions, even a cricket ground which had been laid out years ago for the Regent when he was still Prince of Wales. The broad avenue of elms, their branches almost interlocking overhead, made a tranquil walk and she could easily imagine herself in the country even while the town busied itself around her.

Today they had hardly reached the beginning of the walk when music came drifting to them on the breeze.

'Oh, Miss Marianna, do let's go and look.' Flora was jigging up and down in her eagerness. 'It's the military, I'm sure. I can hear the drums.'

The prince's own regiment, the 10th Light Dragoons, was based at the Church Street barracks and in the absence of another French invasion, spent their time mounting guard on the prince's estate and occasionally taking part in parades, grand reviews and mock battles as part of the town's seasonal entertainments. Marianna felt a surge of interest. Italian opera might leave her cold but a military parade was another matter.

'I'm sure you're right, Flora,' she said happily. 'The soldiers must be practising for the Regent's birthday – it can only be days away now.'

'What do you think they're planning to do?' The maid screwed up her face in concentration, as though by sheer force of will she could conjure up the mystery entertainment.

'My father said there was to be the usual parade but he thought something quite special, too. Possibly a re-enactment of the battle of Waterloo.'

At this intelligence, Flora could contain herself no longer and began tugging at her mistress's arm in a fashion which Carmela would instantly have decreed unseemly.

'Quick, miss, let's go and see!'

They hurried along the wide avenue until suddenly it opened onto a large clearing. Here a dazzling display of deep blue and gold met their eyes. The soldiers were a moving panorama, the brilliant gold braiding of their tight-fitting jackets glowing in the morning sun, their ebony shakos sitting proudly atop their heads. A cluster of curved swords gleamed wickedly as they were raised in the air. Nearby, the drums they'd heard earlier beat out an insistent time as the soldiers moved smartly first one way, then another, wheeling and spinning in such orderly fashion that to the dazed spectator they seemed not five hundred single men but one dashing entity.

'Ain't that just a sight, Miss Marianna,' Flora breathed, forgetting her acquired polish in a moment of wonder.

'It certainly is,' said an amused voice a short distance away. 'Flora, isn't it?' A smiling man doffed his high-crowned beaver in the maid's direction.

'Yes, sir.' Flora bobbed a nervous curtsy.

Joshua must have been at the far end of the parade ground where officials from the prince's household were gathered, and Marianna had not noticed him until he was nearly upon them. As always the deep blue coat he wore was moulded like a second skin to his body. Beneath, she glimpsed a paler blue ornamented Venetian waistcoat and the palest and most close- fitting of fawn pantaloons. On his feet were glossy black hessians with little gold tassels that swung jauntily as he came towards them. Her eyes drank him in.

'And Miss Marquez,' he said, his voice coolly welcoming. 'How delightful to see you here.'

She took her cue from him. They were to meet as acquaintances, nothing more. Was this for Flora's benefit or was he wishing to forget the kisses of a few hours ago?

'So what is the verdict – soldiers or sopranos?' His golden eyes, now laughing, smiled down at her.

'Soldiers, I fear.' Flora looked perplexed, but Marianna glowed inwardly. The mutual joke had brought him closer.

'Why fear? They are a splendid sight are they not, and so much easier on the ear?'

Laughter bubbled within her. 'I doubt the *ton* would agree.'

'They would not or at least not admit to it. A preference for low pursuits denotes an instant loss of face. I seem to recall that when the circus visited town, opinions were most scathing!'

'When was that?' Marianna's face lit up at the mention of a circus.

'It was a while before you arrived in Brighton, but I'd place a heavy wager that if they were to return, you would be first in the queue.'

'I would! I visited Astleys when I lived in London and

saw an equestrian ballet,' she added guilelessly.

'And you enjoyed it?'

'Immensely. It was an amazing spectacle.'

'I imagine it would be. I've never managed to visit Astleys myself, but I've heard legendary tales of their performances.'

Her cheeks flushed with remembered excitement. 'I think it was the very best event I ever attended.'

She was the most enchanting child, he thought, all youthful eagerness despite the womanly curves that filled the figured muslin so becomingly. Adorable, but he must keep a sharp watch on himself. He had stayed in his studio last night, painting until the small hours, and this morning emerged serene. Now all he need do was keep his distance.

'Did Lady Foyle take you?' he asked, disconcerting her for a minute. 'I would not have thought it to her taste.'

'Do you know my aunt?'

'Only very slightly,' he said smoothly. 'So who was brave enough to escort you?'

'Just a friend.'

Her tone was awkward and she seemed keen to change the subject. He wondered if it was the same friend who had spurned her youthful love and married elsewhere. She was a girl of great spirit but also intensely vulnerable. He must tread very carefully.

'Flora and I were speculating.' She gestured towards the soldiers who had now come to a standstill and were awaiting commands from a scarlet-sashed officer. 'We thought the soldiers must be practising for the Regent's birthday celebrations. Do you know what they intend to present?'

'There will be the usual parade of course, but I'm not allowed to discuss the *pièce de resistance* – it's a state secret!'

She laughed aloud, her dark eyes alive with mischief, and he gazed at her for as long as he dared. Then seeing Flora's enquiring expression, he looked quickly away.

'Have *you* had a hand in this great surprise, Mr Marchmain?' Marianna asked.

'I was dragged into the early planning and I'm supposed to oversee rehearsals, but other than that I can't claim to have taken a very active role. I enjoy the dash and colour of the military, but that's about it. I'm looking forward to seeing the final performance though – it will make a splendid finale to the summer season.'

She looked at him questioningly. When he responded, his voice was stripped of expression. 'Prinny is planning to leave Brighton the week after his birthday. I'm due to accompany him back to Carlton House and from there travel on to Norfolk.'

He saw the shadow skim her face and there was a part of him that rejoiced. 'You will be leaving for Spain at the same time, I imagine.'

'I will.'

Chapter Nineteen

Silence fell. They stood side by side, looking blankly into the distance, hearing their own words but not quite able to accept them.

'Our stay has passed very swiftly.' Her tone was wistful and her high colour betrayed her feelings. Joshua pretended not to notice and almost immediately she continued in a brighter voice, 'I'm surprised that you intend to visit Castle March so soon. I thought you would make a stay in London.'

'It's time I returned. I've been away too long, though I doubt I'll be there for many weeks. Just long enough to hang my da Vinci before the Norfolk weather drives me to warmer climes.'

'That is a shame. Houses need to be loved, I think. But if you dislike the place so very much, why do you not sell and buy an estate you find more congenial?'

'I have little love for the house, it's true, but I'm grateful to my great uncle and feel bound to keep it. He bequeathed me Castle March at just the right time.'

'And when was that?'

'When I'd grown tired of being a vagabond. And a

country seat is not to be sniffed at. A gentleman with a large estate always commands respect!'

While they were talking, Flora had sauntered away to mingle a little timidly with the soldiers who were now relaxing at the side of the parade ground.

'I'm sure it does,' Marianna agreed. 'But it's sad you'll not be there long. Still, perhaps you will spend time with your brother before you leave England?'

'Most unlikely.' His tone verged on the curt. 'My brother has a family of his own now and I can only be a discomfort to him.'

'But why?'

She was persistent, he would give her that. 'He is convention made flesh,' Joshua said, trying to make light of a difficult subject. 'I was a constant thorn in his flesh while I was growing up and once I hit town, my conduct was – well, unpardonable!'

'Whatever you did to make your family disown you is long past.'

Her sweet concern touched him, but the truth was brutal and he'd no wish to hide behind pretence. 'For him, Marianna, the scandal lives on. Believe me, it is for everybody's good that I keep away.'

'What did you do exactly?' she asked shyly.

'I failed two people who were dear to me and who deserved better. Failed them badly.'

She looked dismayed and he said tersely, 'It isn't a pretty tale and my family was justified in packing me off to Europe as soon as they could. But you must not be thinking I was a victim. They made sure I had a decent enough allowance.'

'But still...'

He shook his head. 'My parents are dead and I've regained a little respectability by inheriting Castle March. Life is easy for me, and my brother can be forgiven for wishing to keep a hundred miles between us.'

He watched her closely to see the effect of his words. He'd not wanted to have this conversation but since they had, he hoped it would serve to keep her at a distance. Last night had been a very bad mistake and she was still too close for his comfort. But he couldn't stop himself wanting – to see her again and again. And found himself saying, 'What's this I hear about the Cunnnghams' extravaganza on Thursday evening? Something quite out of the ordinary, I believe. Are you invited?'

Lady Cunningham was generally despised as an empty-headed woman who greedily extracted gifts from the Regent and flaunted them in public. But because of her influence over George and because of the opulent nature of the hospitality she provided, her parties were never short of guests. Marianna had not liked Lady Cunningham when she met her nor had she wished to be involved in her lavish preparations: the idea that ladies might perform on stage for their

peers seemed to lack propriety. But a combination of Carmela's horrified response to the invitation and Ernesto's reassurance that these days the most respectable of ladies took part in such informal entertainments, had persuaded her to agree.

Her father had suggested she appear in a tableau as a grand Spanish lady. He'd preserved a single dress of her mother's, a dress Elena had worn when she was not much older than her daughter. When Marianna saw the dress for the first time, she'd gasped. It was a dress as red as passion and as soon as she put it on, she felt its power. It had needed little alteration, fitting her curves to perfection, and no addition other than a scarlet flower for her hair and a pair of high-heeled black shoes. It was a revealing costume that had caused her some disquiet, but now the thought that Joshua would see her in it, made her face flame.

'We have had an invitation,' she said, trying to sound unconcerned, 'and my father wishes to attend.'

'Then I shall see you there. Meanwhile I must report to the palace on the progress of the birthday plans.' Lifting his hat once more in salutation, he turned and walked away.

She was left a prey to conflicting sensations. His confession of wrongdoing had upset her. But so, too, had learning of his family's conduct and his brother's determination to remain estranged. Whatever Joshua had done in his youth, the two were still flesh and blood, and after all these years he must surely have expiated his crime. He had failed those he loved, he'd said, had not treated them as they deserved, but wasn't that true of many others? Was this brother so pure that he had done nothing wrong in *his* life? She was guilty herself of sufficiently bad things not to judge: gambling illicitly, falling into debt, falsely eloping with Dominic when they were both minors. The list was worryingly long.

And now the Cunningham party was looming and bringing a new set of anxieties. The dress was magnificent and, wearing it, she felt a warrior queen. But how warlike would she feel with Joshua in the audience? And Charlotte Severn and Amesbury, too? Their threat was always present and Joshua had warned her to be on her guard against them. If she drew attention to herself at the party, what wickedness might that encourage? But unless she told her father of their continued persecution, she could not refuse to perform her part in the evening's entertainment. And to tell him would be to reveal the whole sorry business of her previous stay in England.

∽

Her father had reassured her that all she would have to do was to walk across a small stage, a painted Spanish fan in one hand and a pair of castanets in the other. In general, he said, English people were woefully ignorant of other nations and even a simple appearance in traditional dress was sure to be greeted with interest. But when the time came to leave on Thursday evening, she had worked herself up into a ball of terror.

Seeing the dread in her mistress's face, Flora ushered her quickly to the corner of the room and angled the cheval mirror. 'You should take a look, Miss Marianna,' she said encouragingly. 'Everyone will say you're all the crack!'

Her maid's attempt at *ton* slang made Marianna smile faintly. Plucking up courage, she looked at herself in the mirror for the first time. The garment's red taffeta fell in ruffled tiers to the floor, each tier ornamented with sparkling crystals. A plain bodice covered her bosom, but her arms were left bare, framed by more ornamented frills. The dress itself moulded her figure so closely that every undulation, every softness, was accentuated. She caught her breath when she saw the stranger looking back at her. Could she really be this sensual creature? She drew herself up to her full height, made prouder by the heeled shoes, and tossed the frilled skirt this way and that in sweeping gestures. Her dark eyes began to glow with anticipation and when Flora placed a scarlet blossom in the black curls, now free from restraint and flowing to her shoulders, she smiled back at her reflection, captivated by the image she saw there.

Flora gave a sigh of pure ecstasy. 'You don't look like yourself, miss. You look like...' She struggled to put her feelings into words. 'Like a Spanish princess.'

'Dear Flora.' Marianna hugged her. 'I fear that a genuine Spanish princess would be far too scandalised to wear such a gown!'

She ought to be scandalised as well, she thought, as the dress nipped at her curves and caressed the flowing lines of her young body. But she wasn't. Instead a strange exultation rippled through her. She practised a few turns, swishing the deep frills of the gown from one side to another. Then holding the castanets aloft, she began to experiment with dance steps, gradually recalling the flamenco lessons she had taken without her aunts' knowledge. Another transgression. But it might serve her well this night. Marianna wanted to perform splendidly and she knew why – though she might never be part of Joshua's future, she would be part of his past. She would leave him with a memory he would never forget. All she needed was the courage to carry it through.

⌒

Once arrived at the Cunningham mansion, Marianna and her father were parted. He was ushered into a large salon, decorated an overpowering gold and filled with rows of delicate gilt chairs set out in a semi-circle. The first part of the evening's entertainment was to be the tableaux got up by the young ladies Sophia Cunningham had importuned. Later, there would be an informal dance to the strains of a professional quartet. Before selecting his seat, Ernesto handed the musicians the gypsy music that would accompany his daughter across the stage. He felt relaxed. Knowing the Regent had declined the Cunninghams' invitation, he had no fear the prince's conduct at the Pavilion would be repeated, and taking part in something a little different would keep Marianna busy and out of trouble.

Meanwhile she had been whisked to an adjoining room, already awash with nervous young ladies and their personal maids making last minute adjustments to what appeared to be highly elaborate ensembles. Marianna herself had little to do but remove the black velvet cloak which covered her flamenco gown. She glanced around at the whirl of activity and was comforted by the sight of costumes a great deal more revealing than her own.

It seemed to take an inordinate amount of time for the gaggle of nervous girls to make themselves ready, but at last they were being shepherded towards the rear part of the drawing room which had been curtained off to form the wings of an improvised stage. In no time the space was filled with a bevy of eager girls: Greek goddesses, Virgin Queens, Cinderellas, even a Boadicea. As they fussed and mingled around her, several of the girls looked askance at Marianna's unfamiliar costume. That only made her hold her head a little higher.

Ripples of polite applause could be heard behind the curtain as each of the girls made their way across the stage to the gentle strands of violins, posing a while to enable the audience to absorb their finery, some of them embellishing their walk with a twirl, a curtsy or even more daring, blowing a kiss.

One Cinderella, clad in stylish rags and dolefully sweeping the floor with her birch broom, received a particularly rousing reception. Then following her, three girls dressed as Greek goddesses drifted onto the stage and formed a small circle. For some minutes they danced together, their floating gauze robes weaving a fragile pattern. A murmur of surprise, not all of it appreciative, travelled around the room. One goddess had been ill-advised enough to wear a damped and transparent petticoat beneath her gauze and the more august members of the audience showed their disapproval of such flagrant exposure by looking pointedly at their feet.

But it was Marianna, far more robustly clad, who burst upon the audience with a thunderclap. She crossed to the centre of the stage in one fluid movement, her heels already beginning to click and rap to a strong beat, her arms gesturing in dramatic flight and the castanets enforcing a compelling rhythm. The beat sounded at first slowly, then more rapidly, first quietly then more loudly, alternating in tempo but always there, throbbing, insistent. The musicians accompanying her threw themselves into the moment and music and dancer became one.

Gradually the more forceful beat began to dominate, working its way to a crescendo while the dancer's feet stamped and twirled across the floor. Marianna's supple, young body flexed and swayed in one direction while the red taffeta frills swished and coiled in another. The audience were silent, hardly daring to breathe. She had them wholly in her power, thrilled by the mastery of her dancing. At first the dance had appeared so daring that they could hardly believe they were watching it in a lady's drawing room, even Lady Cunningham's. But as the black heels weaved their sinuous pattern across the stage and the lithe scarlet form twined and turned in sympathy with the music's yearning, they forgot where they were and gave themselves up to the fantasy.

Standing at the back of the room, Joshua lost his calm detachment. He was caught in the music's powerful rhythms, caught by the sensuous ebb and flow of Marianna's body, so that he felt he was with her, moving with her, away from her, against her. He wanted to be there, he belonged there, but just when he felt he could not remain apart a second longer, the music reached its crescendo and with a last stamp of her heels, a last flourish of castanets, she was still. The applause was tumultuous. Emerging from her trance, Marianna realised it was for her and smiled shyly back. Then as quickly as she could, she left the stage.

After her performance there was little appetite for further tableaux and with one accord the guests began to move towards the dining room where a substantial buffet had been arranged. She felt unable to face her fellow guests immediately but instead took shelter in a secluded corner of the salon. She had seen Joshua at the back of the room and had danced only for him. Very soon they would say goodbye, but if they were destined never to meet again, she wanted him to hold this memory of her. She had danced to entrance him, to seduce him. Her cheeks flamed as she thought of the invitation she had offered, but she could not be sorry.

Chapter Twenty

And now, he was at her side. 'I won't ask you where you learned to dance like that,' he murmured. 'I imagine your father knew nothing of your talent.'

She looked towards the doorway at Ernesto, still wearing a dazed expression, and inundated with extravagant compliments on his daughter's performance.

'Papa insisted I wore a flamenco costume,' she excused herself feebly.

'Then Papa got what he deserved.'

'The dress was my mother's, you see, and Papa wanted to see it come alive again.'

'He certainly had his wish granted.' A wry smile lit Joshua's face.

'Yes, I fear he did,' Marianna said quietly, and then more emphatically, 'I should not have danced. I was supposed only to walk across the stage to the music, but when I heard the first notes...'

'You have dance in your soul, Marianna. You should not be sorry – you were magnificent!'

She glanced up at him. 'I *was* good, wasn't I?'

He laughed aloud. 'You *were* good, my little one. By

God, you were good!'

Hearing his laugh as she entered the dining room, the Duchess of Severn glared in his direction.

'That chit goes from strength to strength,' she remarked sourly to Lord Amesbury, a few steps behind. 'She appears to lead a charmed life.'

Robert handed his companion a glass of wine and said thoughtfully, 'She's a deal too close to Marchmain for her father's liking. Watch his face.'

They both glanced across at Señor Marquez. He was looking with concern at his daughter, smiling softly at the exquisite figure beside her.

'Can we do nothing?' The duchess's voice was sharply edged, her frustration spilling out despite her best efforts. 'I despair of ever confounding the girl.'

'I understand she is to be married off to some Spanish grandee in the very near future. Marchmain will be history.'

'Before that happens it would be pleasant to torture her a little. I feel I deserve some small satisfaction.' Charlotte's mouth twisted into an unpleasant grimace, surprising Amesbury by its ugliness.

'Hell hath no fury?'

'Not just for a woman scorned, Robert, but a man baulked of his prey,' she reminded him.

'It's true that I haven't yet settled my score with the little upstart. But I've been giving it some thought.'

'Dare I say, it's about time? Since that debacle with Prinny, you've been remarkably silent.'

'Marchmain skewed our pitch in that instance – ' Amesbury began.

'Not just in that instance,' she interrupted bitterly.

'The joy of this plan, however, is that Marchmain cannot ride to the rescue. In fact, he will be the very problem. We can use his name against her.'

The duchess was looking sceptical and, stung by her lack of enthusiasm, he put down his glass on a side table and drew closer to his companion.

'I have a little knowledge of the señorita's past history which might serve our purpose,' he whispered in her ear.

'Such as? I hesitate to remind you, but we have already employed your knowledge of her past and failed.'

'We won't this time. She does not yet know the truth about our friend Marchmain and when she does, it's certain to give her great pain. Her father, too – he will be most anxious to return her to Spain where she belongs.'

'Tell me!'

Amesbury readily obliged and an unholy smile wreathed the duchess's face.

'Excellent. But why now? We could have used this ammunition weeks ago.'

He gave an impatient shrug. 'Now that Marchmain has well and truly caught her, it will be a great deal more effective. Always keep your powder dry until you really need it, my dear.'

The duchess said nothing but her smile broadened.

⌒

By this time, a number of couples had been encouraged back into the salon where the chairs had been cleared and a small dance floor established. The musicians were striking up for a cotillion and Joshua, still standing by Marianna's side, immediately offered her his arm.

'Will you join us mere mortals?'

'Are you asking me to dance with you?'

'Yes, Marianna, I'm asking you.'

Her first dance with Joshua would stay in her memory for ever. It was as though she moved through it in slow motion, every second etched on her being. The musky male scent, the feel of solid muscle beneath her hand, the heat of his body as he drew close to her, their figures touching and parting in the graceful movements of the cotillion.

The dance meant they were separated for long periods, but always they returned to each other, their limbs warm and eager, their hands caressing fleetingly. For Joshua it was torment. Each time they were forced apart by the pattern of the dance, a voice screamed through his head that this was the stupidest thing he had ever done. But then – the wonderful moment when they came together again, his body touching hers, lightly, gently, promising delights he must not think of.

The music stopped and partners were bowing graciously to each other, yet neither of them moved. They stood in silence, in thrall to the spell they had created. It was Joshua who gathered his wits, realising the spectacle they'd become. Hastily, he ushered Marianna from the dance floor and led her towards one of the curtained windows overlooking the wide spaces of the Steine. Its bay formed a small enclave, the crimson velvet drapes closing behind them.

'The temperature in this room must rival that of the Pavilion,' he managed to joke. He pushed the casement doors wide open and they walked out on to the small ironwork balcony.

She smiled a little shakily. After the intimacy of their dance, her knees felt ready to buckle. He was feet away, though, and seemed intent on keeping a distance between them.

'Marianna –' he began, but then he was by her side and she had walked into his arms. His lips brushed across her curls and touched her cheeks. Then his mouth found hers. As though in a dream, she reached up and stroked his hair, destroying its modish style, and pulling him ever closer.

His kisses were long and hard, at first his tongue gently exploring, then growing more urgent until she tasted him to the full. His hands found the gentle swell of her bosom and his lips the bare skin of her breast, flickering fire through every nerve and fibre. She closed her eyes and gave herself up to him.

But once more he was the first to come to his senses. What madness! In the middle of the Cunninghams' drawing room with a hundred people a curtain's thickness away. And after he'd sworn never to touch her again. Her dancing had roused him to a passion he was powerless against. Powerless to stop his arms from enfolding her, to keep his lips from her mouth and her body. It was ridiculous. A man of his experience, to be overwhelmed by emotions he could not control. He had to fight this insane desire or he would wreck her on the rock of scandal. For himself, the gossip mattered not a jot. The whole world knew him to be dissolute; people would simply shake their heads and say what else do you expect? For Marianna, though, it would mean utter ruin.

While she remained in Brighton, he must stay her friend but nothing more. Yet he had never before felt such raw hunger as when she'd pressed her slender body into his and offered herself to him. Blame the dress for that, he muttered silently to himself, but he knew it to be a poor excuse.

He led her back into the drawing room as discreetly as he could and went to procure drinks. But her father was before him. Ernesto had been unnerved by the sensuality of his daughter's dancing and, watching her disappear into the window embrasure with Joshua Marchmain, his fears had grown. He had been on the point of following the couple when they emerged from their shelter. He noted the tell-tale flush on Marianna's face and Joshua's dishevelled hair, and suspected the worst. He must remove her from Brighton immediately.

First there had been that unpleasantness with the Regent and now this man – less exalted perhaps – but still of questionable morals. He knew enough of Marchmain to fear for his daughter's reputation. The aunts had been right. He had been too indulgent. Carmela had been right. For weeks she had been warning him of just such a disaster but he'd refused to believe her. Now he had seen the truth with his own eyes.

Joshua, returning with glasses of fruit punch, was in time only to receive a hurried curtsy from Marianna and a curt nod from her father. A few minutes later, they had bid Lady Cunningham goodbye and the front door shut behind them.

The thunderous look on Señor Marquez's face meant

only one thing, Joshua decided. Marianna would be shipped back to Spain before she'd had time even to pack her wardrobe. In a day she could be gone and he would never see her again. He quickly downed the punch and as swiftly bid his hosts a gracious farewell. In a moment he was in the Steine and strolling towards the sea. He wanted fresh air and he wanted space. The evening was closing in, but the heat of the day had not yet disappeared and the town had a subdued hum, lightly clad couples hastening to and from the different entertainments.

He needed to think. He had to see Marianna again before she left, had to tell her... what exactly? He hardly knew. Only that her kisses had marked him enduringly, that their lovemaking had mattered to him. He stood stock still, an arrested expression on his face, neither seeing nor hearing the constant murmur of water as it washed against the pebbled shore. It *had* mattered!

Was it possible he'd fallen in love? He dared not think it. He had loved before, just once, and the affair had ended in catastrophe. His lover then had been young and passionate, too, and given herself willingly. Together they'd broken every rule of society and made themselves pariahs, cut dead in the street by friends and enemies alike. They had lost reputation, lost the world they knew and broken their parents' hearts. And for what? A few months of madness, for he'd not had the courage to see it through. He had betrayed his best friend, then left the girl he loved to face condemnation alone.

After that, how could he live with himself? The answer, of course, was that he couldn't. He'd become a different person and lived with him instead. And now, after he'd suppressed every painful memory, had thought himself incapable of tenderness, he was in danger of falling in love with this enchanting child. But Marianna's youthful innocence was not his to spoil. She would never be a mistress and he would never be a husband. The man she married should be as carefree and innocent as she.

Dusk had fallen and the lights of the small boats anchored just offshore winked out at him, but he made no attempt to move. Instead, his hands began to drum against the promenade railings in an impatient tattoo as his mind beat in unison. Their roles were already determined and there would be no deviating from the script. He could offer her nothing but the shell of the person he'd once been – and she would return to Spain to marry a man she did not know. Nevertheless he had to see her again, if only to bid her a final goodbye.

Chapter Twenty-One

Marianna cast a concerned look at her father as the carriage rolled its way homewards. His face was impassive. She wished he would say something, anything, but he remained mute. It was clear he judged her conduct unbecoming, but his refusal to speak meant she had no defence against the crime he was silently accusing her of. He might not say anything but she was sure he would act: her return to Spain looked imminent.

And what exactly was her crime? The answer was simple – she had fallen in love with a rake. She was in love with Joshua and that was improper. It didn't feel so. It felt warm and wonderful. Naturally it would, she counselled herself. Rakes don't become rakes by not giving pleasure, by not being able to kiss. And he could certainly kiss. Moments ago she had burnt in a firestorm of passion and she'd wanted more, much more. She had wanted to throw reputation to the winds and satisfy this fierce consuming desire. And she still did.

One thing was certain. She could no longer marry the nameless husband waiting for her in Spain. On the morrow she would go to her father and tell him that when she returned to Madrid, it would not be to choose a bridegroom.

⌒

When the morning arrived, however, it brought two surprises. A letter had been delivered the previous evening and sat waiting for her on the hall table. Neither she nor her father had noticed the envelope on their return from the Pavilion since they'd been too absorbed in their own thoughts. But this morning it was the subject of animated discussion between Flora and the upper housemaid. Such personal missives were rare in what was an official residence. Flora placed the letter carefully on a tray alongside the mug of hot chocolate and made haste to her mistress's bedroom, eager to hear its contents. But Marianna was not in a confiding mood. She thanked her maid and, ignoring Flora's evident disappointment, told her she might go.

Once alone, she examined the envelope with curiosity. The handwriting was vaguely familiar, but it was not until she had extracted the two sheets of stiff paper and spread them flat on her lap that she realised the identity of her correspondent. The charming note had travelled the long distance from Cornwall and brought unexpected news of Cassandra Trelawny.

Since Cassie's marriage to Luke, Marianna had written once or twice but it had never felt easy. She'd been the one to bring the couple together: she had known even before Luke that his happiness lay with Cassandra, and she'd wanted him to be happy. But her own disappointment had remained raw and she'd resolutely refused all invitations to Madron Abbey, contenting herself with sending the occasional letter.

Lady Trelawny, it seemed, was in an interesting condition and her husband and family were most anxious for her to consult a doctor in Harley Street. Her father would accompany her to Brighton, she wrote, and she hoped that her dear friend, Marianna, would lend her support for the short journey up to London. Before that it would be a great treat to spend a few days in the Regent's seaside paradise.

Marianna's feelings for Luke had faded and all sense of strain miraculously disappeared. For the first time in their acquaintance, she felt she could meet Cassie without pretence and make a true friend of her. She badly needed to confide in someone and Cassandra, a seasoned married woman, would be the very best confidante. She wanted to tell her about Joshua.

⌒

When later she knocked at the door to her father's office, it wasn't to tell him she no longer wished to marry a man of her aunts' choosing, but to request that she might entertain a friend she had made during her previous stay in England.

For a brief moment her father looked nonplussed. Overnight he had perfected a plan to despatch his daughter immediately to Spain and had been on the point of sending a courier to warn the aunts of her arrival. But he could not be inhospitable. It was an annoying hiccup but when he thought more on it, he could see advantages to the visit. Lady Trelawny was a mature and experienced woman, and a pregnant one at that. She was likely to offer sensible advice to her younger friend and their time together would be spent largely within the confines of Marine Parade, and not in the dangerous territory beyond its doors.

It would be beneficial for his daughter to enjoy new company – Carmela was hardly the most joyous presence, nor was a middle-aged parent who had too much work. The lack of suitable companionship, he reflected, might be one of the reasons that Marianna had gone astray. A woman nearer her own age, but sensibly married, could be just what was needed. Lady Trelawny could help prepare the girl for the wifely role that lay in front of her. If she were able to bring Marianna to a more rational frame of mind, he might never have to raise the distasteful subject of her conduct last night. He would infinitely prefer to forget the whole disturbing series of events that had culminated in their tense ride home together.

Feeling happier than he had for days, he made his way to Raggett's, the town's most prestigious gentleman's club, and a useful place for garnering the latest political gossip. Equally happy, Marianna returned to her bedroom to reply to Cassandra's letter.

She had just laid down her pen when the second surprise of the morning arrived. A scratch at her door revealed Marston, looking perplexed.

'A caller is below, Miss Marianna.'

'A caller?'

'He asked particularly for you, miss.' She noted the reproachful expression which the butler could not quite conceal.

'And does this caller have a name?'

'He is Mr Joshua Marchmain.' The butler's voice was expressionless, but she knew that little went unnoticed by Marston and he would be well aware that Joshua was not a welcome visitor.

Without wasting further words, she slipped past him and ran lightly down the stairs, her heart beating a little too loudly. But when she reached the hall, it was empty. The front door was open and she crossed quickly to the doorway and looked along Marine Parade. Sure enough, there he was at the corner of Chapel Street and about to retrace his steps. He was leading two horses, walking them up and down to prevent them taking cold, for the day was sunless and there was a chill in the air.

At that moment, he saw her and waved cheerfully. 'I'm glad to find you at home. I took a chance in hiring a horse for you. See, it's the pretty mare that you rode before.'

Marianna blushed slightly at his reference to the ill-fated race, but there were more important concerns. She was bemused by his presence and needed some answers.

'What are you doing here? And with horses?'

'Riding? I thought you might appreciate a morning on the Downs. It should blow the cobwebs away.'

'But I'm not dressed for it,' she said weakly, indicating the simple dress of jaconet muslin that she had donned in anticipation of a day at home.

'I'll walk the horses for ten minutes – I'm sure Flora can work wonders in that time.'

Aware of a disapproving Marston behind her, she ignored this sally and sought another pretext. 'My father is away from home right now and I shouldn't leave without his knowledge.' It was convenient to forget all the times she had.

'We won't be gone long,' Joshua said encouragingly. 'And no-one will be around to tell tales – it's too early for most people. We might even manage a gallop!'

She wavered. After her father's severity last night, it would be prudent to ask his permission, but he was not in the house and Joshua was on the front steps. He saw her hesitation and pressed home his case.

'It's a morning for being out of town, Marianna, and I wish very much to talk to you. Where could be better?'

The prospect of private conversation was too tempting to refuse and she flew up to her room calling to Flora on the way. Together they managed the change into riding dress in record time. Her costume of pomona green velvet, ornamented with gold epaulettes, was tailored to mould itself to her lithe young form and she was aware of Joshua's appreciative gaze as she came down the steps to meet him.

The town was soon left behind and in minutes they were riding single file along one of the many narrow chalk paths that led upwards to the smooth contours of downland. The chill in the air had turned the sky slate grey and once they reached the expanse of open grass, their genteel trot was abandoned for a headlong gallop. On and on for several miles, Marianna's curls streaming loose behind her like a waving banner until, exhausted, the horses came to a halt at the top of a particularly steep rise in the ground. Below, the town of Brighton stretched itself lazily towards a dreaming sea, not a breath of wind rucking the water's surface.

They sat for a moment, regaining their breath and

taking in the sweep of grey stone and white cliffs. Above them gulls dipped and called, seeming almost to hang in the air. Then Joshua slid from the saddle and secured his horse to the branch of a solitary tree. As he did so, a shaft of sunlight broke through the leaden sky, catching them both in an illuminated circle. She smiled down at him, her face radiant with pleasure, her unforced joy evoking an answering smile.

Before she could join him, though, he'd turned aside and picked a small bouquet of wild daisies and cowslips and presented them to her with a courtly bow. 'Does Spain have its own language of flowers?' he asked. 'Here the daisy means innocence and the cowslip winning grace – what could be more apt?'

She blushed at the extravagant compliment, but said lightly, 'I believe the language of flowers is universal.'

'Shall we rest the horses and walk a little?' He reached up to help her dismount.

Taking his proffered arm, she strolled with him in companionable silence, wending their way over the springy turf and along the ridge of the hill. When he spoke at last, there was some hesitation in his voice.

'I was hoping you would accept my invitation. I wanted to apologise for the way in which the evening ended yesterday. I imagine your ride home wasn't the most pleasant.'

Marianna coloured. 'There's no need to apologise. I was as much to blame for...' She was looking straight ahead, her cheeks now bright red. 'For the incident.' She paused for a moment. 'And I can't complain – I escaped any scolding.'

'I'm relieved to hear it. I was worried you might already

be on your way back to Spain. But your father seems a most level headed gentleman. You are fortunate – families are not always so sensible.'

'You are thinking of your own?'

When he didn't respond, she said gently, 'I can understand why you should. They seem to have been very quick to judge you.'

'They had past history on their side.'

'Then you must have been in some very bad scrapes while you were growing up.'

His smile did not quite reach his mouth. 'I was.'

'But why?'

'Why? That's a strange question.'

'Not really. Boys are naturally a little wild but why were you *that* wild?'

She felt his figure tense beside her and there was a moment before he answered. 'I was given little attention. I wasn't much use, you see. My parents already had a perfectly satisfactory heir – indeed a paragon of an heir. And then ten years later another son came along at a time when I imagine they must have thought themselves clear of child rearing.'

He had never before revealed so much of what must still be hurtful. She slid her arm from his and took his hand in a warm clasp. 'You're saying that you were unwanted.'

'I'm saying there was no point to me.' His tone was deliberately light. 'It didn't seem to matter what I did. So I guess that goaded me into exploits which became more and more outrageous.'

'Including breaking faith with those dear to you?' She

knew she was venturing into dangerous territory, but it seemed important.

'That was the final icing on the cake.' The light tone had vanished and his voice was riven with bitterness. 'My perfidy ensured my parents disowned me. My brother, too – the scandal jeopardised his betrothal to an earl's daughter.'

'But his marriage went ahead?'

'He married, but the bride's family made it clear that the wedding would only happen if I disappeared for good.'

'And so you went abroad?'

'And so I went abroad. It was the perfect solution. I'd ruined my parents– I was responsible for their early demise or so my brother maintained. I'd injured my sibling. And destroyed my best friend and my first love. Going to Europe and staying there was the best thing I could do.'

The atmosphere had become bleak with memory and in an attempt to break through the grey cloud, he said in a falsely cheerful voice, 'Hopefully *your* journey to Europe will be a happier one. You will be leaving very soon.'

She said nothing but her silence told him he was right. 'Before you do, Marianna, there's something I need to say.'

She felt apprehensive but also strangely excited. She was not foolish enough to think there could be a future with Joshua – he would not be not looking for a wife or even, she imagined, a permanent liaison. Yet could it be that he cared for her enough to prevent, in some way, the bleak future that lay ahead of her?

The faint hope was immediately extinguished. 'I respect your decision to return to Madrid and to your aunts' protection,' he said, 'even though I may not agree with it.'

He put up his hand as she tried to interrupt and repeated quietly, 'I respect your decision, Marianna. But before you leave, I need you to know something. Something important.'

'Yes?'

'I need you to know that I meant every one of those kisses last night.'

Chapter Twenty-Two

She was baffled. This morning he'd sought her out and brought her to this deserted spot for private conversation. But why? What was he saying exactly? That he was happy to see her go as long as she realised his feelings had been honourable?

Her silence seemed to urge him to another attempt. 'I've not led the most creditable of lives, as you know, but in all my dealings with you, I've been honest. Unusually so. It matters to me that you know I've been sincere.'

Marianna was still uncertain whether her heart should be leaping skywards or plummeting to earth. To gain time, she repeated, 'Sincere?'

'Genuine. A difficult word for me – I am a rake after all!' His tone was jesting but when he spoke again, there was a new heat to it. 'I *meant* those kisses.' And added swiftly before she could respond, 'You must not worry. I won't disturb your life in any way, but I couldn't allow you to leave England without confessing what knowing you has meant to me.'

She turned to face him, grasping his hands in an impulsive movement. 'You may disturb my life as much as you wish, Joshua. Should I return to Spain, it will not be to live with my aunts.'

It was his turn to look baffled. 'When did you make *that* decision?'

'Last night,' she murmured shyly.

She could not bring herself to confess the whole truth of her feelings. Some small vestige of doubt held her back. The memory of Luke's rejection still played on her mind and she doubted she could bear the far worse pain that would accompany Joshua's.

'Why this decision?'

She prevaricated. 'My aunts are insistent that I wed a man of their choosing, but I find I can no longer contemplate an arranged marriage.'

'What has changed?' His amber eyes seemed to probe deep into her heart and she felt her stomach tie itself into the severest of knots.

'There are reasons.'

'And I am not to know those reasons?' he asked softly.

'They're unimportant.'

Joshua would not want to hear words of love, words he could not reciprocate. But though she could not speak the truth, she reached up to touch his face, her finger lovingly tracing the scar on his cheek.

He stood stock still for a moment, then in a sudden movement pulled her roughly into his arms, showering her hair and face with a torrent of kisses, until they were both breathless and forced to stop. For a moment they stood immobile, holding hands and laughing foolishly at each other. Then he wrapped his arms around her once more and kissed her again, this time slowly, tenderly, savouring every touch and taste of her. She breathed in his familiar scent and closed her eyes. The memory of last night's kisses still lingered on her body and she wanted his lips back where they belonged.

An instant and she had her wish. The gold-flecked eyes were dark now as he hungrily sought her lips once more, bruising them in his need. His mouth began to trail slow kisses down her neck. Then expertly unbuttoning her riding dress, he raised the satin skin of her breasts to his lips. She gasped with pleasure and fell back against the tree they had stopped beneath. is handHer He teased her with his tongue and she pressed into him, moulding herself like a second skin, her soft warmth cleaving to him.

'Love me,' she whispered.

But suddenly he'd stepped back. He met her bewildered gaze directly, but when he spoke it was as though the words were being dragged from him. 'I cannot...' His voice trailed away.

Marianna looked at him uncomprehendingly. A minute ago, a second ago, she had told him as plainly as any woman could, that she needed his love in all its fullness. And it seemed he'd wanted it. But now, suddenly, he was walking away. Rejection, humiliation, desperation – a deluge of the most horrible feelings.

He gazed blindly into the distance, then grabbed her hands and pulled her towards their waiting horses. Without a word, he tossed her into the saddle and turned his mount towards the town. They rode in silence until they were once more outside the house in Marine Parade. He dismounted swiftly, springing up the front steps to summon Marston to the door. Ashen-faced, Marianna slid from her saddle and brushed past him into the open hallway. With a brief bow, he turned and led both horses away.

∽

Once in the privacy of her bedroom, she allowed the tears to flow. Walking together this morning, she'd felt closer to Joshua than ever before. He had never hidden his dislike of his family, but today she'd realised for the first time the powerful hold the past still had on him. He had let down his guard and confided in her. She'd felt sad and distressed at his story. Angry, too, at his parents, at his brother, even the friends he'd betrayed. None of them, it seemed, had really loved him, not enough to save him from himself. She'd even begun to understand why after that last catastrophic event, he had fallen into a rakish life. He must have thought himself permanently tainted, a bad omen for anyone unwise enough to get too close. But after all these years, he *had* allowed himself to get close – to her.

He'd sworn the kisses they'd exchanged had touched him deeply, but his fine words had been meaningless. They had been a sham. At the very moment they could have sealed their love, he'd rejected her. Was he concerned that if she did not leave for Spain as he'd expected, she would be a nuisance to him? Was this his way of ridding himself of a clinging woman?

She, too, could do some ridding. From now on, she would smother her feelings. More, she would destroy them utterly, cut them off at their very roots and never let them bloom again.

Joshua slammed shut the door of his studio. He had no intention of painting, but he had to be alone and this was the only room in the palace he could be sure of privacy. The news that Marianna did not intend to return to her aunts' chaperonage had struck him like a lightning bolt. She could no longer wed a man for whom she had no feeling, she'd told him, and that meant only one thing. She loved elsewhere – and he was the man she loved. He was still trying to absorb this when she was in his arms and asking to be seduced.

He'd been carried away by the sheer physical delight of wanting her but, when she'd breathed that command, when she'd asked him to love her totally, the reality of the situation had hit him, and hit him hard. He'd paused long enough to realise that what they were doing was madness. He could not let her give herself without thought for the future. A girl who lost her purity was damaged goods – even worse, an outcast in society. He cared for her too much to let that happen.

But now in the quiet of his room, with time to think and think deeply, he grew certain that though he'd pulled back, it was already too late. He knew little of Spanish society but enough to realise that in its eyes Marianna had committed a grave sin. Whether she was a virgin or not was irrelevant. She had allowed a man to kiss her in a way that only a husband should. How could he have been so stupid as not to realise the true import of his actions? She'd not realised either, but she was young, trusting, blinded by love. It had been his responsibility to keep her safe and he'd failed miserably. She would say it was unimportant, that she had no wish to marry any man, but he knew from long experience of women that such vows rarely held. There would come a time when she did want to marry and she would have to confess to her intended husband something at least of her past. Joshua was pretty certain that however mild the confession, it would damn her irrevocably.

Swept with remorse, he strode across the room to the open windows. An unkempt profusion of honeysuckle and dogwood looked back at him. How could he ever make it up to her? He could not. It was impossible, except... a mad notion of asking her to be his wife flitted through his mind and was immediately dismissed. For years he'd spelt disaster for anyone who came too close. There was no way he could ask her to marry him.

Or was there? He paced up and down the floor, wooden boards creaking and cracking beneath his feet. To live as he had these last six years was undemanding and free of pain. Dared he embrace a different kind of life? One over which he had little control, one of unknown pitfalls and sorrows? But she needed him. He may have burned his fingers but he'd burned hers, too. And he had to put it right.

Chapter Twenty-Three

Marianna's resolve to erase Joshua Marchmain from her world was put to the test almost immediately. She had slept little and was making her way bleary-eyed from the breakfast table when a disapproving Marston put a small posy of wild flowers into her hand: blue bellflowers and pink eglantine roses interweaved with strands of ivy. She carried them into her small downstairs parlour and sat staring at them for what seemed an age. There was no note, but she knew from whom they came. Reluctantly, she turned to the bookshelf and took down the dictionary of flowers she'd discovered earlier, flicking through the pages and finding the entries for each plant: bellflowers for thinking of you, roses for a wound to heal and ivy for friendship. And this was his response to her complete humiliation!

She threw the book on to the table and strode into the hall, grabbing the posy on the way. One of the undermaids was busy dusting a console table and bobbed a small curtsy as she saw Marianna approach.

'Lizzie, isn't it?' The maid nodded nervously, wondering if her dusting was at fault. It was usually Miss Carmela who took her to task.

'I'd like you to have these, Lizzie. They will brighten your bedroom.'

The maid gaped and Marianna said in a voice which brooked no argument, 'You will need to put them in water – now.'

The hall clock was striking eleven as the maid scurried away and Marianna, still trembling slightly, walked back into the parlour. Almost immediately she spied his figure through the small square panes of its window: Joshua walking slowly back and forth along the promenade. He was waiting for her, she knew. Her anger had begun to cool and in its place the impulse to run to him was gathering strength. Determinedly, she beat it back but it cost her dear, forcing her to retreat to her room which faced the garden rather than the seafront. An hour later she returned to the parlour and saw that he was gone. She felt empty and aching but knew she'd done the right thing.

A slow twenty-four hours brought another bouquet. She ignored Marston's deep frown and took them from him in silence. But her anger was reignited and she stomped through to the back kitchen and plunged the posy unceremoniously into the rubbish bin. She had no idea what Joshua's intended, but if he thought that two bunches of wild flowers would erase the pain he'd caused, then he was more arrogant than she'd ever believed. She felt proud she had shown resolve, but a small, hard nut of anguish had settled itself firmly within and she knew it would be her companion for years to come.

For three days she dared not venture beyond the front door for fear of being waylaid, but when no more offerings arrived and there was no further sign of Joshua, she thought it safe to leave the house. A travelling fair had come to Bartholomews and Flora was eager to attend. Its unsophisticated pleasures were not likely to entertain Marianna, but she knew she could not stay indoors for ever. Donning a simple sprig muslin and a plain straw bonnet, and with Flora chattering by her side, she began the walk along Marine Parade towards the Steine. They had barely walked fifty paces when at the corner of Chapel Street, an immaculately attired Joshua stepped into their path and forced them to a halt.

He cannot have known we would be walking here today, Marianna thought. He must have been waiting nearby for days.

He bowed deeply and she nodded briefly in response, edging around him in an effort to continue her journey. Already she could feel her traitorous body working against her.

'Would you allow me to escort you this morning, Miss Marquez?' he enquired formally.

'Thank you, Mr Marchmain, but as you see I have my maid and she is all the protection I need.'

He bowed again and she could see him looking searchingly at her face. She hoped he would not remark on her pallor and the dark circles beneath her eyes. The longer he stood there, the harder it was to avert her gaze from his beautiful person. And she needed to.

'We are a trifle short of time this morning, sir. If you

would excuse us...' She edged a little further ahead.

'So short of time that you cannot spare five minutes?'

There was something in his voice that made Marianna pause. He was dressed in his usual elegant fashion, his skin lightly tanned and his hair glinting gold in the late summer sun – as ever he looked the perfect man. Yet there was something different, she felt. Could it be that he was nervous? Surely not!

Flora had been looking from one to the other, her mouth opening and closing like a fish searching for water. Marianna could see she was confused and now the flush on the girl's cheeks signalled her annoyance at Joshua's unwanted intrusion. She looked likely to find her tongue at any moment.

Marianna made a swift decision. 'Go ahead, Flora, I will catch you up.'

'But will you be all right, Miss Marianna?'

'Perfectly. I shall be with you in a few moments.'

Joshua watched the maid walk unwillingly towards the town before he spoke. 'I sent you flowers.'

Marianna said nothing.

'I hoped you would understand their message.'

'I did'

'Then why did you not respond?'

She would have liked to favour him with her opinion of his message, but instead settled for scorn. 'Since when have I had to account to you for my actions?' Her voice trembled only slightly.

Joshua wasn't deterred. 'I wanted to speak to you, Marianna – badly.'

She raised her eyebrows and he was quick to continue. 'I've been a fool. I was a fool on our ride. Not because I escorted you home – that was the right thing to do – but because I should have told you...' He paused uncertainly. 'Told you what I'm about to say.'

Her eyebrows climbed even higher. She had no idea what he meant, but decided she would hear him out.

'You told me you are no longer willing to accept an arranged marriage?'

Marianna nodded, unsure of where this was leading.

'So you are free to make your own choice of husband?' Her head tilted to one side and she looked perplexed. Then came the bombshell. 'I think your choice should be me.'

'What!' She was stunned.

'I think you should marry me.'

'Is this some kind of perverted joke?'

'I can't blame you for judging me harshly. But it's no joke, though it may seem so. In truth marriage to a hedonist is unlikely to advance your social standing.'

She was incensed and hurt in equal measure. His false proposal was yet another dagger to her heart.

'I do not deserve your mocking, sir. If this is no joke, then it's a Banbury story. If I were foolish enough to accept your offer – which rest assured, I am not – you would be certain to decide that your proposal was after all an unfortunate mistake.'

'I am sincere, Marianna. However much to the contrary it may appear, I've always been sincere.'

She was still recovering from the shock of his announcement and could hardly take in what he was saying. Bewilderment made her cutting. 'You would not know the meaning of the word.'

'I've always had your best interests at heart. I hope you will believe that at least.'

'And now you have my best interests at heart by asking me to marry you? Forgive me if I'm sceptical!'

'Of course, you are. But I've done a deal of thinking over these last few days and I know this is right.'

'And when did this improbable revelation visit you exactly?'

'I've made you angry and I'm sorry for that. But try to understand. I didn't think I was the one to make you happy – I carry too much of the past with me. I should have kept away, but somehow I couldn't and now that you've given up all idea of marrying to please your family, I'm asking you to please me.'

Seeing her desperately trying to make sense of his words, he pressed home his case. 'I don't ask you this lightly. Believe me when I say that I want to live with you, to make a home with you – if you'll have me.'

Marianna was weakening. He sounded so earnest, but this change of fortune was too much to swallow. 'It's not possible. You cannot want to marry, Joshua.'

He looked at her so fiercely that she was almost afraid. 'But I do.' Then in a weak attempt to return to the Joshua she knew, 'If we marry, I may even allow you to hang my precious da Vinci!'

The quip faded and his expression took on a rare seriousness, 'You should know, Marianna, that if you take me as a husband, you will do yourself little social good and are sure to upset a great many people. Marriage to me may be a step too far.'

'It's a step I never thought to take,' she said slowly.

But her face had gained colour, the cream of her cheeks lit by an inner glow. This morning had brought a miracle, she told herself, and like any miracle it needed faith to believe. How Joshua had come to this decision was unclear, but she was sure now that he meant every word. This was no cruel jest, no mocking overture. He'd asked her to marry him and all she had to do was say yes.

'You know that you've turned my life upside down.' She paused. 'But you are the only man I could ever wed.'

'And?'

'And if your proposal is honest, you have my answer.'

He held out his arms and for long minutes they were locked in an embrace. But then the unwelcome thoughts began to arrive.

'What about my father?'

'You haven't told him that you're not returning to your aunts?'

'Not yet. It would have been difficult enough – but now this!'

He stroked her arm very gently. 'We'll see him together. Tell him we are wishful of marrying.'

'If only it were that simple.' She hesitated, unsure of how to phrase the unpalatable. 'Papa is aware of Court gossip. He holds some strong opinions.'

'Don't let's sham. He knows me for a rake and will be horrified that his beloved daughter has chosen to throw her lot in with such a loose fish.'

'So...'

'So I will have to prove him wrong, prove that my inglorious career belongs to the past. That you are now my future.'

'That could take some time.'

He pulled her towards him again, burying his hands in the tangle of curls and lifting her face to his. 'Another year is neither here nor there, my darling.'

'A year!'

'Have patience. Before the time is out, my charm offensive will have him begging me to marry you.'

She smiled a little wanly, a furrow still creasing her brow. 'There are my aunts too – they will be completely opposed.'

'Aunts are no problem. I can deal with any number of aunts,' he said easily.

'You will be very busy then.' A smile flitted across her face at the thought of Joshua "dealing" with those fearsome matriarchs. 'They will do anything to protect my fortune.'

'I have a fortune, too,' he pointed out. 'Not, I imagine, of the same magnitude but still a cool ten thousand a year. Who could want more? You can sign your inheritance over to the aunts and never have a thing to do with it.'

'They willl still be unhappy with the match and I fear they'll make sure my father refuses his consent.'

'But if we wait until you are twenty-one, you can marry whom you wish.'

'I don't want to upset Papa.' She sounded miserable.

He hugged her more tightly. 'Don't despair, Marianna. Let me talk to him, get to know him. Make him see I will look after his little girl.'

She looked dubious but Joshua was encouraging. 'I'll invite him to dinner and then the theatre – just the three of us, if you can bear to leave your duenna behind. It will help to break the ice.'

'However will you get him to agree?'

She doubted if anyone could persuade her father to spend an evening with Joshua Marchmain, let alone include his daughter in the arrangement. Yet persuade him, Joshua did.

Chapter Twenty-Four

The following Thursday on the stroke of eight, he arrived at Marine Parade in a carriage hired for the evening. As always he looked complete to a shade, satin knee breeches and black tailcoat throwing into relief the dazzling snow of ruffled shirt and cravat, the latter arranged in precise and intricate folds. A silk-lined cloak completed the picture.

Her father greeted his host with a stiff little bow, but Marianna curtsied to her lover with a mischievous smile on her face.

They were to dine at the Old Ship, the oldest hostelry in Brighton and one that frequently accommodated the Regent's guests. The previous month Marianna had attended a ball at the Ship's magnificent assembly rooms and marvelled at the ninety-foot long ballroom with its spectators' and musicians' galleries. But tonight Joshua had bespoken a private parlour, equally luxurious, but a good deal more intimate. He had gone to a great deal of trouble in planning this evening, Marianna thought. Not only was the room he'd chosen the perfect backdrop for a congenial dinner, but the meal itself had been carefully ordered to appeal to the tastes of a middle-aged gentleman.

A modest but delicious repast ensued, beginning with a turtle soup served alongside a series of entrées, including the omelettes her father loved. Ernesto ate well but remained aloof. For a while the talk was general: the beauty of the Sussex landscape, the benefits of sea air, the numbers of dandies parading Brighton's seafront with their ridiculously padded shoulders and collars so high they were unable to turn their heads. It was not until the serving of a second course of goose, lobster and a braised ham, with chafing dishes of French beans, peas and asparagus, that Señor Marquez made mention of his unexpected invitation.

He lay back against his chair, slowly sipping a second glass of wine. 'I must thank you, Mr Marchmain, for a superlative dinner.'

'I'm glad the meal meets with your approval, sir,' Joshua responded politely. 'It is always hazardous to order for another whose tastes you can only guess.'

'Would it be discourteous of me to ask why my particular tastes interest you? Why, in fact, you have invited me to accompany you this evening?'

'Not discourteous at all. On the contrary, I find it understandable and very simple to explain. I wish to marry your daughter.'

The announcement, quiet and measured as it was, did not prevent Ernesto choking violently on his wine. When he recovered sufficiently to speak, his voice seemed not to belong to him.

'You wish to marry Miss Marquez?'

'I do. I am hopeful of winning your consent and thought

it right that we should further our acquaintance as soon as possible.'

'Marry!' her father repeated. Then turning to Marianna, he said in a voice barely above a whisper, 'Can this be right, my child?'

'Yes, Papa. I love Joshua. He is the only man who will make me happy.'

'But – '

'I am aware of the misgivings you must have,' Joshua interrupted smoothly. 'And naturally I'm happy to give in private whatever assurances you need, but Marianna and I are resolved. We will marry – whether it's next month or next year.'

Her father proudly drew himself up, looking every inch a Spanish nobleman.

'You may not realise it, Mr Marchmain,' he pronounced haughtily, 'but my daughter's choice of husband is of the greatest significance. Through her mother's family, she will inherit a very large estate when she reaches the age of twenty-one. That may influence your decision.'

'I cannot see how.'

'You would not, I am sure, wish to be seen as a fortune hunter.'

'Papa!' The ebony curls framing Marianna's lovely young face gave an angry toss.

'You are right, Señor Marquez. I would not. But since Marianna's fortune is neither here nor there, I think it unlikely. I have a considerable inheritance of my own and am more than happy to share it.'

His cheerful insouciance appeared to sting Ernesto.

'When I said a very large fortune, I doubt you have any idea of its size.' His tone now was even haughtier.

'Papa, don't you see, neither of us is concerned with my inheritance.' Marianna was incensed by her father's wilful lack of understanding. 'Joshua has a splendid country estate of his own and enough money to keep us both in comfort.'

'Not concerned with a massive fortune? What nonsense is this?' her father spluttered. She leaned towards him, her tone placating. 'Could not my aunts devise a new plan for how best to use the money? I know them to be involved in any number of charitable causes and my fortune would be well spent.'

Ernesto struggled to digest this heresy and there was an uncomfortable silence.

'Papa, dear Papa.' Marianna reached across the table and took her father's hand in hers. 'I love Joshua. That surely is what is most important.'

'And I will look after her, you can be sure,' Joshua put in. 'Who better, after all, than a reformed rake?'

Marianna gave him a sharp glance feeling that her lover's intervention was hardly helpful. But Joshua's words had set Ernesto thinking. This match was the very last thing he desired for his daughter and his instinct had been to grab her by the hand and incarcerate her immediately within the confines of Marine Parade until arrangements could be made for her travel to Spain. Lady Trelawny, when she arrived, would have to get on as best she could without her young friend.

But what Marchmain had said made a kind of sense. Who better to look after a young and naïve girl than a man who was thoroughly experienced in the wiles of the world? If she were compelled to marry a man she did not love – not that he would insist on such a thing but the aunts could be very forceful when they chose – what kind of trouble might result? He had seen with his own eyes, the power of Marianna's budding sexuality. He shuddered to think of the likely outcome of an unsuccessful marriage. And as for the fortune she would inherit, Marchmain seemed genuinely unmindful: no doubt the marriage settlements could ensure the rightful disposition of such a large estate.

The third course of creams, jellies and a basket of pastries went virtually untouched, but the mood was mellow as they made their way to the Theatre Royal where Charles Kemble was once more the star of the stage. Fifteen years ago, the actor had launched the new theatre with a stunning performance of *Hamlet*, but this evening he was playing comedy at which, it was universally agreed, he excelled.

The box Joshua had reserved ensured them an extensive view of the auditorium. Marianna surveyed the gold and glitter of the fabulous building with pleasure, its elaborate decoration scintillating beneath the newly installed gas light. An ocean of faces and a thrum of excited chatter filled the entire space, from the Royal Box housing members of the palace household, to the cheapest seats in the highest tiers. She had never before attended a performance at the Theatre Royal since Carmela naturally dismissed acting as a pretext for sin. To do so this evening and beside the man she loved, was double enchantment.

The squabbles of Beatrice and Benedick were soon

filling the auditorium as *Much Ado about Nothing* unfolded the foolishness of its hero and heroine. Sitting close on a matching gilt chair, Joshua stole glances at his betrothed whenever he thought himself unobserved. She was enthralled by the play, face alight and hands clasped together in excitement. *She has forgotten that I exist*, he thought wryly.

Then she took her eyes from the stage and looked across at him with a smile so radiant that his heart almost stopped. The doubts which had plagued him momentarily disappeared. *This had to be right.* He smiled back at her and a wave of emotion rippled between them.

As if sensing a disturbance in the air, Señor Marquez shifted his position, re-arranging the red velvet cushions better to support his back, for this latter part of the evening was proving something of a trial and he was barely managing to keep his eyes open. When the curtain came down for a short interval, he was more than willing to stretch his legs alongside his host in the galleries behind the auditorium.

Marianna, though, declined to accompany them. This was an opportunity, she realised, for Joshua to advance his acquaintance with the man he hoped to make his father-in-law, but barely knew. Instead she set herself to study her theatre programme. She was not to be left in peace for long. Almost as soon as the door closed behind her father, it opened again – to a female figure in rustling taffeta skirts and emanating a powerful, musky perfume. Marianna looked up surprised.

'My dear,' the duchess cooed, 'forgive me for disturbing you, but I was sure you wouldn't mind. I thought it high time we renewed our acquaintance.'

With Joshua's warning ringing in her ears, Marianna smiled politely but said nothing. She would like to believe Charlotte innocent of plotting against her, but common sense told her otherwise. Joshua had made clear to the duchess that he wanted nothing more to do with her, and at the same time made clear he wanted a great deal to do with Marianna. It was hardly conducive to mutual friendship.

'I haven't spoken to you for such a long time and we seem to have become estranged,' the older woman murmured, skating smoothly over the debacle of the Lewes race. 'But that is certainly not my wish.'

She slid into a gilt chair and continued to flatter. 'You look so beautiful tonight, my dear, so young and vital, it makes me sad.'

Marianna closed her ears. Did the duchess really think her compliments would renew trust?

'It is such a shame.'

This time the words penetrated and the young woman became alert. 'A shame?'

'Yes, my dear, a dreadful shame. That's why I am here, you see. I want to help.'

'I am afraid I don't see, Your Grace.' Marianna felt a gnawing anxiety begin to take hold.

'Charlotte, please. We know each other better than to stand on ceremony, I hope.'

Marianna was silent. Whatever Charlotte Severn had to say, she was not going to help her say it.

'Yes, a shame,' the duchess repeated for the third time.

'But you are still very young and you have spirit enough to overcome any temporary unpleasantness.'

Marianna could not stop her brow furrowing. The cat and mouse game the duchess was playing was beginning to find its mark.

'If I did not think you would recover easily,' the woman continued silkily, 'I would say nothing, even though I feel you are entitled to know what might be vital for your future happiness.'

The duchess's voice had assumed the cloying sweetness which made Marianna feel slightly sick. She sat mute, perched rigidly on her chair, and waited for the blow to fall.

'Of course, it may not *be* a problem,' Charlotte said. 'The man may mean nothing to you. But I cannot take that chance. You are too precious.'

Marianna screwed her hands into a ball so tight, her fingers became locked. If only Joshua and her father would open the door and put an end to this dreadful encounter.

'If you care nothing for him, then all will be well, but otherwise...' The duchess allowed her voice to fall away in mock concern.

'Who are we talking about?' Marianna managed. As if she did not know.

'Who? Why, Mr Marchmain, naturally.'

'And why should that interest me?'

'Would it be foolish to point out that you are here this evening with him?' Charlotte queried archly.

'I am here with my father. We are both Mr Marchmain's guests.'

'How very civilised. I should not disturb what is so

obviously a delightful evening.' And she got up to leave, her skirts rustling noisily behind her.

Marianna wanted to scream – what is it, what do you know that is so bad, but she managed to maintain a posture of indifference. The duchess's hand was on the door handle when she turned back to face her quarry.

'I understand you have a dear friend who now lives in Cornwall or perhaps we should say, a former dear friend.'

Cassandra? What on earth did Cassie have to do with anything? Marianna's mind skittered in confusion, but she willed herself to maintain an impassive face.

'Her name is Cassandra Latimer, although she is now a Trelawny. But, of course, you know her name,' Charlotte purred. 'After all, how many dear friends would you have in Cornwall?'

'What of Lady Trelawny?'

'An extraordinarily beautiful woman, I believe, and one with an unusual past. A little colourful shall we say.'

'I fail to see what such tittle tattle has to do with me.' Marianna's voice was glacial. Whatever this woman was engaged in, it was tawdry.

'Let us see, shall we?' Charlotte Severn let go of the door handle and walked back a few paces into the room. She looked Marianna in the eyes and a derisive smile lit her face.

'When Cassandra Latimer was engaged to the man who is now her husband, she allowed herself to go just a little astray.' The duchess mockingly drawled the "little". 'And who could blame her with such charming temptation at her feet? Thank goodness that it ended well. But the man who enticed the ravishing Cassandra from her fiancé and who – I blush to mention this in a young girl's hearing – who seduced her and then left her amid a mountain of scandal, was the man you have made your particular friend. In fact, *our* particular friend. Joshua Marchmain.'

Chapter Twenty-Five

It seemed the theatre walls were closing in on her, heavy and threatening. Crystal chandeliers shook in her face and the wall sconces, with their too bright gas jets, ripped themselves from their moorings and came crashing down on her. A huge weight seemed to be breaking her body in two. Yet she knew she must respond to this wicked woman. After what seemed an age, she managed to speak, her voice steady from sheer force of will.

'You are misinformed, Your Grace. Mr Marchmain is not a particular friend of mine. The tale you tell is indeed sad but is of no interest to me.'

'I am delighted to hear it,' the duchess returned, and with one last false smile of condolence, she whisked herself through the door.

Marianna hardly realised her visitor had left. She was staring into an abyss, a dark, hollow nothingness. She felt herself hardly able to breathe. She had to get away. She had to get out of this place. She jumped to her feet, upsetting the delicate gold chair and stumbled out into the gallery. Her father and Joshua were making their way back to the box, ready to resume their seats. She saw but didn't see their startled expressions: she was looking through them, falling down into a black and endless void. She had to get away, get away, get away.

'Marianna?' Her father approached her uncertainly.

But she rushed past him along the gallery, down the sweeping staircase and out of the front door. Carriages had not yet been called for and New Road lay peaceful in its solitude. A moon rode high in the sky, here and there obscured by tattered fragments of cloud. In the ghostly light she ran for shelter like a small, frightened animal.

Marine Parade was reached in minutes and a surprised Marston summoned to the door. Not a word did he get from his young mistress. At the sounds of arrival, Carmela appeared from the drawing room, her embroidery still in her hand. She called something to Marianna but Marianna did not see or hear.

Up the stairs, past a dozing Flora on the landing, and finally to sanctuary. Only now could she rest, here at the bottom of the dark pit that had swallowed her whole. She fell on the bed, dry eyed, too stricken to cry.

How long she lay there she had no idea, minutes perhaps, hours even, before Ernesto's anxious face appeared in the doorway.

'*Querida*, what on earth is the matter?'

'I'm sorry, Papa,' she whispered. 'I felt unwell and had to get home.'

'But why did you not tell us? Mr Marchmain would have ordered the carriage immediately. He is most worried about you.'

She could not bear even to hear his name.

'Papa, will you forgive me, but I feel too ill to talk this evening.'

Her father looked stern. 'How can this be? We left you perfectly well and out of nowhere you become so ill that you behave with the utmost discourtesy. I demand to know what has happened, Marianna.'

'Nothing has happened, Papa. I am simply unwell,' she repeated in a failing voice.

'But to rush off like that! What will Mr Marchmain think?'

'I no longer care what Mr Marchmain thinks,' she said in a stronger voice.

Ernesto's face expressed surprise, but he did not press the matter. 'At least allow Flora to help you undress.'

Marianna agreed, hoping by doing so, that she would be left alone. But the misery of the evening was not yet finished since her father was the bearer of more unwelcome news.

'Did Carmela tell you that while we were at dinner, Lady Trelawny arrived.'

'Lady Trelawny?' Her voice shook.

'The friend you very much wished to see.' Her father's tone was unusually tart.

'But she is not due for another day.'

'That too was my understanding, but it seems she decided not to stay in Winchester overnight but to continue to Brighton. Her father is already on his return to Cornwall. He did not wish to be long away, I believe.'

'Cassandra is here!' Her voice broke with wretchedness.

'She is, my dear, so whatever ails you, it would be wise to find a swift cure. Carmela reports that Lady Trelawny was tired from the journey and decided on an early bedtime.

But she is looking forward to seeing you on the morrow for she has a good deal to tell you and is sure that you will have much to tell her.'

And with that, her father called Flora into the room with instructions to help her young mistress to bed. Marianna was hardly aware of the maid's presence and submitted mechanically to being undressed and slipped between the covers. Left alone she lay prone, her newly brushed hair wild across the pillow and her eyes staring blankly ahead. She felt nothing. If she pinched herself, and she did, her flesh was numb. That should scare her, but it didn't. Nothing scared her, nothing touched her, nothing ever could touch her again.

Three years ago she'd lost the man she loved to Cassie. It didn't matter that Luke had never returned her love, didn't matter that her love now seemed juvenile. It had hurt so badly then, cut her into such tiny little ribbons that she'd thought she would never be whole again. But over the years she'd remade herself and finally found the man to help her fashion the rest of her life. Now he was gone, too – another love lost, but this so much greater than the first. This time she would not be able to stick the pieces together again.

And how had she lost the man who was to crown her life with romance and adventure, love and joy? Why, she'd lost him to the very same woman. Indirectly perhaps, but without a doubt she'd lost her love to Cassandra once more. Such bitter irony!

⤸

Flora brought her the message while she was still abed. Her chocolate had grown cold on the bedside chest and hot water cooled in its basin. But she'd not stirred. She had no wish ever to leave this room, no wish ever to move again.

'I think you should read it, Miss Marianna,' the girl dared to suggest, aware that something dreadful had happened and guessing at its cause.

A man, the maid reasoned, the one who'd stopped them on their way to the fair just a few days ago, the one who'd come to the house early this morning and handed her a letter with strict instructions to place it in her mistress's hands. She tried again, this time pushing the envelope into Marianna's listless grasp.

Left alone once more, Marianna glanced indifferently at the message. She knew its author and knew she'd no wish to read it. But something impelled her to rip the seal open and scan the few words within. It was brief and to the point.

Whatever has gone wrong, I need to know, he wrote. *I hope you will feel able to tell me in person. I shall be by the groyne directly opposite your house at noon this morning. Please meet me there.*

It was signed simply *Joshua*.

He had named the very same place they'd first met all those months ago. Two months ago to be precise – was it only that long? Marianna felt she had lived a lifetime since then. An undercurrent of excitement had permeated that first meeting, but also a distinct unease. Joshua had been mockingly persistent, seeming to care little for her discomfort. Surely that had been an omen. But deceiving her so wretchedly about his past was of a different order. He had destroyed her trust, her belief in herself, and left her vulnerable to the cruelties of a woman like

Charlotte Severn.

Yet it made no sense. Hadn't Joshua also protected her, rescued her from the same woman's clutches, not just once but several times? He'd warned her to be on her guard against the duchess and Robert Amesbury. So why last night had she not been? Why had she chosen to believe Charlotte? The frailest whisper of hope began to bloom. The duchess had lied before and proved unscrupulous, even malicious. The tale she'd told at the theatre could be another attempt to destroy, a fabrication concocted when every other of her despicable plans had failed. The more Marianna thought of it, the more likely it seemed. It was such a far-fetched story.

True, Joshua had lived a profligate existence – she was well aware of it – and aware that as a young man he'd failed his friends badly and been exiled for his wrongdoing. But it would have to be a diabolical coincidence that those friends had been Cassandra and Luke. Why then had she been so willing to believe the worst? Was it because she feared deep down that being loved by him was too much of a miracle? That she was not special enough for a man like Joshua to change his life so completely?

She'd been foolish! Joshua's feelings were genuine, he loved her. From all the women he'd known, he had asked *her* to marry him. She *was* special! And what had been his reward? To have his chosen bride believe a scurrilous story from a corrupt woman.

Marianna started out of bed. She must meet him and make an immediate apology. And he would have the chance to deny Charlotte Severn's evil words – his answer to a simple question would set everything to rights. She pulled the first gown she could find from the wardrobe and dressed quickly, her face a pale oval against the gown's drab olive. Slipping unseen from the house, she made her way swiftly towards the groyne.

The sky was overcast, all trace of summer having for the moment disappeared, but the breeze was light and the water unnaturally calm. She clambered down the sea-stained steps to the lower promenade. Then she saw him.

Out of nowhere, last night's harrowing events were back and landing with a sickening thud. Her stomach churned, but she carried on picking her way across the beach, stone by stone, until she stood a few feet from him.

'I cannot stay long.' Her earlier certainty was deserting her and nerves made her brusque.

'Then I must be grateful for the few minutes you can vouchsafe me.' He spoke lightly but his eyes wore a puzzled expression.

It was better to ask the dreadful question at once, she decided, clear the air and be comfortable together again. But her voice when she spoke was hesitant. 'Please accept my apologies for the way I behaved last night. I heard a disturbing story and it upset me greatly.'

He was still looking baffled. 'Last night, Marianna, we were at the play and enjoying ourselves, as I thought. What could possibly have disturbed you?'

'The Duchess of Severn,' she said baldly. 'She visited me in the interval.'

'Dear Charlotte. And what have I to thank her for now?'

Chapter Twenty-Six

His tone was so much one of levity that Marianna was convinced in that instant that the duchess's spiteful story was a complete falsehood. There was not the smallest shadow of guilt in Joshua's face. Instead he was smiling gently at her, waiting it seemed for her to come to her senses.

In the face of his good nature, she was finding it difficult to continue and her words came haltingly. 'It was a dreadful tale that she told – and it concerned you.'

His look was still one of bland enquiry. She tried again, her words so quiet they were hardly audible against the soft swell of the tide. 'Some years ago, the duchess said, you seduced a young woman on the eve of her wedding. And you were the bridegroom's best friend.'

She was watching him closely as she spoke and saw his eyes narrow. A terrible premonition began to burn through her. Did he know the rest of the story? She turned as white as the chalk cliffs which rose in the distance.

'Say something, Joshua,' she pleaded. 'Say that it's not true. Surely it's not true?'

'Alas, my dear, for once the duchess is telling the truth.

But it's an old story and I wonder how she came by it. No doubt Amesbury could tell us.'

Marianna was speechless, her rekindled trust shattered in one savage blow. She'd mentioned no names but still she knew that her worst fears were confirmed. Joshua had confessed, yet he was shaking it off as if it meant nothing. The vision she held of him crumbled into dust. A different person stood in his place, a person she could neither trust nor revere. She felt the dark abyss opening again beneath her feet, but this time she did not run away.

Gathering every ounce of resolution and with a voice that hardly wavered, she said, 'Mr Marchmain, I regret that I cannot marry you.'

'What! What are you saying?'

'I cannot marry you,' she repeated dully.

'This is a nonsense, Marianna. Last night we were to wed. Last night you were eager to persuade your father that I would make an excellent husband!'

'Last night I also learned of your past. And it is a past I cannot forgive.'

His head was shaking in disbelief and he began to stride back and forth, crunching the pebbles beneath his boots. After minutes he came to a halt in front of her, his gold-flecked eyes keen and lacking any trace of their usual lazy amusement.

'My dear.' He made a move towards her but she stepped nimbly to one side, evading his touch. 'My dear, you knew of my past, if not its details. I'm too old and have wandered the world too long not to have a history. But that's all done with. You are my only concern now, the only woman I need or desire.' His expression had clouded but he spoke calmly.

'This is not to do with *your* needs, but everything to do with mine. I cannot marry a man for whom I feel contempt.'

It was a most terrible thing to say. Had she meant it? She must have done, since the blurted words had come involuntarily. And they had their effect. Joshua appeared thoroughly shaken. His face darkened and when he spoke his voice was edged with anger.

'I am not proud of my past, but tell me what exactly has earned your contempt?'

'The people you hurt were dear friends of mine and you hurt them, not by accident, but simply in pursuit of your own pleasure. The woman's name was Cassandra Latimer and the man she was to marry was Luke Trelawny.'

'Cassie and Luke Trelawny!' His brow furrowed for a moment and then she saw a dawning comprehension. 'And was Luke the man you loved so hopelessly?'

He was mocking her, but she ignored the provocation. 'It matters not. He was your friend and you betrayed him. Then you betrayed Cassandra.'

'I repeat, I'm not proud of my actions. But it happened many years ago, a product of my shallow youth. You said yourself I should be forgiven for crimes committed as a stripling. You were unhappy with my brother for the very conduct you seem intent on emulating.'

'That was before I knew what you had done.'

'You knew what I had done. I told you the day we met on the Level.' His jaw jutted pugnaciously as though he was damned if he would let her rewrite their conversation to suit her own quixotic ends.

Marianna was beginning to unravel, but she pulled her defences together and fought back. 'You told me you had failed friends. I did not know then the manner of that failure or that it was my very dear friends you had treated so wickedly.'

'So your moral code is relative, is it? My actions are forgivable, but only if they involve people for whom you have no care.'

She realised he was right and that her stance was illogical. But it did not change the way she felt. She'd known too well the damage done to Luke, known how helpless she'd been to comfort him.

Her long silence seemed to encourage Joshua and he softened his voice in persuasion. 'Cassie and Luke are happy now, are they not? Isn't that what's important? It was a bad deed but good eventually came from it.'

A great deal of good had come from it, but only eventually. So much unhappiness and suffering had gone before.

'If they are happy, can we not be happy too?' Joshua continued.

That was simple to answer. 'I can never be happy with a man who would deliberately cause such heartache.'

'You refine too much on what is long past.'

'How can you dismiss your wrongdoing so casually?'

'I don't. I am well aware of my sin. But I was a stupid boy – and now I've grown up. My life is different.'

'Precisely how different?'

Marianna was regaining courage. If he'd shown true remorse, pleaded with her, asked for forgiveness, she might have found it impossible to resist. But he'd done none of those things. Instead he'd been at his most mocking and combative.

'Have we returned to my improper life and my fearsome reputation? Now let me see... you haven't exactly minded consorting with a rake these past weeks. And more than consorting, I could say, if I were being ungallant.'

'How dare you!'

'And nor did Cassandra mind,' he continued inexorably. 'Don't forget it takes two. What happened was not my fault alone.'

'You should have known better and acted better.'

'I agree, but then so should she. She was, after all, the one who was betrothed.'

Marianna hitched the skirts of her gown clear of the uneven strand and turned to go. 'I've no wish to continue this argument,' she said in her quietest voice. 'It is much too painful.'

He seized on the phrase. 'That suggest you still care for me.'

She said nothing and he pressed her. 'If that is indeed so, why are you doing this?'

'I have told you.'

Exasperated, he burst out, 'Are you sure it's not because you still love Luke Trelawny and wish to punish me for the fact that he married elsewhere?'

It was an unkind stab. She turned back to him and in a voice that wobbled only slightly made her final adieu. 'I have nothing more to say, Mr Marchmain. This is goodbye. Please don't attempt to contact me again.'

And with that she was gone.

❧

Left alone, Joshua stared sightlessly out to sea. He'd offered his hand in the best of faith, only for her to walk away on a whim. It had to be a whim. It was absurd. He was no angel. He'd behaved badly, once very badly, but that had been years ago, years when he'd been barely more than a fledgling and had understood nothing, neither who he was nor what he wanted. Surely youth offered some mitigation.

They had been years of heady excitement, of feeling that every day as he ventured forth he could renew his world. He'd certainly done so when he met Cassie. Renewed her world and Luke Trelawny's, too.

Fresh-faced and inexperienced, he'd launched himself on the town the very same month as Luke, and they'd become firm friends. A few months on, Luke had left for his home in Cornwall and returned with Cassandra on his arm. A single look and Joshua had fallen instantly under her spell. She'd been so eager to seize life, so alluring, so tempting and tempted. He'd cast caution to the winds, ignoring every demand of friendship. There had been nothing deliberate about the passion that had flamed between them; it had simply been too wild to control. That was no excuse, but why couldn't Marianna forgive such an old tragedy?

He could make a guess at the answer, and his rancour began slowly to subside, dissolving into the sea air and on the cry of the gulls. He'd destroyed her belief in him. It had taken time but gradually she'd begun to see beyond the label society had bestowed, to see him for the man he was. And it turned out that the man she saw fitted her so perfectly that she'd tumbled into love with him. Now the image she held had been shattered by a moment of careless talk.

But how careless, he wondered savagely. It had all the marks of spite, the marks of the vendetta waged by Charlotte Severn since first she became aware of the girl as a rival. The woman was stupid as well as vindictive. How could she not realise that the affair between them had ended months ago, that the plots she had been busily engineering against Marianna were pointless? He would never return to her.

Maybe not, but she had wreaked all the damage she could possibly desire. It mattered not to Marianna that Cassie and Luke were content. He had caused them pain and there could be no defence. But if they had suffered, so by God, had he! For years he'd wandered Europe, taking solace in the beauty he'd found, trying to erase the ugliness he'd known. Women had come and gone, his physical needs satisfied, but always there was beauty to strive for, a beauty just beyond his reach.

He'd begun to paint in the hope that there at least he would find what he so desperately desired. The endless seas he painted, with their limitless horizons, were an escape from the unlovely life he led and the person he'd become. But there was no escape. For a brief moment, the need to care for Marianna had offered the prospect of a new wholeness, but that too had turned to ashes. He was not made for beauty. His decision to marry had been foolish, a transgression duly punished. The doubts that had bombarded him ever since he'd proposed were justified. He took a deep breath and began the climb back to the promenade. He would go to hell in his own way, he thought grimly. For years he'd been doing just that, and with some success.

Chapter Twenty-Seven

'Mr Marchmain and I have bid each other farewell, Papa.'

Marianna stood a few paces inside her father's office, ready to flee as soon as she was able. She was humiliated at the confession she must make – that she no longer wished to marry the man that only a few hours ago she'd been mad to wed.

'Farewell? What do you mean, *querida?*'

'We have decided that after all we do not suit,' she said as composedly as she could.

'This is... unexpected. Are you quite sure, my dear?'

'Yes, quite sure.' Sure that her heart was breaking and at any moment her father must hear the pieces falling to the ground.

'You do not wish to marry him?' Ernesto repeated almost to himself.

He suddenly felt a good deal lighter. Marianna's determination to wed a man he considered grossly unsuitable had shocked him. It had been a struggle to appear complaisant, not wanting to be alienated from his only child. But now it looked as though those plans had come to nought and he would not have to suffer Joshua Marchmain as a son-in-law.

'No, Papa, I no longer wish to marry him.' Please, she begged inwardly, please don't ask me why. Then thinking she should offer something more to her long suffering parent, added, 'I'm sorry to have caused you trouble.'

'No trouble, my dear. You are right to draw back if you have doubts. And it seems that you do.'

She nodded, her face etched with unhappiness. Her father got up from his desk and put his arms around her in a comforting hug. 'You have made a sensible decision,' he said consolingly. 'But now you must put it out of your mind and think what is to be done. Have you had a chance to consider?'

She had no idea now what her life was to be. How very different to just a day ago! But she must not upset her father and, freeing herself from his arms, she fixed him with what she hoped was a steady look.

'Lady Trelawny will soon be travelling to London to consult a practitioner in Harley Street. She is wishful that I accompany her before I return to Spain and I've decided to do so.'

'As her friend, that is naturally a kind thought.'

'I will make arrangements to leave with her, but Papa – Lady Trelawny is to know nothing of this.' She gestured vaguely in the air. 'I mean nothing about Mr Marchmain. It cannot interest her and may cause her distress if she feels I am upset.'

'I will say nothing, you have my word. But *are* you upset, *querida*? You seem very calm.'

'I know that I am doing the right thing,' she answered obliquely. Her heart was rent in two, but her father must never know.

The stay with Cassandra in London would be brief and beyond that she hardly dared think. Once her papa was back in the capital, he would no longer need her services since Lady Foyle would again act as his hostess. And she had no desire to linger in a place where at any moment she might come upon the man she most wished to avoid.

She supposed that she would return to Spain – where else could she go? – but it would not be to marry as her aunts wished. Of that she was sure. After Luke she'd been indifferent, ready to marry the husband they chose. Yet that was no longer possible. The sorrow of youthful infatuation had given way to an all-consuming passion, but for a man she could not marry. And if she were not to wed Joshua, she would wed no other.

Trying hard to shake herself free of such dismal thoughts, she realised her father was speaking again. 'I shall not be far behind you in leaving Brighton, Marianna. But there is an important event to consider before we are finished here – the Regent's birthday festivities. I am sure you won't have forgotten that the palace is throwing a grand dinner and ball in the prince's honour. Friday's celebration is to be the most sumptuous of occasions, I believe, and we have been greatly honoured by an invitation. Fortunately, you will not have left for London by then.'

The gentle reminder left Marianna anguished. Her mind shrank from the idea of ever setting foot in the Pavilion again, but her father clearly expected her to accompany him. And after the upset she'd caused, she felt she owed him that at least. If he had an inkling of her true feelings, he would not wish her to go within a mile of the palace, she knew. But he saw a composed face and heard a calm voice and suspected nothing.

She felt a constriction in her throat and swallowed hard. 'I shall be pleased to attend, Papa,' she said.

'Then it is settled. After the ball you and Carmela will accompany Lady Trelawny to London. From there, you can journey with your cousin on to Spain. I shall make sure that I am back in town in time to see you both safely on your way.'

Her father walked back to his desk and began to leaf idly through a sheaf of messages. Marianna judged it time to go. She was thankful that the interview was at an end, but there was still Cassandra to face. And that encounter would be far more difficult – women possessed antennae that were so much sharper. Somehow she must prevent her friend catching any hint of the distress that was crushing her.

꙳

She was to be allowed a few more hours of grace. Cassie had endured a disturbed night and did not appear in the drawing room until almost noon and, when she did, Carmela was in attendance. From the moment Lady Trelawny had arrived at Marine Parade, Carmela had taken the expectant mother under her wing. Delighted to have a charge to coddle, she was busy now fussing over the likely need for shawls or slippers or footstools. She seemed intent on wrapping their guest in thick coils of cotton wool.

'You will never go to the parade, Lady Trelawny,' she

said in a shocked tone, when Cassie mentioned that she was looking forward to visiting the Level that afternoon to view the Regent's birthday parade.

'I don't see why not.' Cassandra's musical voice held a note of amusement. 'I cannot sit indoors for ever, and I'm quite sure that my young friend will be looking forward to the spectacle as much as I.'

Her young friend, coming into the drawing room at that moment, felt herself grow heavy with despair. She had counted on hiding herself away until Friday, when she must endure the Regent's party, before a final escape to obscurity. But apparently it was not to be.

'You would like to go, Marianna, would you not?' Cassandra asked coaxingly.

'Naturally we must not miss such a display,' she returned bravely. 'We can stroll to the Level after luncheon. I believe the ceremonial marching is to begin around two o' clock.'

In fact, they arrived well before that hour, hoping to secure a good vantage point. Alarmed at Lady Trelawny's imprudence, Carmela had insisted on accompanying them, dressed as ever in unadorned black – an almost laughable contrast to the flamboyant colour that was everywhere around.

The square on which the soldiers were to parade was the Regent's old cricket ground, but now transformed by a hard covering underfoot and decorated with flags and bunting of every shape and hue. Crowds were gathered along the intersecting pathways leading there and a tiered stand had been built at one end for the more genteel visitors. The little party made their way to seats on the front row from where they would enjoy an uninterrupted view. A military band already playing with gusto added to the sense of anticipation. The sun was bright for a late August afternoon, but a cooling breeze blew inland from the sea and the striped canvas awnings overhead stood ready to protect delicate complexions.

Cassie looked around her in appreciation. She had been living retired from *ton* society so long that she had forgotten the exciting hum of people intent on pleasure. Glancing to right and left at the fashionable silks and satins, the poke bonnets, the little pieces of gauze and tinsel masquerading as hats, she began to feel a complete dowdy. Life in the countryside was wonderful but it had its drawbacks, particularly for one who had long been considered a diamond of the first water. She must make sure that she returned from London with new gowns as well as medical advice.

She need not have worried. Whatever she wore, she was instantly the centre of attention. Her flame-haired beauty ensured that. A number of people recognised her and she nodded in response, while a woman three rows back craned her neck to see who it was accompanying Marianna Marquez.

Their fellow spectators, though, made no attempt at conversation – the stirring music made talking impossible – and Marianna was thankful. She had lost all desire to socialise. Her anxious scan of the stand had revealed no sign of Joshua and she could only hope that his role in planning the event had been backstage. Either that or he had deliberately absented himself, guessing she would attend. He would not know of Cassandra's presence, of course – Marianna had been careful to avoid any hint that his former lover had arrived in Brighton. And it must stay that way. The thought of a meeting between the two was unbearable.

'Isn't that the Dragoons?' Cassandra leant forward in eagerness as the band struck up an altogether more martial note.

The Light Dragoons had arrived, resplendent in their ceremonial uniform. They marched proudly towards the square, a thousand limbs moving as one. A drum major strode at their head beating time with his golden mace. Their show of military prowess began with a display of intricate marching, patterns dizzying in their complexity and breathtaking in their co-ordination. There followed individual feats of daring and skill until finally the stupendous conclusion of a mock battle, complete with enemy infantry and a troop of cavalry. An hour slipped easily by before the last hurrahs of the crowd were sounding and they made ready to leave.

'Marianna, my dear. How agreeable!' A perfumed figure crossed their path. 'I forgot to ask when we last met if you intended to come to the parade, but somehow I knew the uniforms would bring you!'

Carmela glared at the newcomer and Marianna bowed stiffly. 'As you see, Your Grace, we have been enjoying the display.'

Slightly to the rear of the group, Cassie caught up with them at that moment. She smiled shyly at the duchess and

Marianna had no alternative but to introduce her.

'Your Grace, this is Lady Trelawny.'

'Trelawny?' the duchess queried faintly.

'That's right.' Cassie's voice was warm. 'Cassandra Trelawny. How do you do? Was that not a most magnificent spectacle?'

Bewilderment, mortification, naked fury, flitted across the duchess's face in rapid succession. But her rigid training stood her in good stead and a mask of indifference slipped into place.

'The Dragoons can always be relied on for a superb exhibition,' she replied airily. 'The dear prince dotes on them, you know.'

Cassandra marked the note of condescension but, as the woman appeared to be a friend of Marianna's, she felt it incumbent to be courteous. Her two companions seemed to have been struck temporarily dumb and she waded gallantly into a smooth stream of small talk. The duchess played her part in the charade ably, automatic responses issuing with ease from her practised lips, while all the time questions laid siege to her mind. Why was Lady Trelawny here? Surely after what she had divulged to Marianna Marquez, this woman should not be her friend! Something had gone badly wrong.

She broke off what she was saying and looked wildly around. She needed to see Robert Amesbury urgently.

Cassandra was nonplussed by the older woman's evident disquiet but, hoping the duchess would soon recover her composure, she persevered. 'I spend my life in the depths of the Cornish countryside so you must know that today has been a most wonderful treat.'

Charlotte Severn pulled herself together with enormous effort. 'And what brings you to Brighton at this time, Lady Trelawny?'

A last hope had flashed into her mind and she was clinging to it. Cassandra had come to Brighton to commiserate with Marianna, to reiterate that she too had suffered from Joshua Marchmain's iniquity. She had come to tell her that the man was bad through and through and that Marianna was right to separate from him forever.

'I'm on my way to London,' Cassie said happily. 'My husband insists that I see someone in Harley Street though goodness knows why. Everything,' and she patted her expanding stomach lovingly, 'seems to be progressing just as it should.'

The duchess's hope flickered and died. 'And will you also be travelling to town, Marianna?'

Desperate to appear unperturbed, Marianna found her voice at last. 'I will, Your Grace. Lady Trelawny's arrival is timely. We can enjoy at least a sennight together in London before she returns to Cornwall.'

The duchess digested this. 'Then you are staying in England?'

'I imagine so,' she lied.

'And not returning to Spain?'

'Not for the moment. My father has need of me still. And I'm enjoying my stay greatly and would be loathe to cut it short.'

Marianna had the satisfaction of seeing the duchess blanch. Let her think that she and Joshua were still together, that the return to London signalled a deepening of their relationship. This spiteful woman had recounted her poisonous news for one reason alone. She had wanted to ensure their separation. She had succeeded, but Marianna would never give her the pleasure of knowing it. Let her feel chagrin that her plan had not worked, let her feel anguish that Joshua would never return to her.

In time, of course, he would. That was inevitable, but every moment of pain inflicted on this malevolent creature was worthwhile. The strength of her own venom shocked Marianna. But if she could have heard the duchess's embittered conversation just a few hours later, she would have prized the small triumph.

Chapter Twenty-Eight

'It hasn't worked!'

Robert Amesbury looked ruminatively at the furious woman opposite him. 'Why is that my sweet one?' he asked drily.

'Don't call me that.'

'I cannot think why I did.' He glanced at the sour expression distorting her face. 'Anything less sweet would be hard to imagine.'

'It hasn't worked,' she spelt out angrily. 'Cassandra Trelawny is here in Brighton and quite clearly friends with that chit. The girl has no shame! Wasn't she supposed to be desperately in love with Luke Trelawny? Yet she is happy to consort with the woman who broke his heart and unconcerned that Joshua was the willing accomplice. She is shallow beyond belief.'

Amesbury raised his eyebrows and seemed about to comment but then decided otherwise.

'I know what you are about to say. Don't! I may be shallow, but at least I'm consistent. The girl is happy to entertain Lady Trelawny in her own home, more than that, happy to accompany her to London in a few days' time.

What would you wager on her being equally happy to see Marchmain there, whatever ill she knows of him?'

'Let it go, Charlotte,' he advised her roughly. 'I would like to punish the girl as much as you, but we have failed at each attempt and done nothing but made ourselves look foolish. It might be as well simply to let her disappear to Spain.'

'That's because you haven't heard the best of it. The chit is staying in England!'

Amesbury's brows knit together in annoyance but he spoke calmly. 'So what do you want to do?' His equanimity infuriated the duchess.

'Do! Do! I want to get rid of the girl for ever. You know what I want to do.'

'Then we must make a final throw of the dice. No hesitation this time. No misgivings.'

'You are right. I have been too kind to her.'

Lord Amesbury grimaced, but the duchess went on, 'Far too kind. I have allowed her to flourish instead of nipping the life out of her from the very outset. We will do what we've had in mind for weeks. Are you ready?'

'I can be ready at any time, dear lady.'

'Good. Then, the Regent's ball the day after tomorrow?'

He took her hand and slowly brought it to his lips. 'A perfect occasion, I feel. A splendid finale to an overlong drama.'

⁓

By the time they had wended their way back to Marine Parade, Cassandra was feeling very tired. It had been an entertaining afternoon, but a long walk and prolonged sitting had taken their toll. Once in Marianna's small parlour, she cast off her bonnet and sank gratefully into a comfortable chair.

'You should rest in bed, Lady Trelawny,' Carmela scolded. 'It cannot be good for the baby to be forever on your feet.'

'Thank you for your concern,' she replied sweetly, 'but I can rest here.' She reached for a cup from the tray that had just arrived. 'Tea is sure to restore my energy.'

'But Lady Trelawny...'

'I will stay.' Cassie's voice was firm. 'Such a delightful room – it must catch every glimmer of sunlight and its view of the sea is unmatched. I can understand why you chose this for your own, Marianna. And it's perfect for a comfortable coze.'

The last thing Marianna wanted was a comfortable coze. She hoped her cousin would stay with them and put paid to any chance of intimate talk, but Carmela rose almost immediately, announcing that in that case she had many things to do, and all of them urgent.

'This afternoon has been wonderful,' Cassie said, as the door shut, 'and thank you for taking me. It felt strange to be among a fashionable crowd again but thoroughly enjoyable. Not that I would ever forsake Cornwall!'

'I don't imagine you would. Tell me about life at the Abbey.'

If Marianna had hoped to deflect her friend, she hoped in vain.

'The best thing about this afternoon was sharing it with you.' Cassie beamed at her. 'I've been waiting a long time for you to come to Madron and discover the house for yourself.'

'The moment never seemed right.' Marianna hedged. 'I was in Spain and my aunts would not have taken kindly to my travelling abroad again. They only permitted my return to England because Papa needed help.' A small white lie would not hurt.

'Perhaps once the baby is born, you will feel able to make the journey to Cornwall.'

Marianna smiled non-commitally. By then she would be back in Madrid and there would be little opportunity to venture abroad.

'We never had time to know each other really well,' Cassandra was musing. 'But I'm sure if we had, we would have become the closest of companions. One thing of which I *am* very sure – I have you to thank for my happiness.'

Her friend flushed and made haste to disclaim any such thing. 'My dear, yes!' Cassie insisted. 'If it had not been for you, I might never have felt able to trust Luke. And with what result! We could not be happier together and this child will only bring us closer.'

Marianna felt genuine pleasure. A few months ago, a few weeks ago even, her enjoyment would have been compromised by regret but that had melted like summer snow. She had a new and far heavier burden now.

'It's wonderful to see you so happy.' She pressed Cassie's hand. 'But my role was very small – a silly letter only. You were always destined to be with Luke.'

'You made me see that and I cannot thank you enough. I was guilty of great foolishness and you made me see I could have a different future.'

Marianna said nothing, but picked up a spoon and began swiftly to stir her tea.

'It seems that no matter how badly one has behaved,' Cassandra continued thoughtfully, 'and I did behave badly, the past doesn't have to ruin one's life.'

When her companion again made no response, Cassie paused and looked intently at the girl seated beside her. 'I hope you'll forgive me for saying this, my dear, but you've not been looking quite as carefree as I remember. I wonder – is there anything wrong?'

Danger leaped out in mile-high letters. Marianna knew she must steer the conversation away from this treacherous ground. 'There's nothing wrong. I am just a little tired. Brighton is a town made for leisure and that can be hard work! This summer has been very busy.'

'I can imagine,' her friend said sympathetically. 'Wherever the Regent is in residence, it's unlikely to be peaceful.' She paused again, as if wondering whether or not she should say more. 'But *should* anything be causing you unease, Marianna, my best advice would be to face it bravely and then not look back.'

'There is nothing, I assure you.'

'I'm glad to hear it. You are far too young to suffer anxiety.' She leaned back in her chair and gazed through the bow windows at the rolling sea beyond. 'But truth to tell I was only your age when I managed to fall into a maelstrom of trouble that took years to resolve.'

Marianna could hardly speak. If Cassandra intended to confess her youthful folly, she did not want to hear. Or did she? There was a part of her that needed to know why this woman had abandoned an honourable man like Luke, the part perhaps that needed to excuse her own all too easy fall into the arms of the same philanderer.

'How many years?' she heard herself ask in a constricted voice, though she knew the answer well.

'Six wasted years. I thought I could never forgive myself for what I'd done nor forgive the man involved. But I was wrong.'

'How did you forgive?' Marianna's throat was dry.

'I was foolishly naïve, on the town for the first time in my life. And so was he. We were both too young and heedless to bear the responsibility of our actions.'

Her words were almost an echo of those Marianna had heard from Joshua himself.

'And you didn't blame the man?' she ventured. 'Should he not have taken responsibility?'

'But why? We were both to blame. In fact, I can thank him now. Until I met him I'd taken Luke for granted. I was sleepwalking into marriage. A short-lived affair, for that was all it was, may have destroyed my betrothal but it made me realise I'd forsaken a deep, abiding love for a momentary passion, one which had no substance, no depth. If I were ever to meet the man again, I would shake him by the hand and thank him truly.'

Marianna was shocked. How could Cassandra speak so lightly of an event that had almost ruined her life and even worse, almost ruined Luke's. Six wasted years, she'd said. But here she was exculpating Joshua and willing to share blame for the catastrophe, even grateful to him for showing her the true nature of her feelings!

Cassandra replaced her teacup on the tray and rose to leave. 'Carmela may have been right,' she said softly, perhaps sensing that her words had in some way hit home. 'A rest in my room before dinner will refresh me. I will see you later, my dear.' She bent her graceful form towards Marianna and dropped a light kiss on the top of her head.

Left alone, Marianna wrestled with the words had passed between them. A blissfully happy Cassandra could afford to forgive the past, she thought churlishly. But it is *her* past to forgive, a small voice murmured, not yours. What have you to forgive? Cassandra's sorry story was played out when you were not much more than a child. She is happy, Luke is happy. Why can't you be?

But she knew she was confusing the symptom for the cause. The overwhelming nature of her distress came from one crucial fear – that Joshua Marchmain was the dissolute man everyone said he was and that she could never trust him to be otherwise. For a short while she had believed him capable of changing. But how short that time had been. Knowledge of the wicked path he'd trod six years ago had brought home to her the magnitude of his offences – his flagrant immorality, his uncaring selfishness – and had damned him in her eyes for ever. Joshua had not changed, would never change, and if she gave herself to him, she would live a lifetime of heartache.

⌒

Fortune favoured her the next day when Carmela decided to forsake her household duties and devote herself to the expectant mother. It was her cousin who escorted Cassandra on a shopping expedition to Bartholomews market and her cousin who sat with their visitor sewing and reading in the small parlour. Marianna was able to disappear for long stretches of the day, citing the necessity of helping Flora to pack her wardrobe. It was a job that appeared to take an inordinate amount of time, and while she sorted muslins and silks she tried to keep her mind a determined blank. The grand dinner and ball at the Pavilion was one more trial to face, the final trial, and she needed to keep at bay the thoughts that constantly harried her.

When she met her friend later in the day, she greeted Cassandra with a guilty warmth. 'It's a great shame that you cannot come to the ball. Papa would have been happy to obtain a ticket for the dance, if not to the dinner.'

Her visitor gave a rueful grin. 'Marianna, look at me, I am in no case for dancing! But you must not fret. Carmela and I will go on very well at home. And if I can be of any help in your preparations, send your maid to let me know. I shall not be sleeping – merely waiting for the call!'

Marianna, though, was not to need her friend's expertise. Since coming to Brighton, Flora had improved as a lady's maid by leaps and bounds and tonight's grand occasion was to be the fitting climax to her apprenticeship. When her mistress presented herself in the drawing-room a few hours later, conversation stopped and her audience gazed wonderingly at her.

'Dear Marianna, you look gorgeous!' Cassandra was lavish in her praise.

Her father nodded, his chest seeming to expand with pride. Even Carmela gave her a brisk smile of approval.

'You are sure that you're happy to stay home?' she asked her friend, needing only one answer. If Cassandra remained at Marine Parade, there would be no chance of her meeting her former lover.

'I'm very happy to. Carmela and I have planned a light supper together and then we intend to do a little sorting of baby clothes before an early bedtime. In my present condition, it makes for a perfect evening.'

'Far better than junketing with the most undesirable people,' Carmela could not resist saying.

'Unfortunately, cousin, we are forced to partake of a little junketing, but I promise I shall have Marianna home well before midnight.' Ernesto's voice was cold and crisp as though he too wished the evening over as swiftly as possible.

Marianna had not wanted to dress finely, but Flora had been adamant. This was to be the last grand event of the Brighton summer. In her maid's opinion it was the time to shine, the time to leave a splendid final impression. When she looked at her mistress that evening, she knew Marianna would do just that. The gown of orange blossom crêpe, worn beneath a tunic of bespangled gossamer, clung lovingly to the curves of her lissom young figure. A shawl of spider gauze covered her bare arms and on her feet she wore cream satin slippers ornamented with cream roses. A circlet of orange blossom was threaded through the glossy curls cascading gently around her face. She looked every inch a young princess, destined for a magnificent evening filled with pleasure. Only the pale face gave a glimpse of her true feelings.

Chapter Twenty-Nine

As before, they approached the Pavilion through newly planted gardens and alighted from their carriage in the shelter of the portico. As before, a footman escorted them to the Long Gallery. Here the guests who had been invited to dinner waited to be summoned to the table. With a swift glance Marianna established that Joshua was not among them. Dinner was always served promptly at six in the evening and there were already upwards of thirty people in the gallery. She knew that many more would arrive for the ball, but first a copious meal had to be endured, an essential part of the Regent's evening entertainment.

'This is extraordinary, Papa,' she whispered, as they were ushered into the Banqueting Hall.

The space easily rivalled the Music Room for drama. The biggest chandelier Marianna had ever seen, held in the claws of an enormous dragon, hung from the central dome. A host of smaller chandeliers shimmered around the room, sweeping light across the silver gilt decorations until the room resembled nothing more than a huge treasure casket.

'Extraordinary!' her father whispered back, beginning a search for their place names.

Everything in the room was designed to overwhelm, from the painted canopies with their intricate patterns of moons and stars to the spectacular ormolu candelabra positioned in the centre of a dining table which stretched as far as Marianna could see.

Almost immediately the first serving of food was brought to the table by a dozen uniformed footmen. Elaborate soups were followed by a choice of fish, then patés and meats, followed in turn by a dozen different entrées of meat and game. Should any of the guests feel the need for additional nourishment, seven rosewood sideboards positioned at intervals around the room groaned with platters of cold beef, venison, game and pies.

She cast a worried glance at her father. 'How on earth am I to eat even a fraction of this?' she asked in a low voice.

'Do your best,' was all he could offer.

She picked her way delicately through each serving, taking a very small helping of a very few dishes. After nearly an hour she had done her best and was beginning to relax, when worryingly a second tranche of food began to arrive. Four different roasts with their accompaniments and a multitude of sweet and savoury side dishes were scattered across the massive table. Her spirits sank as she encountered myriad jellies, tarts, ices, meringues and cream puddings. But by dint of engaging her neighbours in animated conversation, she managed to talk more than she ate.

Although many of her fellow guests seemed similarly

disconcerted by the sheer volume of food, the Regent himself ate solidly for the two hours apportioned to dinner and barely looked up from his plate. Marianna was unlikely in any case to catch his eye, seated with her father at the lower end of the table, for which she was thankful. This time there would be no Joshua Marchmain to rescue her from the prince's clutches.

Joshua himself had not appeared at dinner, though the duchess and her husband occupied a prominent place on the left of the prince. And when she heard a sniggering laugh ring out during a sudden interval of silence, Marianna knew that Amesbury, too, was in attendance. Only a few more hours to survive this monstrous evening, she thought. Shuddering inwardly, she took her father's arm on the walk to the ballroom.

'Thank heaven someone has had the presence of mind to open the windows,' Ernesto commented, as the late August breeze, tangy with salt, wafted through the long glass doors of the ballroom. An ornamental front garden lay beyond, cool and green, a welcome foil to the overpowering heat within.

The orchestra, auditioned personally by the prince, was already striking up for a cotillion and dance pairs were being formed. Marianna looked around the room and felt grateful there was hardly a person that she knew. She could sit decorously beside her father and watch the revelling that Carmela so despised from the fringes. But out of nowhere, it seemed, a string of young men materialised at her side. The enchanting young girl, barely known to them, had piqued their interest and become a prize to win. With one accord they rushed to claim her as a partner. In a moment almost every dance on her card had a name beside it.

Almost – not even an indulgent father would oppose her aunts' dictate that on no account must she ever allow herself to waltz. Over the next hour she danced with one young man after another, all of them personable, all of them eager to please: they found a safe place for her gauze wrapper, fetched her lemonade, sat out a country dance with her as she cooled by the open window. Obliging young men, delightful young men.

But she could not dance away the heartache. She must go through the motions, smile prettily, step daintily, and hope for the hour to come very soon when Ernesto would consider that sufficient respect had been paid to the Prince Regent and they could retire. It was during a lively quadrille that she was jolted from her counterfeit calm – Joshua had joined the throng in the ballroom. His elegant figure marked him out from the crowd, his light-coloured satin breeches and dark coat fitting him where they touched. An embroidered waistcoat and lace cravat with one single winking diamond completed the modish ensemble.

He was soon dancing. With the duchess, naturally. Who else? Marianna could see he was eager to talk to the woman whenever the dance brought them together. He would have a good deal to say, she thought bitterly, after wasting so much time on a new and unsuccessful dalliance. But Charlotte Severn would forgive him. She was hardly a stranger to dalliance herself. In no time they would be together again, the lovers they had always been. As the dancers traced the figures of the quadrille, the duchess's flushed face seemed to leer out at her. This was her victory.

Marianna looked quickly away and bent an attentive ear to her partner. The social mask must never be allowed to slip, though her life was in ruins and the ashes of its destruction all around. She stumbled slightly and her partner steadied her.

'I am so sorry,' she apologised. 'I wasn't paying sufficient attention to my feet.'

'You are a most accomplished dancer, Miss Marquez.' The willowy young man guiding her round the floor was nothing if not gallant.

She began to watch her steps fiercely. She must try to concentrate even though her mind was determined to stray. Knowing him to be so very close, Joshua consumed every thought. So close and yet as distant from her as the jungles of Africa. For three long years she'd allowed herself to be governed by a pointless infatuation for Luke Trelawny. And the moment she'd freed herself from that shadow, another had arrived to govern her life, only this time more painfully than she could ever have imagined. It was history repeating itself a hundredfold. The anguish she'd felt in saying goodbye to Luke was in retrospect a mere pinprick. It was Joshua who was teaching her real suffering.

The quadrille had come to an end and Marianna sank down onto one of the ebony chairs dotting the edges of the room. Her partner had left to find a second glass of lemonade, but she knew it would be only a brief respite. All too soon she must return to the dance floor, her feet nimbly performing the correct steps, her face smiling just enough.

But then, as she waited, the orchestra struck up a waltz.

This was the moment she'd hoped her father might deem it fitting to leave. She glanced around the room and found him engaged in a deep discussion with one of the prince's most influential courtiers. He must think she was enjoying the ball and decided to delay their departure – hopefully his conversation would soon flag.

At first Marianna didn't notice the figure. He must have walked towards her in a wide arc and only when he was bowing courteously over her hand, did she realise that Joshua stood before her.

'I hope you will do me the honour, Miss Marquez,' he began formally.

His beautiful gold-flecked eyes were as warm as ever, but his gaze was challenging. She was utterly unnerved. That he should dare to approach her this evening and then behave as though they had never endured a harrowing goodbye.

'Thank you sir, you are most kind, but I do not waltz,' she managed to say, in a voice that seemed not to belong to her.

'I thought it possible,' he conceded, 'but I was hoping you might make an exception.'

Whatever possessed him to think that she would dance any dance with him, let alone a waltz? The answer arrived swiftly.

'We have never danced the waltz together much to my regret, and I imagine this will be our only chance to do so.'

He bent his head towards her and his bright hair glinted in the light of a thousand candles. When his eyes sought hers, she found herself unable to look away. Break the spell, she scolded herself. Keep your mind focussed. Get him to leave.

'I do not waltz, sir,' she repeated dully.

'But for old times' sake?'

He was incorrigible. He was also magnificent. Unwillingly, she registered the power of his body, the satin breeches clinging in all the right places.

'There are no old times,' she snapped. 'And if you had an ounce of propriety, you would not address me in this manner.'

'That's better, Marianna! For a moment I was worried you might have gone into a decline. But I see you are as spirited as ever. Come, my dear, a few minutes only.'

He was holding out his hand and several guests nearby had begun to look in their direction, sensing an unfolding drama. She must get away, leave immediately. But where was her father? She looked around again and could have stamped with vexation when she realised that he and his companion were now nowhere to be seen.

'Marianna?' Joshua's voice caressed her, his warm eyes glinting gold. The strains of the music had begun to thread their magic through her veins and her body was softening dangerously. Where was her father? Why did he not come?

Joshua was still holding out his hand, beckoning her to come to him. And people on either side of them had begun to look even more interested. She felt herself take a step forward and then she was in his arms.

'I will dance,' she said angrily, 'but only because I've no wish to be the centre of a scene.'

'Naturally, why else would you dance with me?' he mocked. 'It was such a long time ago, was it not, that you were happy to do a great deal more than dance?'

'You are insufferable. Why can you not leave me alone?'

'One final dance and I promise you all the solitude you could wish.'

Marianna kept a resolute silence and in response his arms tightened and he swept her into the middle of the floor, manoeuvring her dexterously between couples and clasping her firmly against his chest. She tried very hard to hold herself at a distance, but her body was soft beneath his touch and growing softer with every minute. He smiled down at her, his eyes bewitching in the subdued candlelight.

'You waltz well. That's a surprise. I'd supposed you would not have been allowed to learn the dance.'

'You supposed correctly,' she found herself saying, the corners of her mouth crooking themselves into a small smile despite her best efforts.

'You never disappoint me!'

She was beginning to drown in his magic, but she must resist at all costs. She saw Charlotte Severn standing at the side of the room, her husband by her side. The woman shot her a look of hatred.

'Do you not think, Mr Marchmain, that you would be wise to forgo this dance and ask another to partner you?' Marianna's voice was deceptively steady.

He followed her gaze. 'I think not, Miss Marquez. I had my fill of that particular pleasure many months ago.'

'I find that difficult to believe, so enthused you were earlier this evening.'

'Enthused no, irritated yes.' And his arms tightened even more firmly around her.

'Why irritated?' she found herself asking.

'It is taking Her Grace longer than I'd hoped to understand my changed feelings,' he said diplomatically. 'She did not take kindly to my reminding her.'

Marianna said nothing. So they were not together again. Why did an arrow of delight fly straight to her heart? It should not matter to her, must not matter. And yet it did, crushed as she was to his chest, moving with him to the enticing rhythms of the waltz. Their limbs shadowed each other, touching, separating and touching again. She felt his warmth through the light clothes he wore and savoured his musky smell. His lips brushed the top of her hair then came to rest just behind her left ear.

Slowly, delicately, she felt the tip of his tongue taste her skin. She was melting, melting, diffusing into liquid pleasure. His arm slowly slid down her back and pulled her body even closer until she felt his answering hardness. His mouth trailed kisses down her neck. He was seducing her, here on the dance floor and in full view of a hundred pairs of eyes. And she was letting him! She could not bear it. She broke from him abruptly and fled, leaving him alone in the middle of the ballroom floor.

Chapter Thirty

Joshua was incensed – she had deliberately exposed him to ridicule! – but shrugging off the tittle tattle he knew would already be starting, he made to follow her. As he drew near, though, he saw a servant in the prince's livery approach Marianna with a message, and stopped in his tracks. Reluctantly, he turned back, ignoring the interested stares from around the room.

This whole miserable scene was his own fault. He should have accepted her refusal to dance and walked away. He should never even have asked her. But an angry frustration had taken hold of him. How stupid he'd been to break the unspoken law by which he'd lived for more years than he could remember! The scourging he'd received from the Latimer affair had left him wanting no more such hazards. He might flirt with young women and acquire the reputation of a dangerous man, he might enjoy the challenge of confounding their duennas, but he was always careful never to step across the line. Discreet and sometimes not so discreet liaisons with well-born ladies, bored with their husbands, served his physical needs. Such relationships were often tedious, occasionally joyless and always sterile, but they had caused him not one jot of discomfort.

His life had flowed smooth and unruffled – and then he'd met Marianna. Her youthful spirit had enchanted him, holding as it did the promise of a beauty he'd so long sought. He'd been beguiled even into offering his hand. But the summer had proved a mere dream and after their last tempestuous encounter, he'd vowed to put her from his mind. The fantasy was over and his old life awaited him.

Tonight, though, seeing her once more in all her loveliness, a slender flower of a girl, the craziest desire had overpowered him and all he'd known was that he had to be close to her again. One more time, one final time. And look where that had led. He would be the object of derision in the Court for days, but it didn't matter. Nothing mattered.

⌒

Marianna rushed from the dance floor, her cheeks on fire and her heart hammering. She must find her father immediately: she had to leave this place and never return. But a footman in knee breeches and starched shirt was barring her way.

'Yes what is it?' she asked impatiently, her breath still uneven.

'A message, Miss Marquez, from your father.'

'My father? Where is he?'

'At the eastern exit of the palace. A carriage will be waiting there.'

It was a little odd that her father had disappeared without a word and then sent a servant to fetch her.

'Why has he not come for me himself?'

'I am to say he is concerned you may catch cold and has gone ahead to order the carriage in advance.'

How very like Papa, she thought with sudden warmth, forgiving him his earlier desertion.

'But my shawl and reticule? I must find those first.' She smiled at the retainer. 'They cannot be too far away.'

'Señor Marquez has them already, I believe. They await you in the carriage.'

Her father had been unusually busy. She was surprised since she'd thought him far too engaged with his political friends.

'Then I have nothing to do but find him,' she replied almost gaily, relieved that she was at last on her way home.

She made her way out of the ballroom and along the passage the footman had indicated. The strains of music faded gradually into the distance and the buzz of chatter disappeared. It was a lonely walk with not a soul in sight – yet Marianna had a nagging feeling that she was being watched. How foolish – the alarms she'd suffered that evening were making her too sensitive. The corridor itself was narrow and bare and meagrely lit by a few branches of candles at irregular intervals along its walls. It was an odd whim of her father's to have his daughter traverse the length of the Pavilion to the little used eastern exit. But he was there waiting to take her home. And all would be well.

The colonnade which gave on to the gardens was smaller here and far more enclosed than the portico at which they had arrived. She walked swiftly through the small porch and out of the palace. Tall trees shaded the building at this point and the covering of gravel was a mere path rather than a carriageway. Her father was nowhere to be seen, but in the dusk she glimpsed the outline of a coach and made her way gladly towards it.

Her footsteps sounded unnaturally loud in a silence that filled the air like a palpable presence. She had only gone a few paces when two figures loomed out at her from the darkness. Instantly she started back, but before she could regain the shelter of the Pavilion, they had grabbed her arms and pinioned her between them. Their clothes were unwashed and they smelt strongly of liquor. Terrified, she imagined she had been attacked by thieves, though she had little on her person worth stealing. Their rough hands dug into her flesh as they jostled her forwards. Then she realised – they were dragging her towards the waiting coach. This was not a robbery but an abduction!

In a moment they had wrenched open the carriage door and made ready to bundle her inside. She struggled furiously, but she was no match for two hulking men and found herself being thrust into the coach. Then a loud shout sounded nearby. The hands loosened their grip and she was dumped, spread-eagled across the rear seat of the carriage.

She scrambled to her feet and down the coach steps. The dusk was dense, almost impenetrable, the moon shining only fitfully from between lowering clouds, and she could hardly see a foot in front of her. She could hear though. There was a crack as two skulls were smashed expertly together.

'Run – back to the Pavilion and find your father.'

It was Joshua. As she turned to flee, she saw that her

assailants had recovered their footing only to be floored again, one after another with several punishing left hooks.

'Run!' he repeated.

She needed no second urging and rushed towards the colonnade, desperate to find help. Both attackers lay on the floor, prone and unmoving. Joshua, his cravat askew, stood back ready for a further onslaught. But their loud groans were heartfelt and they seemed unlikely to give more trouble. She was in the Pavilion now and about to retrace her steps along the passageway

when a sudden noise from outside made her turn again. Surely those villains could not have recovered so quickly.

But it was Robert Amesbury who stood to one side of the carriage brandishing a sword.

'Get up blockheads,' he swore at the men. 'And find the girl. Else what use are you to me?'

One of the men made a feeble attempt to stagger to his feet, but then crumpled to the ground again. The other managed to crawl to the colonnade and haul himself upright on its wooden pillars. Marianna felt him grab her skirt as she tried to whisk herself from sight. She had not run, could not run, with Joshua in such danger.

Amesbury gave a growl of annoyance and turned to face his nemesis. 'When will you learn, Marchmain, not to interfere? I draw comfort from the fact that this is the very last time.' He slashed at the air with his sword, its wicked sharpness threatening the unarmed man.

'You are a cur, Amesbury. I don't fight with dogs.'

'Who said anything about a fight, dear friend? You will not have the chance. Regretfully, I cannot allow you to return to the palace and tell your story. It would be too degrading.'

'What then? Or need I ask?'

'I imagine not. Sadly you will be found a victim of robbery. Such dubious creatures hang around the Pavilion these days and it will occasion few questions.'

'And Miss Marquez?'

'My plans for her must change. Your intervention has done her little favour. Instead of a few days' incarceration, she must now be lost for months. She may be allowed to surface in Spain eventually if she proves a sensible girl. By then no-one will believe a word of any story she chooses to tell.'

The moon suddenly swam free of its cloudy cover and a shaft of silver illuminated the scene. It flooded everything in its path, glinting along the horses' glossy coats, embellishing the scratched panels of the coach and flashing its light onto a lone strip of glittering steel. In a second, Joshua had seized the dagger from its resting place in the lining of the carriage door and made ready to defend himself.

'You will hardly inflict damage with that poor object,' his adversary mocked.

'We shall see. Any blade is gold if it destroys a mongrel such as you.'

The fight was ugly. No graceful sword play, but a tense game of cat and mouse. They circled each other warily, each waiting for the other's move. Then Amesbury's sword was swinging through the air and Joshua nimbly retreating out of reach. Amesbury tried again but with the same result. Again and again he struck, and each blow

Marianna expected to be final. Both men were tiring in this inelegant ballet, but only when Joshua seemed sure that his opponent was

sufficiently winded, did he begin to advance. Then it was a swift run beneath Amesbury's blade and a desperate attempt to wound at close quarters. His enemy was too quick, though, and retreated out of harm's way.

Enthralled by the savagery of the fight, the man who held Marianna had loosened his grip. She thought she might manage to pull herself free, but she knew that even if she did, she couldn't leave. She must stay for Joshua, keep vigil as he fought for his life – and hers.

Amesbury was growing ever more furious and began to slash wildly, circling the sword over his head, hurling its blade from right to left. But still Joshua evaded him. Years of practice with the most exigent of fencing masters had taught him the skills of defence as much as offence. And he needed them. He could fight only at close quarters and the sword had a very long reach.

Amesbury, tiring faster than his younger and fitter opponent, determined to make an end of his adversary. He saw his chance when Joshua for an instant came to a standstill. He lunged forward to catch the younger man off guard. In the blink of an eye, Joshua saw his danger and dipped beneath the oncoming sword so low that he almost knelt on the gravel. Then in a swooping movement from the ground he raised the dagger upwards and into the man's right arm. He pinked it neatly and Amesbury's sword clattered to the floor.

'Still so disdainful of a humble dagger?' Joshua's face

was pale, but in the moonlight his eyes glittered with an unholy joy.

Robert Amesbury roared in pain and struggled blindly to free himself from Joshua's iron hold. But footsteps were running towards them from the passageway behind. The ruffian holding Marianna suddenly let her go and loped off into the darkness, the summer growth of bushes shielding him from view.

She was free and her father was by her side. Two of the prince's guards had pinned Amesbury between them and were forcing him back into the palace. Joshua, his beautiful coat rent with sword slashes and his golden hair sadly dishevelled, faced her father.

'Take her home,' he said hoarsely. 'I believe she has had sufficient excitement for one evening.'

Ernesto nodded grimly and placed the spangled shawl around his daughter's shoulders. Together they stumbled through the back corridors of the palace to find again the familiar entrance. Marianna sat back in the carriage, pale and exhausted. Only then did the tears begin to roll slowly down her cheeks.

Chapter Thirty-One

Marianna slept late the next morning. When she opened her eyes, Flora was bending over her, a look of concern on her face. She smiled and Flora smiled back.

'It's so good to see you awake, miss. You gave us such a fright last night.'

'I did?' She struggled to sit up, blinking at the brilliant light that was streaming into the room from chinks in the drawn curtains.

'It was as though you were sleepwalking, dazed like. You didn't seem to recognise any of us, nor your own room. I put you to bed and you slept straight away, real deep too, and you've been sleeping like that ever since and it's past noon.'

'You've sat by me all night, Flora?' Marianna propped herself up on one elbow and pressed her maid's hand affectionately.

'What else would I do, miss? We were so worried.'

'And my father?'

Flora piled the soft white pillows as high as she could and her mistress collapsed back on them with a sigh.

'My father?' she prompted.

'He's at the palace right now. He's gone to enquire of Mr Marchmain. Seemingly he did you a great service last night.'

'He did.' Her voice was barely above a whisper and the tears again began to flow. Her maid's face puckered in fright.

'Whatever is it, miss? You're safe and Mr Marchmain has come off with barely a scratch, or so I believe. That villain, they say, has packed up and gone back to London. He should be in prison, but Quality never goes to prison.' She sounded bitter.

Marianna rallied herself and said in a far stronger voice, 'Are you saying that Lord Amesbury has left Brighton?'

'So Cook says. Her sister works in the Pavilion kitchens and such a to-do. The Regent himself was involved. After your father brought you home, *Lord* Amesbury' – and she emphasised the title with scorn – 'was taken to the prince by the guards and had to confess what he'd been up to. Cook's sister says that Amesbury has been told he ain't welcome any more at the Pavilion nor at Carlton house neither.' Flora's acquired gentility was rapidly vanishing in the face of her honest indignation.

'Where has he gone, do you think?' The thought tormented her that her enemy might even now be waiting, ready to make another attempt on her.

'Apparently –' Flora drew in her cheeks at the thought of the news she had to impart – 'the Regent has advised his friend to go abroad for a space. Lying low I call it. He should be in prison.'

'And all this has happened while I've been asleep?'

'Yes indeed, miss. It's like you were under some kind of spell, but it's so good you're back with us again.'

There was a gentle tap at the door and Ernesto looked into the room, his face drawn, but when he saw Marianna sitting up in bed and sipping her morning chocolate, a wide smile lit his face.

'How good to see you looking yourself again, *querida*.'

'I'm sorry I gave you a fright, Papa. But all's well, as you see.'

Flora sipped quietly out of the door and Ernesto walked over to his daughter's bedside, enfolding Marianna in a stifling bear hug. Her tears began now to fall in earnest and he pulled back, his face once more anxious.

Marianna put her hand in his and squeezed it reassuringly. 'I am well so you must not worry, but I don't seem able to stop crying.'

'You have had a terrible shock, my dear. I am not surprised you are deeply upset. When I think what could have happened!'

She would rather not think, but she was desperate to know from him what had passed at the Pavilion. Had her father learned anything of the shameful history which existed between herself and Amesbury? She prayed not.

'Do you know why Lord Amesbury tried to abduct me?' she asked at last. 'I presume that's what it was.'

'An abduction indeed. It makes my heart heavy to say this about any man, but he is evil through and through. And the Duchess of Severn is no better. She was in the plan, too, it appears. I always thought her an indelicate woman, but I had no idea that she would sink to such wickedness.' He fell silent as he considered the two miscreants.

'But what was their plan and why should they plot against me?'

'Why they should do so, I have no notion. As for the plan, I don't think you need to know it.'

'I want to know, Papa,' she said stubbornly.

'My dear, how will it benefit you to know the depths of their villainy?' His voice was filled with misgiving.

'I have to know, Papa. I have to know the truth.'

He gave a heavy sigh. 'Robert Amesbury planned to hold you in a house that the duchess owns in Worthing, just a few miles down the coast. He would have kept you there some days and allowed the gossip on your whereabouts to flourish. Or so I have learned from the Regent.'

'But how would that have served his purpose?' Marianna was genuinely puzzled.

Her father's face grew grimmer and his mouth tightened into a thin slit. He could hardly bring himself to speak the words. 'When Amesbury released you, he intended to publish to the world that you had voluntarily stayed with him as his mistress. It would be his word against yours and, as a notable member of the *ton*, he expected to be believed. Even if he were not, the mere suggestion that his words might be true would ensure your reputation in England was shattered for ever. No doubt he would spread news of your supposed affair as far afield as he could.'

Her mind swiftly processed this information but she said nothing.

'Do you know why he would do such a thing, Marianna?'

her father ventured at last.

'I believe that for some reason the duchess is jealous of me,' she extemporised. 'Perhaps Lord Amesbury has feelings for her and he planned this dreadful attack on her behalf.'

That at least was partially true. Charlotte Severn must suppose her intervention at the theatre had failed – she would be eager to destroy Marianna's reputation and make her a social outcast. The way would then be clear for the duchess to seduce Joshua all over again.

'The crime seems out of all proportion to the cause,' Ernesto said thoughtfully.

Marianna knew that Amesbury had his own reasons to hurt her, but she was not about to confess them. Fortunately, her father was following his own thoughts.

'But then these people cannot be understood by any normal standards of conduct, so perhaps we should not look too far for a motive.'

She closed her eyes, suddenly very tired again, but Ernesto had not yet finished. 'Lady Trelawny would very much like to see you when you feel able to receive her, my dear. She has been much disturbed by this terrible business and is wishful to be a comfort to you if she can.'

Marianna nodded wearily. 'I would like to sleep a little, but later perhaps we can take tea together.'

'I will tell her,' he said softly, and took a seat to one side of the bed. It was evident her father intended to keep watch as Flora had done through the night.

Marianna sank back on the pillows and closed her eyes. But it was not to sleep. A procession of shadowy figures danced across her vision. Blurred images of Cassandra, her father, the Regent, Amesbury, and in their wake memories of Joshua: Joshua fighting for his life, Joshua fighting for her. Why had he been there? Why had he intervened?

Last night she'd snubbed him ruthlessly and left him to face public humiliation. Yet it had weighed with him not at all. He'd continued to protect her. He must have seen the messenger stop her. Realised something was badly wrong. Seen those brutal men waiting as she walked heedlessly into their trap. And gone into the fray with no more weapons than his own two fists. He could so easily have been killed. Amesbury would have denied all knowledge of the crime, glibly blaming it on the shiftless men who occasionally inveigled their way past the guards and into the Pavilion gardens. *Such unsavoury people gather around the palace these days,* she could almost hear him say. She would have lost her reputation, but Joshua would have lost his life.

As if sensing that she did not rest easily, her father spoke again, his tone hesitant. 'This is a delicate matter, *querida*, but you owe much to Mr Marchmain. I understand that your – friendship – is at an end, but it is still right that you should see him. A few minutes only, sufficient to thank him for his bravery in your service.'

Her heart was beating too fast. She acknowledged how very much she owed Joshua, but how could she meet him again, knowing he had risked his life for her yet knowing, too, that she must still reject him? The dreadful events of last night changed nothing. He was still the man who'd betrayed his best friend, who'd deliberately seduced Cassandra Latimer. He was not the man Marianna had hoped for, the man she'd invested with her dreams.

'You will see him?'

She opened her eyes and saw her father looking anxiously down at her. 'It will be for a few minutes only,' he repeated, stroking her hand reassuringly. 'I can be with you. Or Lady Trelawny if you prefer.'

'No!' She almost shouted the word. Her father looked astonished.

'I mean, Papa,' she said in a quieter tone, 'that it is I who Mr Marchmain has rescued and it is I who should thank him. I will see him alone.'

'Very well, my dear. I will send a message asking him to wait on you tomorrow if that is convenient.'

Marianna closed her eyes again. She was safe, but not at peace. Tomorrow she must see Joshua and offer him her heartfelt thanks, but still stay true to herself. It would be difficult. No, it would be utterly painful: to see his dear face, to look into his loving eyes, to desire his beautiful form and then – have to say goodbye again. She groaned inwardly. The pain was almost physical. But she was tired, so tired. Her eyes shut fast and sleep overcame her.

⁓

It was evening before she woke again and Cassandra was standing in the doorway with a small tray in her hands. 'You've missed tea, my dear, but I've bought a little supper. Sleep is an excellent restorative, but you must eat.'

Her friend placed the tray on a nearby table and drew up a chair at the side of the bed. She bent down to kiss Marianna's cheek and a subtle scent of roses filled the air. 'How are you, Marianna? Such a fright you have given us!'

'So I understand. I'm sorry I've caused such consternation but as you see, I am fully recovered. Almost fully recovered,' she amended, as Cassandra's face registered doubt.

'I could hardly believe my ears when I learned what had happened. It's almost impossible to comprehend. Lord Amesbury must be the most wicked of men. I understand the Regent has banished him from Court for some time. That is mild punishment. He should be in prison.'

Cassandra's normally gentle manner had given way to one of hot indignation, causing Marianna to smile. Lady and lady's maid were evidently in agreement.

'It's so good to see you smile,' her friend said happily. 'You will be back to your old self in no time.'

Marianna thought otherwise, but she had no intention of admitting Lady Trelawny into the deepest and darkest of her secrets. Lady Trelawny, though, it seemed had other ideas.

'And it was Joshua Marchmain who came to your rescue! I have not seen or heard of him for an age and then he appears out of nowhere, your very own guardian angel.'

Marianna held her breath.

'I must tell you,' Cassandra said a trifle self-consciously, 'that I was acquainted with Mr Marchmain in my youth.'

Marianna schooled her face to blankness.

'It appears that he forms part of the Regent's entourage and that you have been in the habit of meeting him regularly. You never mentioned it.' There was a gentle scolding to Cassandra's tone.

'I've met many people from the palace this summer. Mr Marchmain is just one.'

Her friend ignored the dissembling and continued blithely, 'I understand he is to come here tomorrow. It will be good to meet him again.'

Alarm at these words was clearly written on Marianna's face and Cassandra offered a hasty amendment. 'Naturally, you will wish to see him alone. You must have much to say to each other. But I would like to exchange a few words with him before he leaves the house. It's not often an opportunity to lay the past to rest comes one's way.'

Marianna felt her tongue stilled and her face freeze. She eased herself into a sitting position and looked directly at the visitor by her bedside. What exactly did this lovely young woman intend for the morrow? Whatever it was, she feared it could only make her meeting with Joshua even more tormenting. The air between them prickled.

In an attempt to diffuse the uncomfortable mood, Cassandra spoke again. 'I should explain. As a young woman, I fell into trouble. I mentioned something of it when we talked yesterday. Mr Marchmain was involved and I fear that in the end he suffered unjustly for his part in our small tragedy.'

'And you wish to see him again?' Marianna's chagrin fought with jealousy. Were these two old lovers to be reunited and under her roof?

'I turned out to be a very bad mistake for him. I would like to make my peace,' her friend said simply.

Chapter Thirty-Two

Joshua threw down his brush in annoyance. He'd been standing before a blank canvas all morning and getting nowhere. Normally his studio was a tranquil retreat, and painting a path to pleasure. But today the magic wasn't working. He looked gloomily through the long glass windows that overlooked the garden – it was a dreary world. Since midnight, the rain had been incessant, beating a repetitive tattoo on the ornamental roof.

The Regent had risen much earlier than usual, sending a collective shudder through the household, and Joshua had been summoned to his presence before the great ormolu clock in the Long Gallery had struck even ten. A lengthy interview had culminated with the prince's command that Amesbury leave the Court immediately. His lordship had been swift to make preparations for France and at Steine House, Joshua had heard, the duchess was organising a hasty departure to London.

That was all very satisfactory, but this was not: he was unable to paint. If he were honest, he'd been unable to paint for days. Ever since Marianna had made plain that he was not her future. He wondered how she was faring after the frightening events of the previous evening. She was tough, he concluded, she would survive happily enough once the immediate shock had receded. As for him, he had a few bruises from the tussle with those ruffians, a few aches and pains, but in days he would be as new. His rawest ache was something that would not heal so easily.

After their disastrous meeting on the beach, he'd told himself that he could resume his old life with equanimity. He could feel free once more. But last night at the ball he'd known himself to be anything but free. He'd wanted to master her, wanted to prove that she was not indifferent to him, no matter how much she might wish it. And he'd succeeded so well that she had fled without warning and left him looking a fool, alone in the midst of the dance floor. He'd felt fury – that she'd rejected him for no good reason, that a chit of a girl should do this to him!

He'd watched her storm from the room, watched her met by a liveried servant he didn't recognise. That was strange in itself and in a wrathful mood, he'd begun to follow her. He wasn't sure why – perhaps it was simply an inability to let go. But thank God he had. When she had taken the little used passageway, his instinct for danger had been alerted. And how right he'd been!

Two burly thugs had set upon her as soon as she'd emerged from the palace and he'd seen what they intended almost immediately: a coach and pair stood waiting in the shadows beyond. He hadn't seen Amesbury, the third villain of this blackguardly trio, but it would have made no difference if he had. Two men, three men, he would have fought for her no matter how many. He would have fought for any woman so threatened, but his blood had run cold when he saw it happening to the girl he loved.

And he did love her, he knew that now. His wish to marry stemmed from love, not guilt. He'd pretended otherwise but after all the excuses, the justifications, the weasel words he'd told himself, he loved her. The minute he'd seen her threatened he knew that she had all of his heart. But his case was hopeless: she would not forgive him.

He'd been surprised, therefore, to get Ernesto's message asking him to call at Marine Parade. Unsure, too, whether or not he should obey the summons. The thought of seeing her again made his heart jump, yet such a meeting would be distressing for them both. As for himself, it would be an elegy, a melancholy closing of the one good chapter in his life. The Court was busy packing for London and the leaves in the Pavilion gardens already turning gold. It was a time for endings, an ending that would have no new beginning. He would see her on the morrow, feel the turn of the knife once more, and walk away. He'd return to his bare canvasses and his bare life. This was the path he'd chosen when he'd betrayed his friend and seduced the girl he was to marry. For a brief moment this summer he'd glimpsed a different life, but that was at an end now. And he must not repine.

$$\backsim$$

'Flora, lay out my cream figured muslin please.'

The maid stared in surprise. 'The cream muslin?' she questioned, thinking she must have misheard.

Marianna nodded. 'And the deep red satin ribbon we bought the other day in Barthlomews. I shall wear it threaded in my hair.'

'Are we going somewhere important, miss?' the maid ventured.

'We're going nowhere, but I'm to have a visitor today and I wish to look my best.'

But why was that? It mattered not how she looked when Joshua came to call. She planned to be with him a few minutes only, before he disappeared from her life for ever. It was mere whistling in the wind. A facade to cover her misery, a boldness when she felt fatally weakened.

Flora scurried around laying out underwear, stockings and the figured muslin along with matching satin slippers. She could see that her mistress was hardly herself, but that was not to be wondered at. Such a dreadful experience she'd gone through. And now this Joshua Marchmain coming. She supposed it was right that miss should thank him prettily for his rescue, but in Flora's view the man meant trouble. It would be better for all of them once they were free of Brighton and free of him.

Marianna dismissed her maid as soon as she could. She wanted time to collect her wits before Joshua arrived. She had formulated the words she needed to say, and he had only to respond in similar vein and their ordeal would be over.

But when an hour later she faced him across the drawing room, the words died on her lips. As always, he looked a picture of quiet elegance, but his eyes, that familiar colour of melting honey, held a reserved expression.

'I'm delighted to see you so well.' His tone was studiedly neutral.

'Thank you, I am well,' Marianna managed to say, and then as an afterthought, 'and you?'

'I've suffered no lasting damage – at least from the fight,' he offered drily.

She tried to keep her mind on the words she'd rehearsed. 'I am so glad you were able to call, Mr Marchmain. I wanted very much to thank you.' Her voice began to break as she met his shrewd gaze.

She tried again. 'I must thank you for your bravery – and of course your skill,' she finished in a rush.

'It's comforting to know that my experience in Italy has proved useful at last.' He fingered his scar and his voice took on a caustic note.

'If it had not been for your intervention,' Marianna doggedly followed her script, 'I would be in a sorry case.'

'We must not think of it.' He brushed aside her thanks. 'You are well and safe and that is what matters.'

She felt stupidly annoyed that he seemed determined to make light of his rescue. How nonsensical. She should be glad that he was willing to pass over the event so quickly, since it could only mean that his visit this morning would be mercifully brief.

'But still,' she persisted, 'I am conscious – my father and I are conscious – that we owe you a great deal.'

'You owe me nothing, Marianna,' he said harshly. 'Unless it's a fair hearing.'

The interview was not going the way she'd imagined. Why had she ever thought it would? A painful silence filled the room for what seemed an age, but when he spoke again, his voice seemed deliberately indifferent.

'May I ask what your plans are?'

'I am to go first to London, and from there travel on to Spain. Carmela will accompany me.'

'Ah yes, to Spain and the unknown suitor. I imagine he has been resurrected.' They were back on dangerous ground and his gaze, she saw, was derisory.

'There will be no suitor.'

'But how can that be?' His eyebrows rose in mockery.

'Surely, Mr Marchmain, you of all people should know the answer to that question.'

'But I don't.' His gaze was penetrating. 'If you no longer intend to marry, it's not because you love elsewhere. A week ago I would have said differently. I would have said you'd sought and found an abiding love. But now? I think you want only the illusion of love.'

Marianna was now desperate to end this dreadful conversation, but was stung into exclaiming, 'You are unfair, sir!'

'I think not. You don't like reality, Marianna. You prefer illusion and when the real world comes too close, you retreat. Your love for Luke Trelawny was empty emotion. And now your love for me has gone the same way. You don't want a flesh and blood man with all the good and bad that implies – you want a man that doesn't exist, a fantasy lover. Trelawny filled that role until he inconveniently married. My tenure was even shorter. I fell from my pedestal almost immediately.'

For a moment the breath went out of her and she looked as though she was about to collapse. Joshua paid no heed. 'If it's not to be the unknown bridegroom, then what?' he asked, as if he'd not just uttered the most wounding words possible. 'A convent perhaps?'

She stared at him. 'Isn't that one of the few acceptable choices for a virtuous Spanish girl? The altar or the cloister – or so I understand.'

Rage fought with tears. How dare he predict her future? What she did was no longer his concern. But suddenly his voice was soft. 'Don't choose a convent, Marianna. You were not made for such.'

He began to walk towards her and she seemed paralysed to move. But before he reached her, the door opened and Cassandra walked into the room. Marianna had thought this encounter could not get worse, but she'd been wrong.

Joshua stared blindly at the vision that had entered. Though well into pregnancy, Cassandra was still able to stun any man who crossed her path. But Joshua's mesmerised gaze was not for the woman he saw before him, but for the one he'd long ago bid farewell.

'Cassandra?' he queried in amazement. 'Cassie Latimer!'

'Cassie Trelawny,' she corrected him gently.

'Of course. Lady Trelawny, my apologies, and my very good wishes on your marriage.' Joshua bowed politely. 'And on your forthcoming happiness,' he added, smiling at the noticeable bump Cassandra carried.

'Thank you, Mr Marchmain. You are most kind, and I am delighted to see you again.'

Chapter Thirty-Three

Marianna remained silent and unmoving, hardly able to believe the turn of events. It was as though she was watching a play unfold, with herself the sole audience. Her friend seem unperturbed. 'Marianna told me you were to call today and I was hoping we might meet.'

Joshua looked slightly dazed, but Cassie was continuing with hardly a pause. 'I'm sure she has thanked you profusely for the service you rendered her. But I would like to add my own thanks. Your bravery saved her from the most dreadful fate.'

He gave a brief nod and seemed poised to leave, but Cassandra had not yet finished and her quiet voice seemed to fill the room. 'Before you go, Mr Marchmain, there is something else I need to thank you for – the service you rendered *me* many years ago. You must have suffered harm from it.'

Joshua was by now looking even more dazed, as well he might thought Marianna, burning with righteous anger.

'If you had not intervened in my life so dramatically,' Cassie went on, 'I would have wed Luke, but for all the wrong reasons. I would not have the happy marriage I have today. I needed to find out where I truly belonged, and you did that for me.'

Joshua's expression was wry. 'You are most kind, Lady Trelawny.'

'I speak only the truth. But what of you, Joshua?' Her voice softened. 'I hope you, too, have found where you belong.'

'I thought I had, but apparently I was mistaken,' he said curtly.

He picked up his gloves from the small table beneath the window and bowed to each of the women in turn.

'I believe it is time I left. Cassandra, Lady Trelawny, it has been a pleasure to meet you again. Marianna, my very best wishes for your future happiness.'

And he was gone. Then the sharp click of the front door, and Marianna could no longer maintain her veneer of detachment. Careless of what Cassandra would think, she rushed from the room and up the stairs to her bedroom, locking the door behind her.

She threw herself onto the bed and buried her face in the pillows. The carefully scripted encounter had gone very wrong. All she'd had to do was express grateful thanks for her rescue. A few words on either side would have sufficed. Instead, what had happened?

Joshua hadn't wanted her thanks. What he'd wanted was an acknowledgement that she'd been foolish. That she had her priorities wrong. His rescue was trivial – it was the rest of her life that mattered and her choices were stark. Worst of all, he'd shredded her heart by claiming she had no idea what love was; that all she was capable of was a pretence of love.

And then there was Cassandra greeting him as a long lost friend, behaving as though they were meeting at some dowager's tea party. Her friend had absolved him, even come close to praising him, Marianna thought savagely, so that he no longer need feel an ounce of guilt for his past sins.

The churn of thoughts brought her to her feet and, unable to rest, she began to pace the polished floorboards. Joshua had done a dreadful thing – he'd almost destroyed the man she'd once loved. An illusory love, Joshua had taunted. And he was right – she'd recognised that weeks ago. Was he also right when he accused her of not wanting a flesh and blood man? Perhaps.

Despite the heartache, Luke and Cassandra were happier than ever and their baby would soon be an added joy. And what of her, Marianna Marquez, heiress and sad girl? What was to become of her? Just a few days ago her world had been full to overflowing, then Charlotte Severn had dripped poison into her ears, and suddenly her life, her future, was changed for ever. The duchess had won their battle of wills.

But why should she? Marianna was allowing her to win – no, willing her to win. She was behaving exactly as Charlotte Severn had anticipated. The woman had judged her to the last inch. How mortifying to be the duchess's creature. But if she were to defy Charlotte's malign calculations...

She paused her restless wandering and gazed out of the

window. For long minutes she stood there, watching the waves tumble to shore. Joshua Marchmain was a fallible man, a man who had lived a far from perfect life. But it was a life that had given him little happiness. She remembered how puzzled she'd been that someone who seemed to have everything could be so discontented. Yet from the moment they'd met, he'd been very different. Was it possible that his days of philandering were over and he'd finally stumbled on happiness?

She rested her forehead on the cold glass of the window pane, thinking, thinking. Minutes ago she'd heard him say that he'd believed he had found where he belonged, but he'd been mistaken. But he hadn't been. He did belong with her and she belonged with him. Not with an unknown husband, nor behind a veil. She belonged with this strong but flawed man, who'd once been an unloved child. Who, before he'd properly matured, had committed an error that determined his life's path. Why could she not accept that?

There was no reason, no reason at all. She snatched up her bonnet and pelisse. The wind was blowing strongly and dark clouds threatened the return of an early autumn storm, but she took no heed. In a minute she was tripping down the stairs as quickly as she'd run up them. Flora was crossing the hall and made to speak to her. She held up a warning finger to stay silent and slipped out of the front door.

The breeze sent her skirts skirling, but she bent her head against its force and pushed on towards the Pavilion. The guard on the gate recognised her from previous visits and, though surprised at her solitary state, allowed her through into the gardens. Quickly, she found her way around the side of the palace, making for where she knew Joshua would be. Where else but in his studio?

⌒

Joshua looked up as she appeared in the open doorway. Her graceful young figure was silhouetted against the stormy sky and she looked heartbreakingly lovely, dishevelled curls framing a luminous face. He drew in a sharp breath but resisted the impulse to reach out to her. He was confused – why was she here?

Today had been altogether mystifying. Meeting Cassandra after so long had been astonishing and his mind was still grappling with her sudden arrival on the scene. He could make little sense of it except that her presence had forced him to be circumspect. When she'd entered the room, he'd almost forgotten his resolve to stay cool and polite. He'd wanted to grab Marianna, shake her, make her see the foolishness of her decision. He would have done it, too, if Cassie had not opened the door at that very moment. In the end, he'd been forced into a cold, mechanical farewell – a fitting end to a doomed love affair.

But now here she was, teetering on the threshold of his studio, her face wistful, her eyes shining. 'I had to come,' she said simply.

'And...' A small flicker of expectancy started deep within him.

'I'm sorry. I was wrong.'

'About?' he prompted, the flicker growing stronger.

'Just about everything. I've been obsessed with what happened all those years ago. You behaved very badly, but so did Cassandra. She has forgotten the bad memories, Luke too, and you – all of you have forgotten. I don't know why it became so important to me.'

'Perhaps because I was not the man you imagined.' His voice was guarded and he remained standing at a distance.

'I've been very stupid.'

She moved closer to him, her gaze clear and unwavering. 'I don't know why I got it so badly wrong. I started out thinking you were irredeemable, the worst kind of man. But then I fell in love and you became the best kind of man there could ever be.'

'And now you know that I am neither?' He brushed away a lock of hair from his forehead, and for a moment he looked tired. Her heart stirred with tenderness.

'I know that you're the only man I ever want to be with,' she said, with a catch in her voice.

He was beside her in a step, his tiredness forgotten. He held out his arms wide and she walked into them.

'Is that true?'

'I've never stopped loving you, Joshua. But for a while I lost my trust.'

'And now?'

'I was wrong to doubt you. The past is dead and it's the future that matters.'

'So... does that mean you still wish to marry?'

'I do with all my heart – though what Papa will make of it, I cannot begin to imagine.'

Joshua smiled down at her, the familiar glint back in his eyes. 'And not only Papa,' he mocked gently. 'How will Carmela survive the news?'

Marianna pulled back a little and said in a thoughtful voice, 'I think perhaps we should wait until she is back in Spain before we formally announce our betrothal.'

'Then let us arrange her travel as soon as possible.'

She could not prevent a small gurgle of laughter. He had thought he would never hear the sound again and pulled her close, holding her fast against his body, his careful restraint destroyed in an instant.

He tipped her face to his and kissed her. Over and over again. At first soft and exploratory and then ever more demanding. Blind to everything around them, they crashed a path through the studio until they came to rest on the well-worn couch pushed against its rear wall. Laughingly, they disentangled themselves and surveyed the carnage. Canvasses lay scattered, an easel had been overturned and paint streaked the floor and soaked though their footwear.

'We seem to have managed a pretty good demolition.'

'Since we've made such a satisfactory start, perhaps we should finish,' she suggested. Her lips curved into a provocative smile.

In response, he folded her tightly into his body. 'Do you not think we should wait until you have a wedding ring on your finger?'

He was nibbling delicately at her ear, but she detached herself sufficiently to take him to task, running a finger lovingly down his face. 'I would never agree to such a foolish notion.'

'Why foolish?' He kissed her eyebrows one at a time.

'Unbelievably foolish! Every girl knows that once she's

caught her rake, she must make it impossible for him to escape!'

'Is that so?' His hands were making light work of the muslin's fastenings. 'I've obviously left it far too late to save myself.'

'I fear so.' Her voice faded into a delighted sigh.

'Sadly your beautiful gown is like to be ruined,' he lamented, as the crushed dress was swiftly undone and cast to one side. Shirt and breeches soon went the way of the muslin.

His lips were moving across the bare skin of her neck in sweet, fiery kisses. She heard her breath coming fast as his mouth reached her breasts and teased them into desire.

'I cannot think of dresses just now,' she panted, small groans of pleasure emanating from she knew not where.

'And why would you?' he murmured, his body hard and hot. 'While I am so very close, what need have you of a gown?'

Epilogue

'Las Meninas has to be the one flawless picture ever painted.'

Joshua was squinting at the large canvas, trying without success to detect an imperfection. The young Infanta Margerita, surrounded by her entourage of maids, bodyguard, two dwarfs and a dog, looked out at him from a room in Philip IV's palace.

Marianna smiled knowingly. 'It depresses you.'

'Only a very little. Nothing so perfect can depress me for long. Do you see Velásquez himself in the painting, just behind this group here, working at his canvas but looking out at the viewer? He's mocking me for my very poor efforts.'

'He's greeting you from across the centuries,' she said consolingly. 'But does his painting always have this effect? You must have seen it many times before.'

'In fact, I'm much less dispirited than usual. That's because you're here with me.'

'Las Meninas looks different with me by your side?'

'Everything looks different.'

'You are a shameless flatterer.' She held his arm more

tightly. 'At least, I assume that was a compliment.'

'It could be nothing else. I've been walking on clouds for the last six months and I want to paint the most exquisite picture that will say everything I feel for you. But Velásquez reminds me how far I am from achieving it.'

She smiled up at him, her face aglow with happiness. 'Whatever you paint for me will be better than anything in the Prado, since it will be done with love.'

Their fellow visitors shuffling their way around the white-walled room stopped for a moment to watch them. A tangible warmth surrounded the couple and everyone in the vicinity felt it.

'An understatement, my darling.' Joshua dipped his face beneath the brim of her bonnet and kissed her soundly.

'Not here!' she remonstrated. 'We're not in London now!'

He took her arm again and they walked sedately on, until she said, 'I'm a little fearful that any time soon you will come down to earth with a bump.'

He shook his head. 'I'm almost sure that you're wrong. I find married life suits me perfectly.'

'Only almost sure?'

'I can't allow you to get too puffed up,' he teased, adjusting the rose satin ribbons of her villager hat and surreptitiously slipping his arm around her waist. He gave her a tight squeeze and an elderly lady encased in black glared at him through her *pince nez*. In response, he smiled sunnily back.

Side by side, they strolled slowly through one salon after another, until they reached the front entrance. The huge door of polished wood stood open and ahead Marianna saw the fresh blue of a spring sky. 'At this time of the year Madrid is heavenly,' she said.

'The city has made a perfect end to our journey,' he agreed. 'But now it's time to head home – or rather, head to my home.'

'Mine, too, now,' she reminded him.

'It means leaving your father behind, my love. You'll miss him.'

A troubled look came into her eyes. 'We will miss each other. We've had such a short time together, but he's very happy with his new post here. I think he found England a little complicated. And he'll be sure to visit us there.'

'And your aunts?'

'They won't stir from Spain. And it's strange,' she conceded, 'I'll miss them, too. I never thought I'd say that, but they've been so welcoming. It must be your charm – you've won them over completely.'

'Though not Carmela, I fear.'

'You never will,' Marianna said sagely. 'For Carmela you will always be the dangerous profligate. But she is truly happy in Santa Caterina – the convent is where she's always wanted to be. Brighton was a horrible aberration. She'll want to forget she ever visited the town.'

Joshua reached over to take their outdoor coats from the attendant and helped his wife into her rose velvet capote, shrugging himself into a greatcoat with upwards of a dozen capes. He took her hand and guided her down the long flight of steps. 'That's something *we're* not likely to do, I fancy.'

'Forget Brighton? No, indeed, though I don't think I

would ever wish to return.'

'But why not? In the end everything came right and since we found happiness there, the town should have a place in our hearts.'

A shiver prickled the surface of Marianna's skin as they began to walk slowly along the wide pavement, the trees on either side sprouting their first greenery of the season.

'The place has as many bad memories for me as good,' she said as easily as she could. 'Lord Amesbury, for instance.'

'He need never concern us again. I forgot to tell you – I received an intriguing message yesterday. It came from an old friend at Carlton House. The duchess has married Amesbury!'

Marianna looked shocked but said with some spirit, 'They deserve each other. But it's very soon after the duke's death. Only a few months. Surely that cannot be right.'

'Charlotte has never been one to spend too much time observing the proprieties.' Joshua's expression was wry. 'I imagine she was desperate to find another husband – marriage at least gives her the semblance of respectability – and Amesbury was free. She grabbed him while she could.'

Marianna remained silent, watching the stream of stylish carriages making their way along the wide boulevard at a smart trot, but with her mind far away.

'And they are in London,' she said finally, the strain in her voice betraying her anxiety.

'Don't fret, my darling. They may be in London, but that's where they'll stay. Being close to power is all that interests them and now that Amesbury has been allowed back into Court, they'll be eager to resume their places in the Regent's entourage. They're sure to hang on to George's coat tails for ever and we're just as sure never to see them again.'

'Norfolk is not that far from London,' she reminded him, still anxious, but willing herself to be convinced.

'It's far enough, particularly in the depths of winter. The climate can be inclement and the roads sometimes impassable. I only hope you won't find it too quiet.'

That galvanised her and she turned impulsively towards him. 'I'm so looking forward to seeing Castle March and setting up house together.'

'A house for someone else, too.' He gestured to the gentle swell of her stomach.

'It will be the perfect place for children to grow up – and for us to grow old.'

'You mean there'll be no chance there of falling back into my wicked ways?'

She nudged him playfully. 'You know I mean nothing of the sort. I'm very sure your wicked ways, as you call them, are long dead.'

'You should be sure, since it's you that's tamed me.'

'I doubt that.' She blushed at the thought of the night they had just spent together. 'Not that I'd want to!'

He bent to kiss her full on the lips, ignoring the scandalised glances of their fellow strollers. 'Together we'll make Castle March a real home, Marianna. At last I can hang my da Vinci! It's the very first thing I shall do. Actually the second,' he corrected himself. 'There's a small matter of carrying you over the threshold.'

'You must make sure you don't drop the pair of us!'

'I'll be taking the greatest care of you both.'

He looked at her blooming cheeks and shining dark eyes. 'You are more beautiful than ever,' he murmured. 'I think we should be thinking of quite a large nursery.'

'Do I get any say in that?' She smiled up at him.

'Not a word. It's already decided. But I do need your advice with something that has me in a puzzle.'

Marianna, still smiling, raised her eyebrows.

'It's a matter of the greatest importance, so take care before you answer. Where exactly *am* I to hang the Leonardo?'

If you enjoyed reading *Romancing the Rake,* do please leave a review on your favourite site. Authors rely on good reviews – even just a few words – and readers depend on them to find interesting books to read.

Other books in the Allingham Regency Classic Series:
Duchess of Destiny (2017)
Dance of Deception (2017)
Masquerade (2018)

Other books by Merryn Allingham:
The Girl From Cobb Street (2015)
The Nurse's War (2015)
Daisy's Long Road Home (2015)
The Buttonmaker's Daughter (2017)
The Secret of Summerhayes (2017)
House of Lies (2018)
House of Glass (2018)
A Tale of Two Sisters (2019)
The Venice Atonement (2019)

About the Author

Merryn Allingham was born into an army family and spent her childhood moving around the UK and abroad. Unsurprisingly it gave her itchy feet, and in her twenties she escaped an unloved secretarial career to work as cabin crew and see the world.

The arrival of marriage, children and cats meant a more settled life in the south of England, where she's lived ever since. It also gave her the opportunity to go back to 'school' and eventually teach at university.

Merryn loves the nineteenth century and grew up reading Georgette Heyer, so when she began writing herself the novels had to be Regency romances.

For more information on Merryn and her books visit:
http://www.merrynallingham.com/

And sign up for her newsletter at
http://www.merrynallingham.com/
and receive *Through a Dark Glass*, a FREE volume of short stories.

Printed in Great Britain
by Amazon